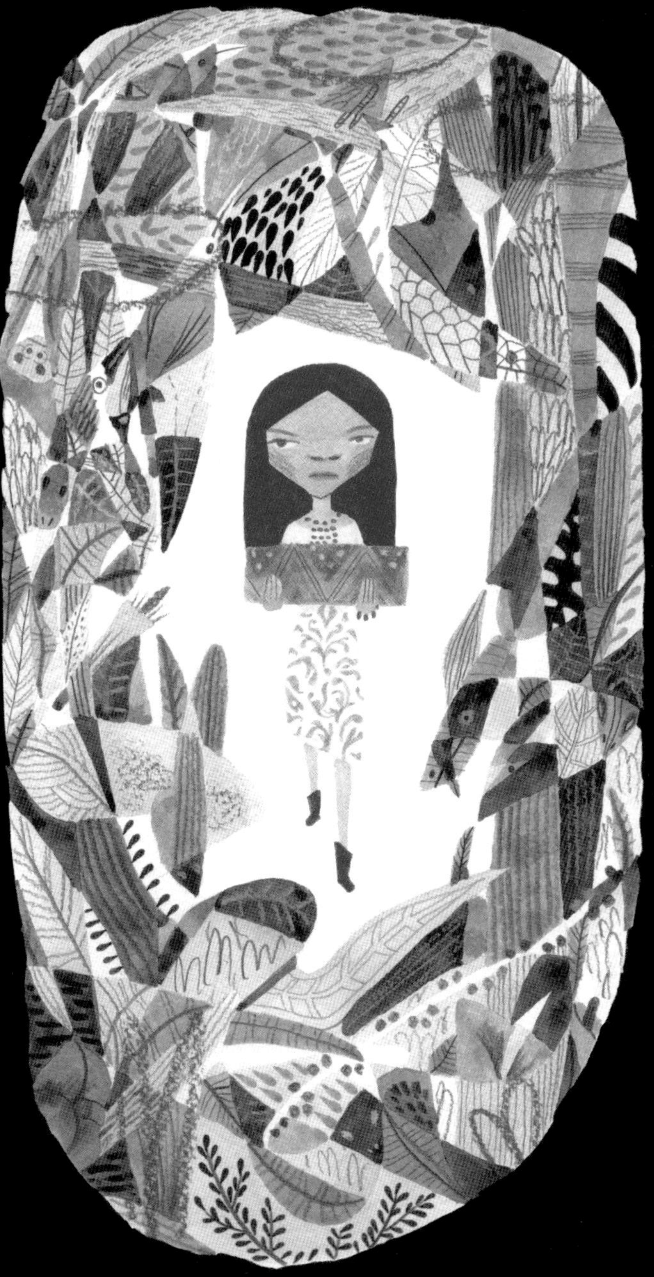

AMAZONA

Dedicated to those who have had to flee, leaving their lives behind
May the light in their hearts never fade

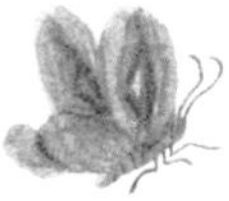

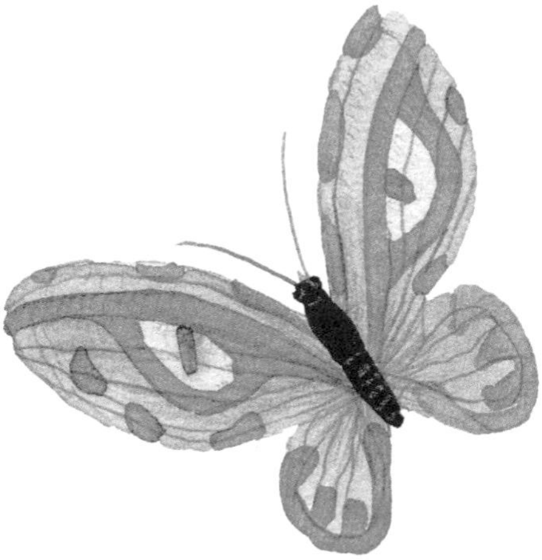

May it light new paths

So its brightness can blind the greedy

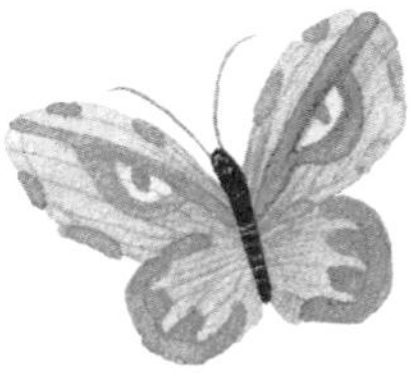

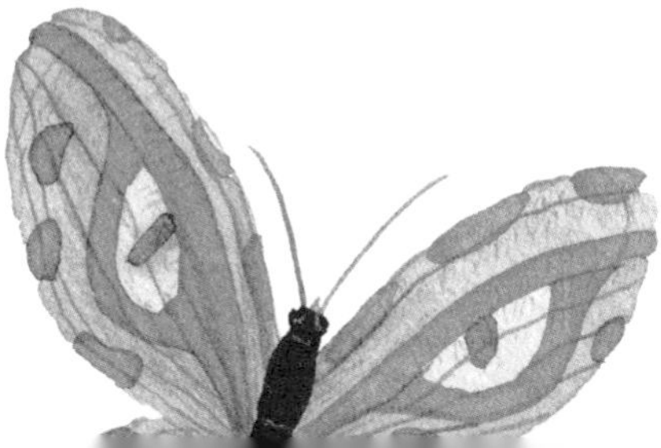

AC/E
ACCIÓN CULTURAL
ESPAÑOLA

This book was supported by a grant from Acción Cultural Española (AC/E)

Story and art by Canizales
English-language translation by Sofía Huitrón Martínez

First American edition published in 2022 by Graphic Universe™

The author will be donating a proportion of his royalties for this book to Resguardo Indígena Nasa de Cerro Tijeras

Text and illustrations © 2019 by Canizales

English-language translation copyright © 2022 by Lerner Publishing Group, Inc.

Graphic Universe™ is a trademark of Lerner Publishing Group, Inc.

All US rights reserved. International copyright secured. No part of this book may be reproduced, stored in a retrieval system, or transmitted in any form or by any means—electronic, mechanical, photocopying, recording, or otherwise—without the prior written permission of Lerner Publishing Group, Inc., except for the inclusion of brief quotations in an acknowledged review.

Graphic Universe™
An imprint of Lerner Publishing Group, Inc.
241 First Avenue North
Minneapolis, MN 55401 USA

For reading levels and more information, look up this title at www.lernerbooks.com.

Main body text set in Dinkle.
Typeface provided by Chank.

Library of Congress Cataloging-in-Publication Data

Names: Canizales, author, illustrator. | Huitrón Martínez, Sofía, translator.
Title: Amazona / Canizales ; translated by Sofía Huitron Martinez.
Description: First American edition. | Minneapolis, MN : Graphic Universe, 2022. | Audience: Ages 14–18 | Audience: Grades 10–12 | Summary: "Andrea, a young Indigenous Colombian woman, has returned to the land she calls home. She comes to mourn her child—and to capture evidence of the illegal mining that displaced her family" —Provided by publisher.
Identifiers: LCCN 2021027632 (print) | LCCN 2021027633 (ebook) | ISBN 9781728401706 (library binding) | ISBN 9781728448671 (paperback) | ISBN 9781728444093 (ebook)
Subjects: CYAC: Graphic novels. | Indigenous peoples—Colombia—Fiction. | Family life—Colombia—Fiction. | Gold mines and mining—Fiction. | Colombia—Fiction. | LCGFT: Graphic novels.
Classification: LCC PZ7.7.C3634 Am 2022 (print) | LCC PZ7.7.C3634 (ebook) | DDC 741.5/9861—dc23

LC record available at https://lccn.loc.gov/2021027632
LC ebook record available at https://lccn.loc.gov/2021027633

Manufactured in the United States of America
1-48222-48809-11/2/2021

anizales (Harold Jiméne
mazona /
022
3305250249442
a   08/09/22

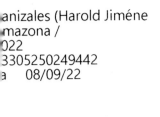

AMAZONA

CANIZALES

TRANSLATED FROM SPANISH BY SOFÍA HUITRÓN MARTÍNEZ

Graphic Universe™ • Minneapolis

No, I'm not a white woman.
No, I'm not half-clothed in pieces of a flag.
No, I don't care about looking sexy while
trying to save my world.

But yes, I am a woman of the Amazon, and I have returned to settle some issues.

The last time I was here, I was running from the bullets of people in fatigues.

They are still here, a few yards away, surrounding our sacred land and ready to spit fire at me the moment they see me.

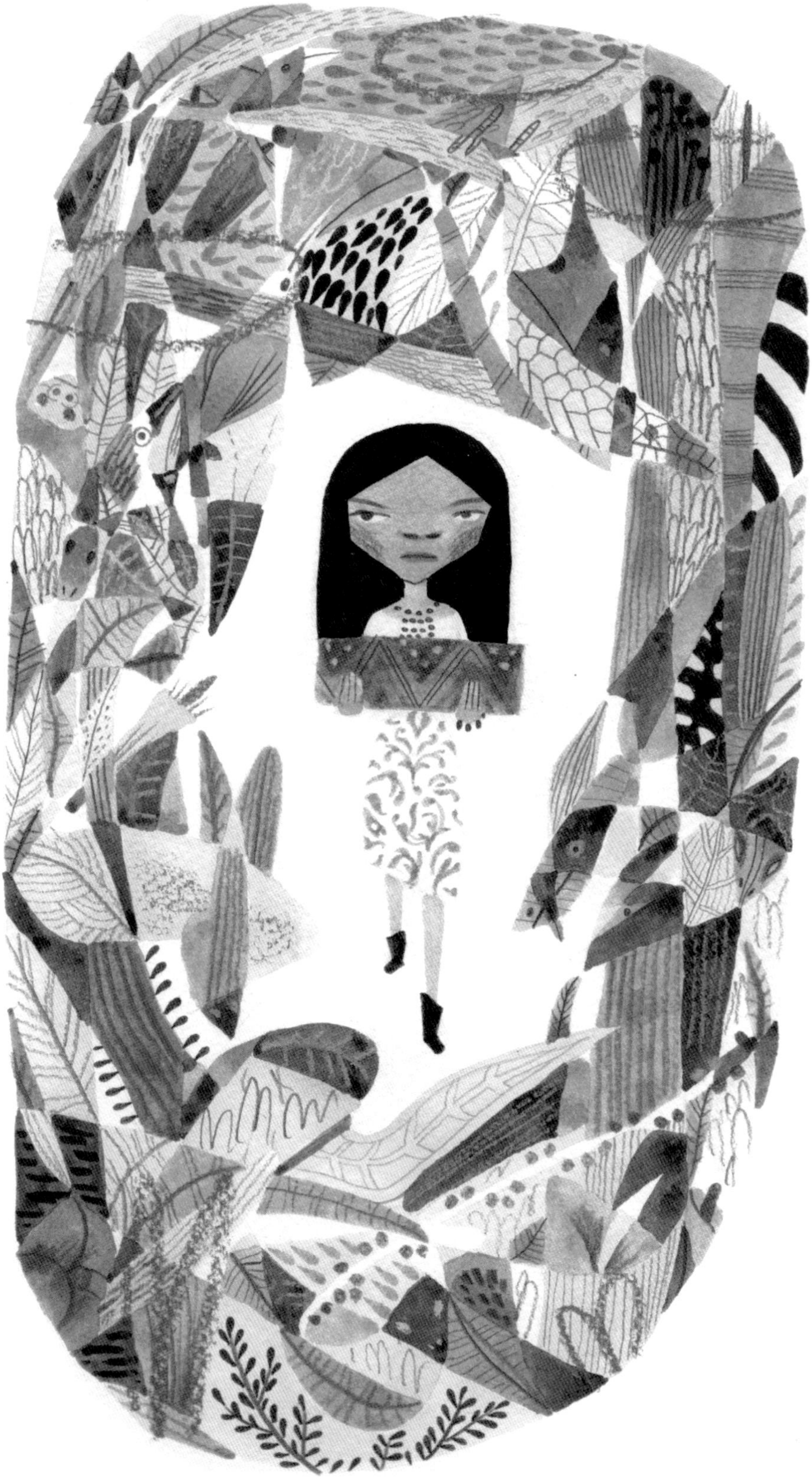

We no longer live in the Amazonia region. We were displaced eleven months ago.
Now we are forced to live in the city of Cali, Colombia.

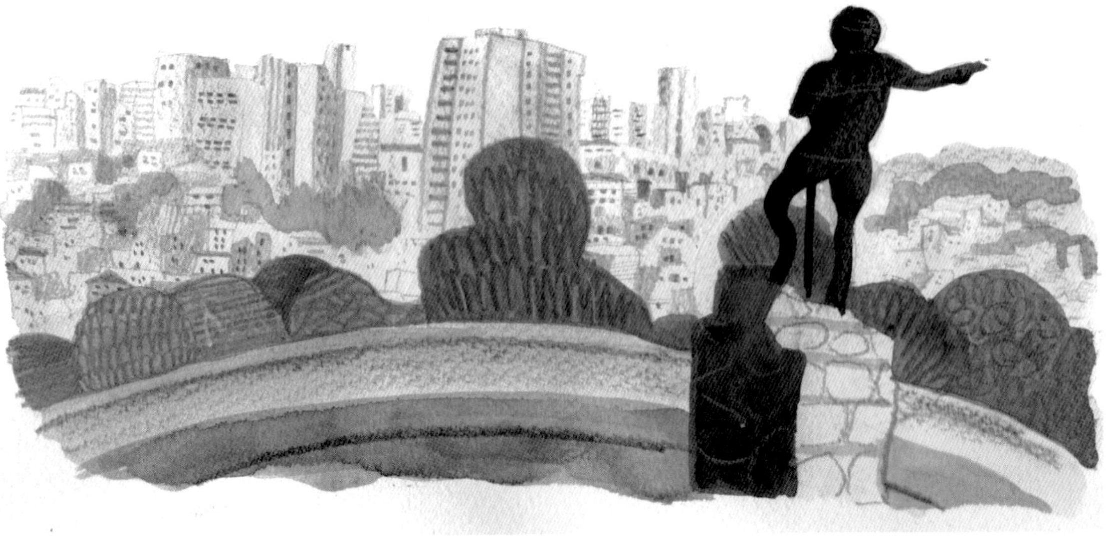

An organization decided it was better to keep us hidden in a dilapidated house in the city center than have us out in the streets, where we would tarnish the city's festive landscape.

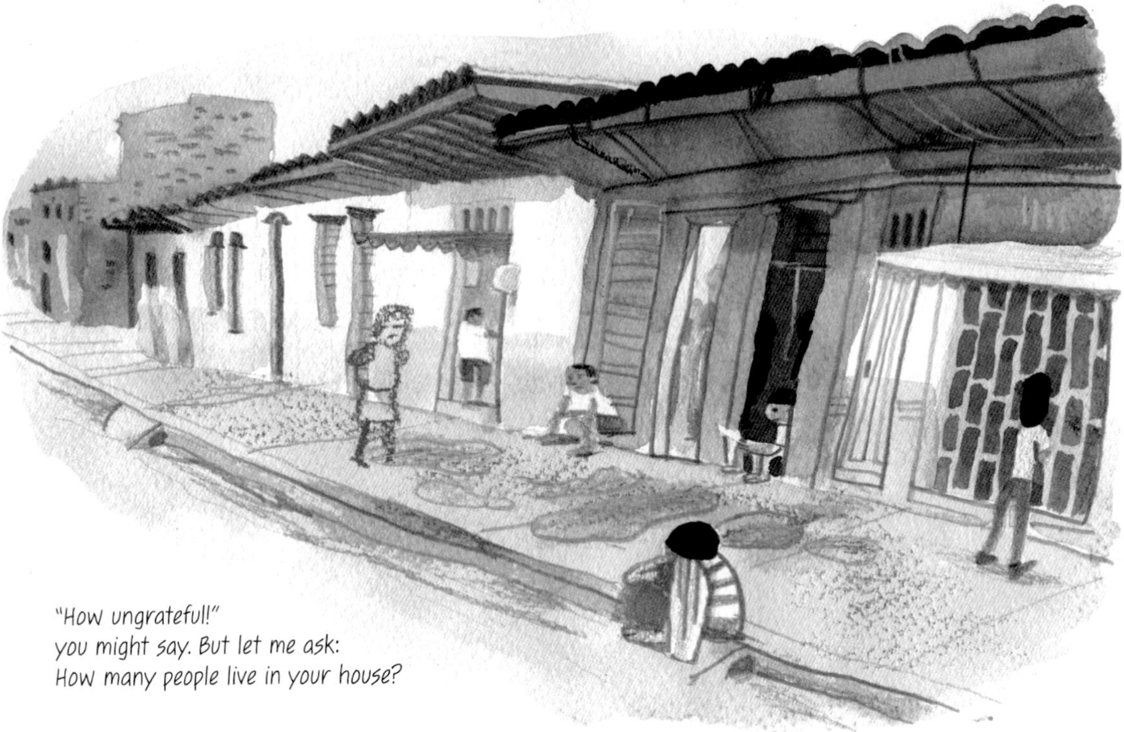

"How ungrateful!"
you might say. But let me ask:
How many people live in your house?

In the place where we live now, and forgive me if I don't call it home, you'll find: my sisters and brothers . . .

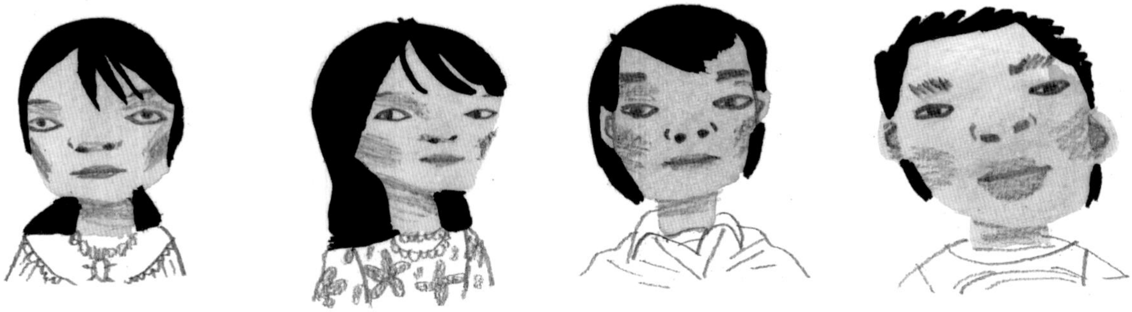

My cousins and aunts and uncles . . .

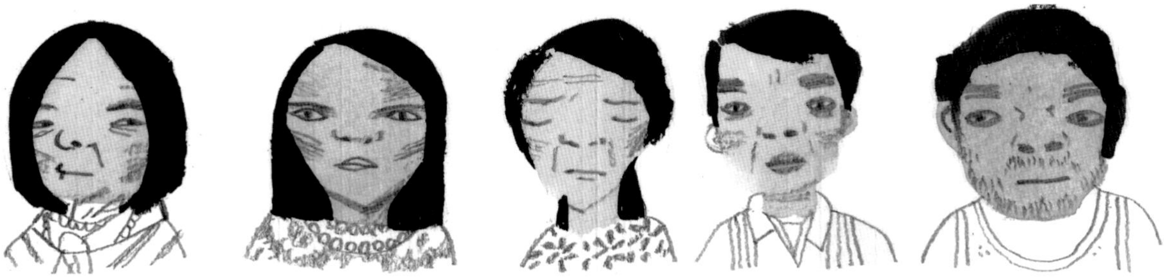

My neighbors, grandmothers, and grandfathers . . .

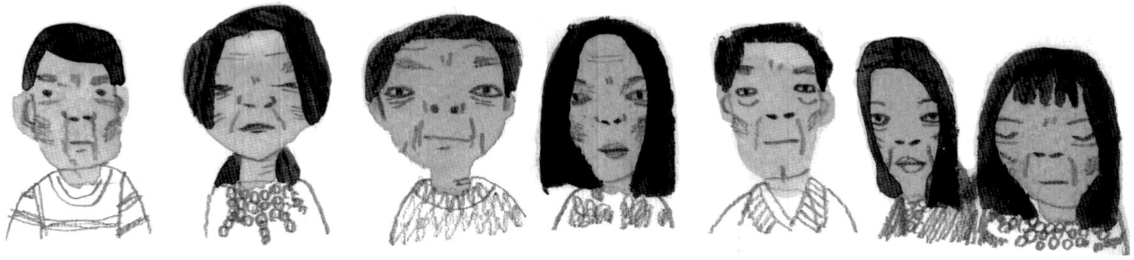

And boys and girls who lost their own families. A total of thirty-eight people sharing a 600-square-foot space. The place is divided into two rooms with no windows, a bathroom with no door, a kitchen, and a patio.

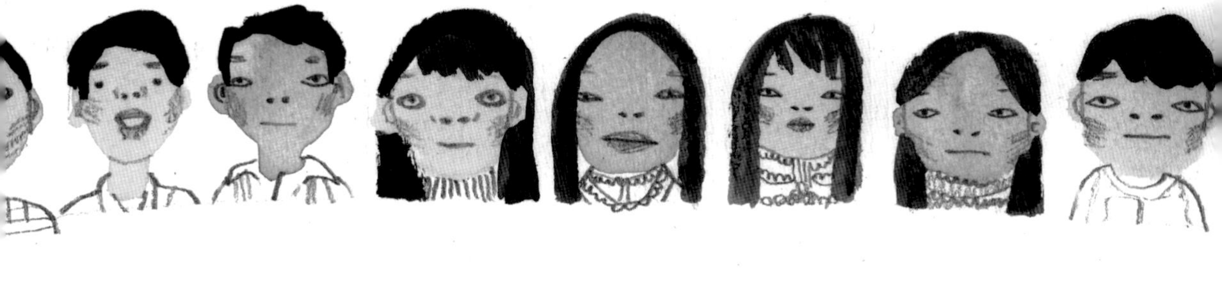

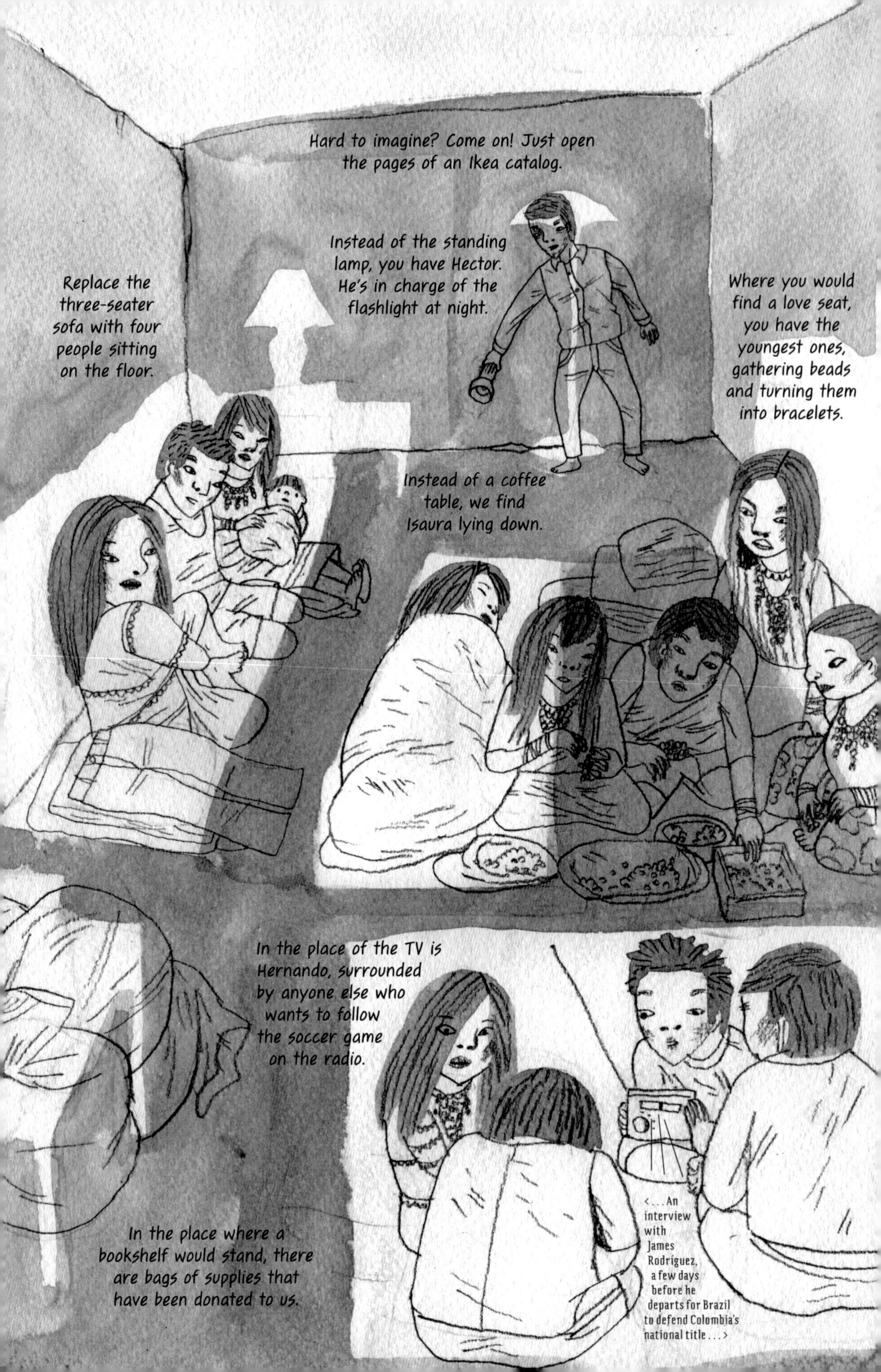
Hard to imagine? Come on! Just open the pages of an Ikea catalog.
Instead of the standing lamp, you have Hector. He's in charge of the flashlight at night.
Replace the three-seater sofa with four people sitting on the floor.
Where you would find a love seat, you have the youngest ones, gathering beads and turning them into bracelets.
Instead of a coffee table, we find Isaura lying down.
In the place of the TV is Hernando, surrounded by anyone else who wants to follow the soccer game on the radio.
In the place where a bookshelf would stand, there are bags of supplies that have been donated to us.
<. . . An interview with James Rodríguez, a few days before he departs for Brazil to defend Colombia's national title . . .>

The local system of commerce is not for us. Money is not a great part of our culture.
Yet without it, something seems to be missing.

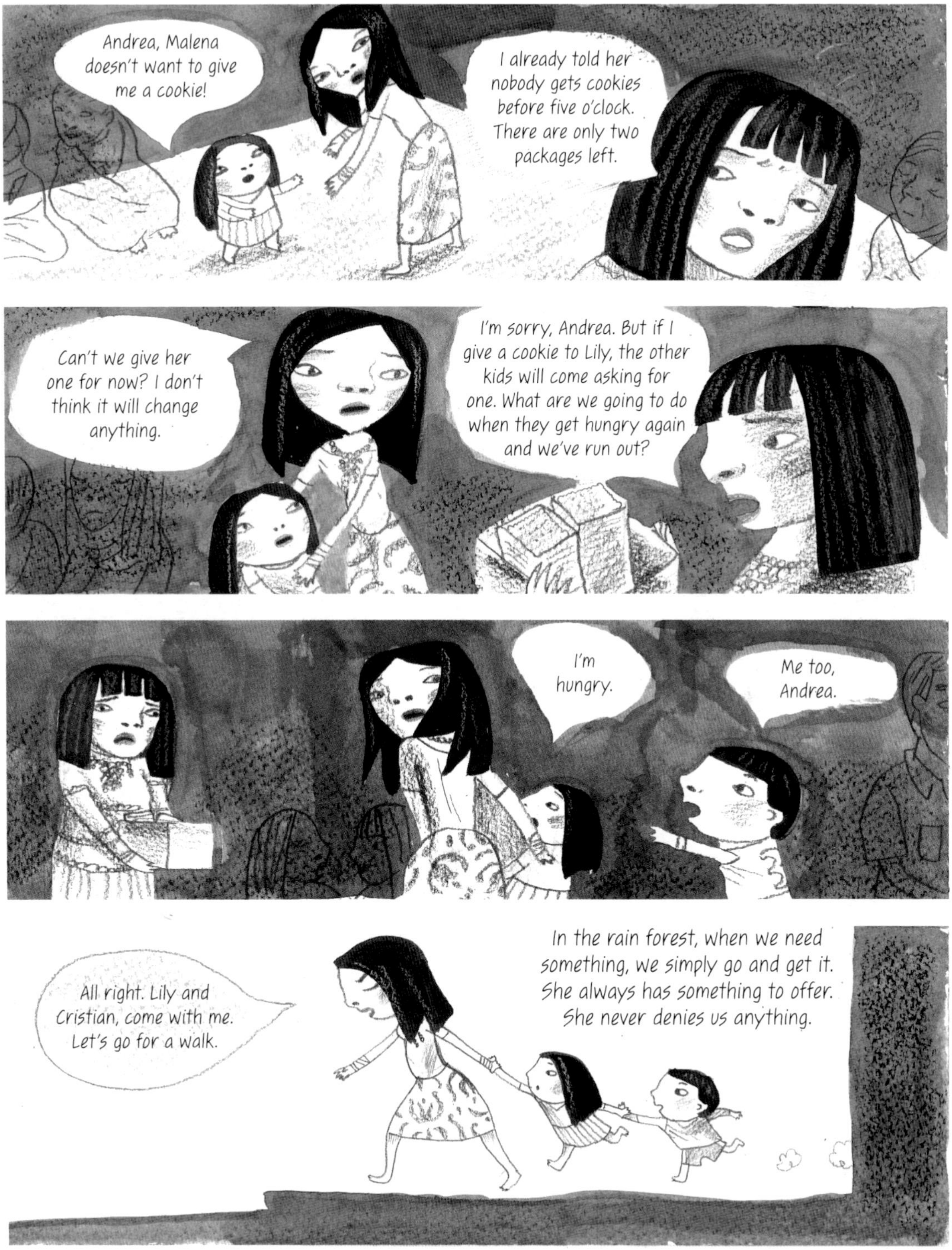
Andrea, Malena doesn't want to give me a cookie!
I already told her nobody gets cookies before five o'clock. There are only two packages left.
Can't we give her one for now? I don't think it will change anything.
I'm sorry, Andrea. But if I give a cookie to Lily, the other kids will come asking for one. What are we going to do when they get hungry again and we've run out?
I'm hungry.
Me too, Andrea.
All right. Lily and Cristian, come with me. Let's go for a walk.
In the rain forest, when we need something, we simply go and get it. She always has something to offer. She never denies us anything.

Things are different here. You either look down and see trash on the ground or look up and see eyes that avoid your own.

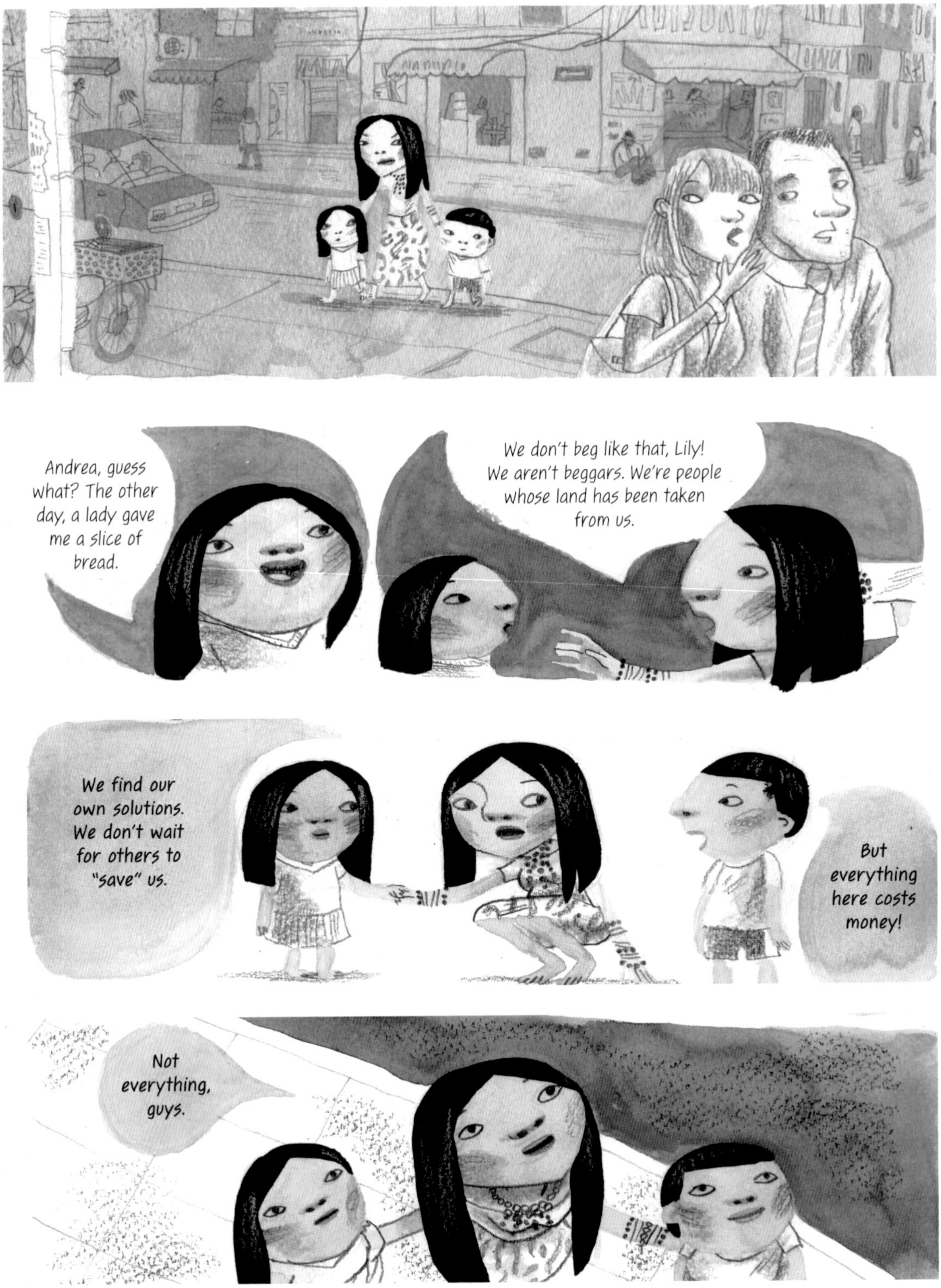
Andrea, guess what? The other day, a lady gave me a slice of bread.
We don't beg like that, Lily! We aren't beggars. We're people whose land has been taken from us.
We find our own solutions. We don't wait for others to "save" us.
But everything here costs money!
Not everything, guys.

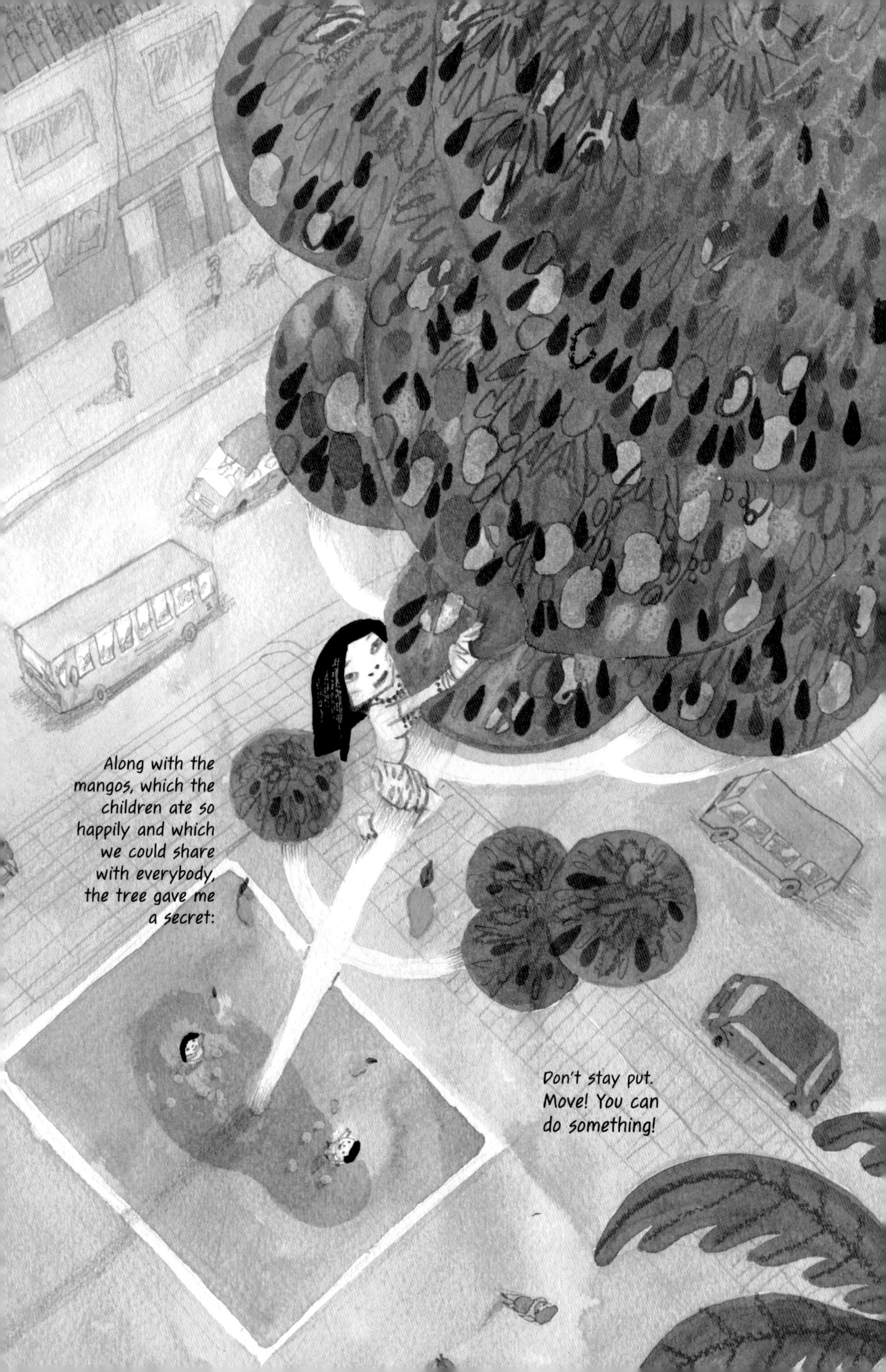

Along with the mangos, which the children ate so happily and which we could share with everybody, the tree gave me a secret:

Don't stay put. Move! You can do something!

Would we be able to go back? The question ate away at my soul.

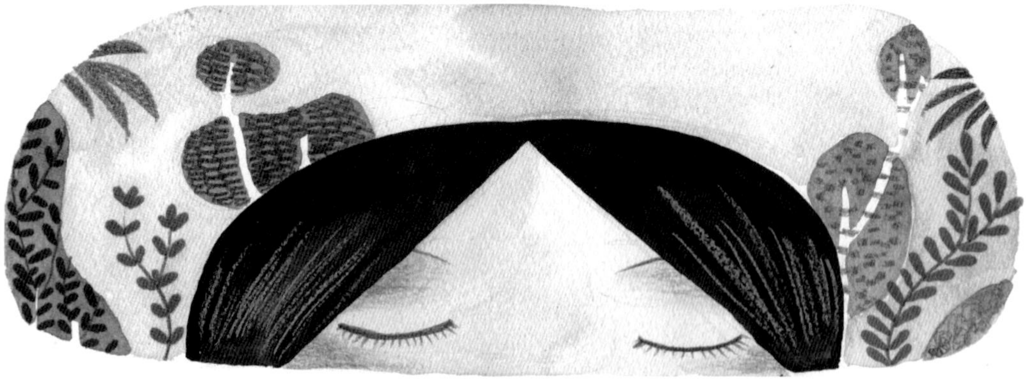

Memories of the trees, the reeds, the frogs, the monkeys, the flowers, the water . . .
became things I could only see in my dreams.

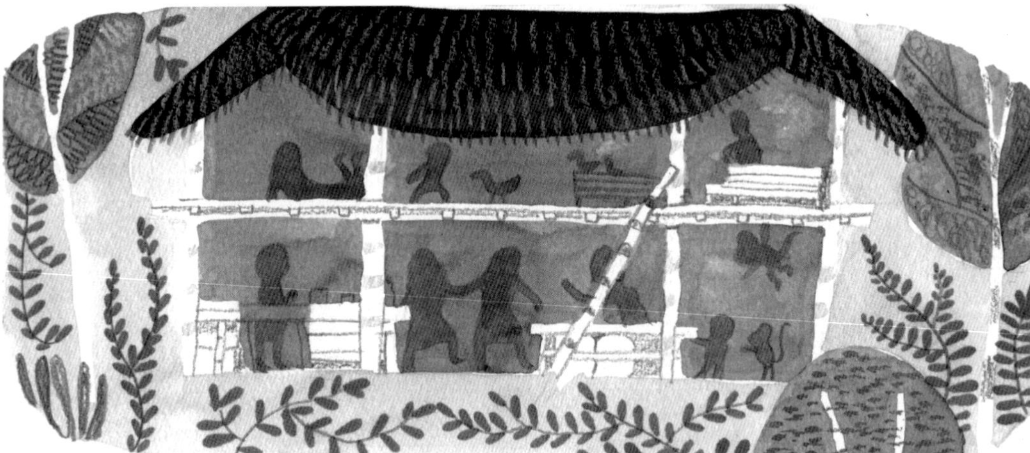

My laughter had echoed throughout our old home, past my father, my mother, my husband, Julian, Esmeralda, and Esteban. Now the only thing in that house is what the bullets have written across it: desolation.

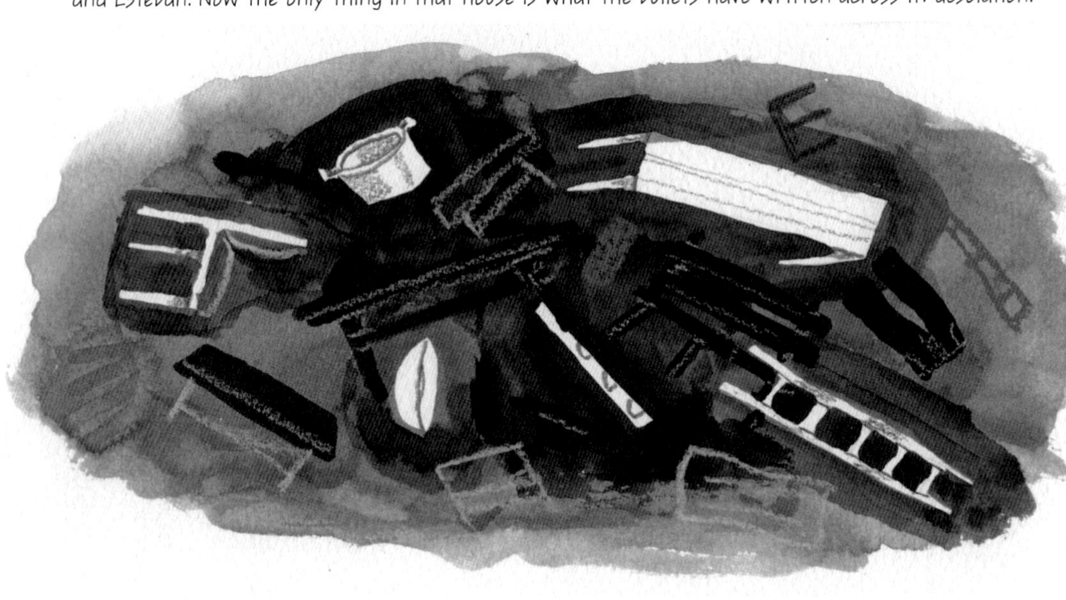

A few weeks after we were forced to leave, my brother Julian dared to go back to our village, without telling anyone. But he could not get in.

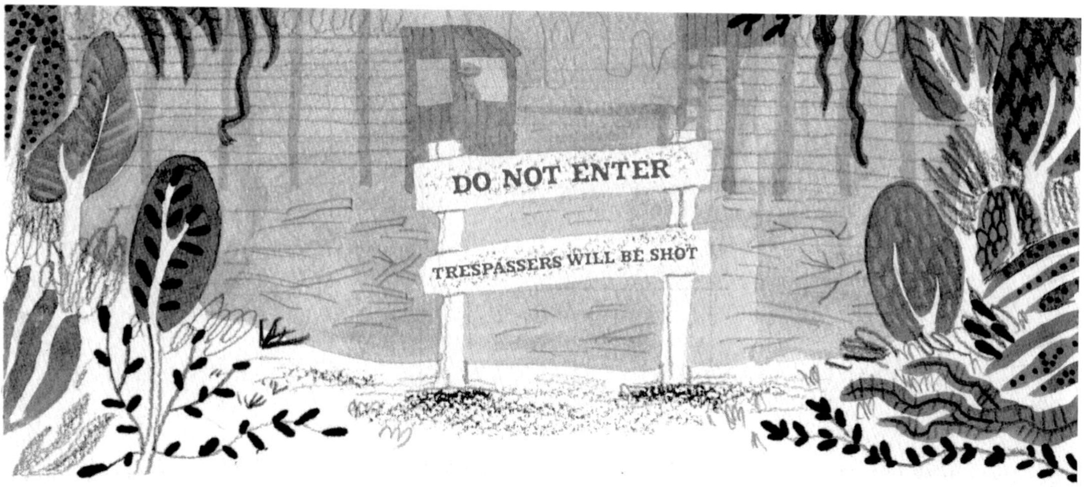
DO NOT ENTER
TRESPASSERS WILL BE SHOT

He told us the place was unrecognizable. The ancient trees had been chopped down. A wire fence surrounded everything, impossible to cross.

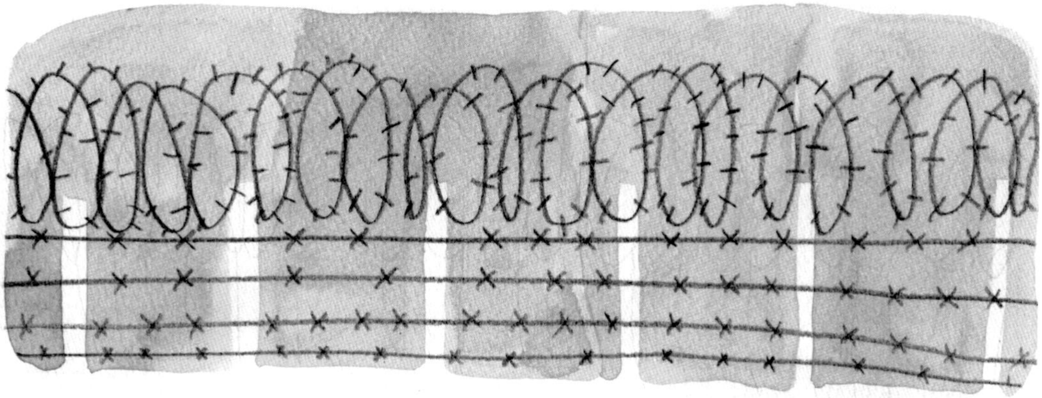

He didn't dare leave his hiding spot between the bushes. Only a few steps away stood outposts with armed guards inside. Their expressions left no doubt that they would shoot at anyone who came close.

Back then, we weren't as far away from our village as we are now.

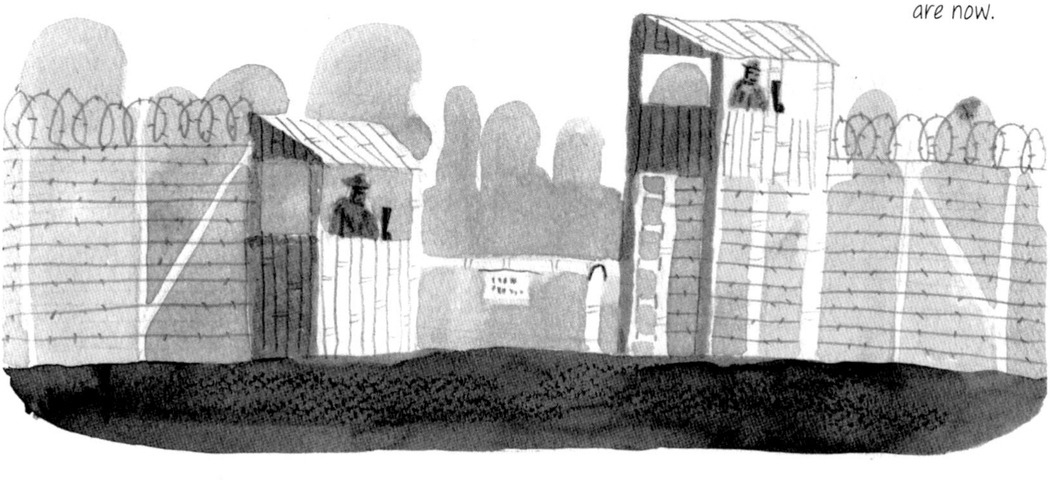

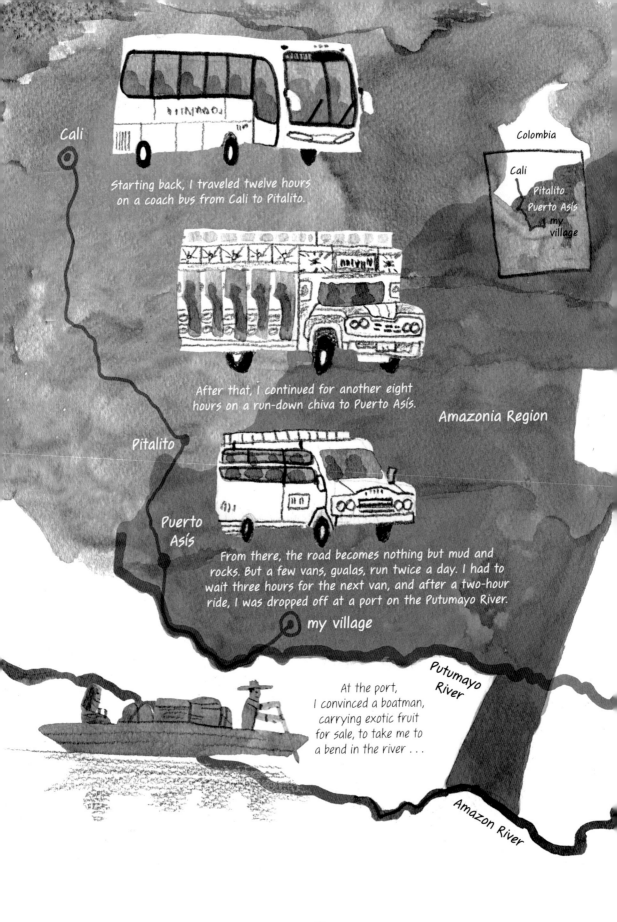

Cali

Starting back, I traveled twelve hours on a coach bus from Cali to Pitalito.

Colombia

Cali

Pitalito
Puerto Asís
my village

After that, I continued for another eight hours on a run-down chiva to Puerto Asís.

Amazonia Region

Pitalito

Puerto Asís

From there, the road becomes nothing but mud and rocks. But a few vans, gualas, run twice a day. I had to wait three hours for the next van, and after a two-hour ride, I was dropped off at a port on the Putumayo River.

my village

Putumayo River

At the port, I convinced a boatman, carrying exotic fruit for sale, to take me to a bend in the river . . .

Amazon River

16

. . . The point from which I've been walking for the last four hours, without a map or a compass.

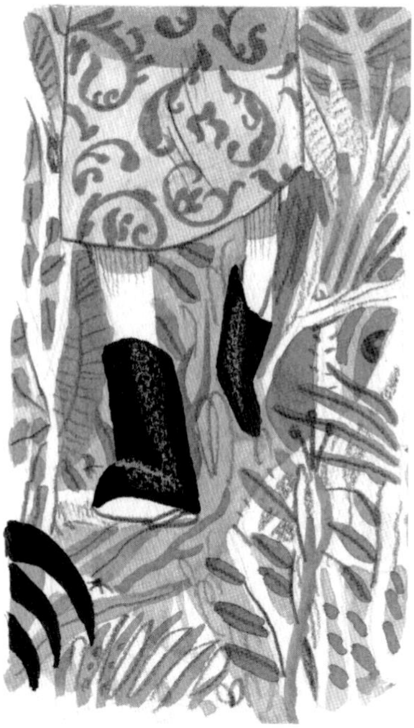

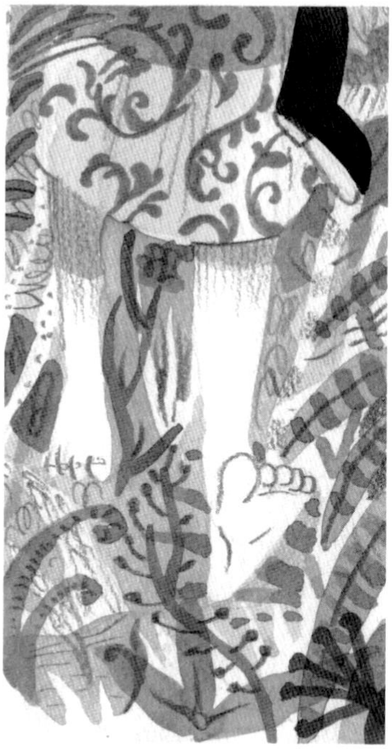

And here I am, feeling the energy of the earth once again. It is wonderful, after almost a year.

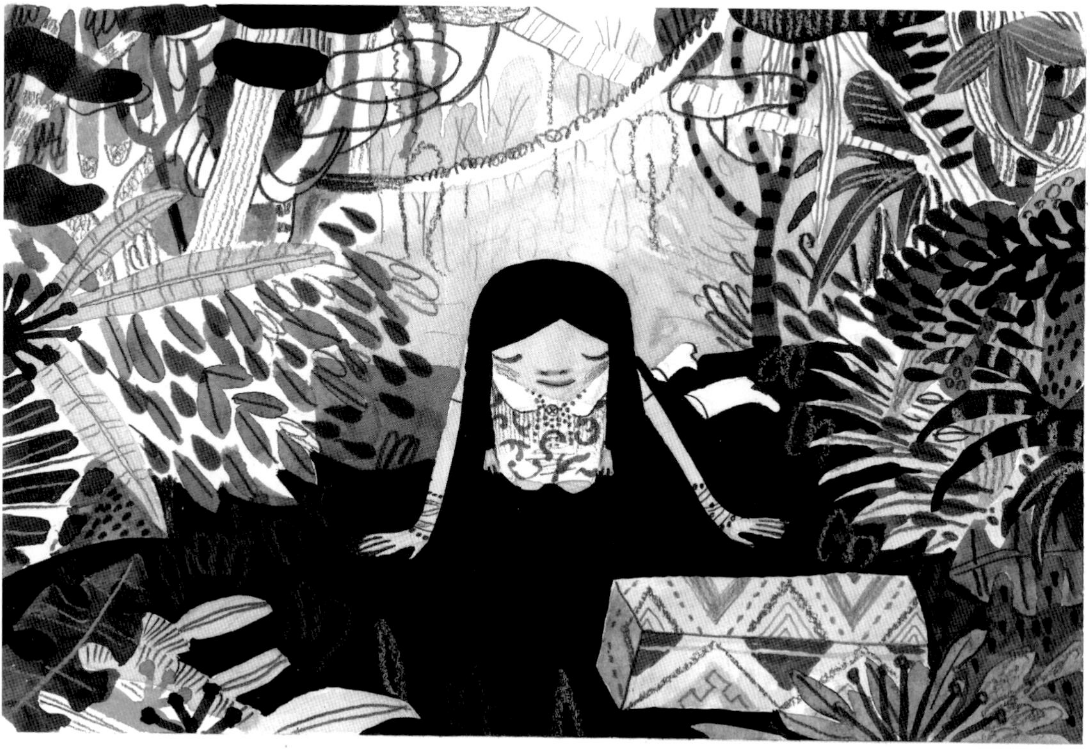

The jaguar is the one
that guided me here.

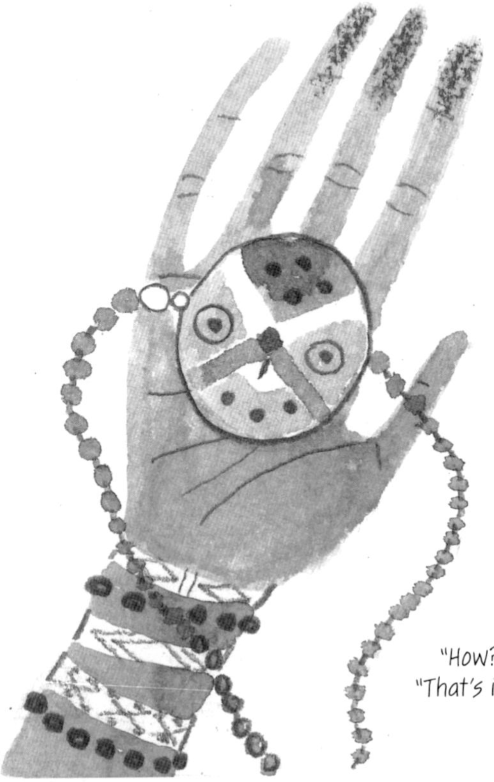

A few days ago, in a
vision, it told me I had to
come back and reclaim
what is ours.

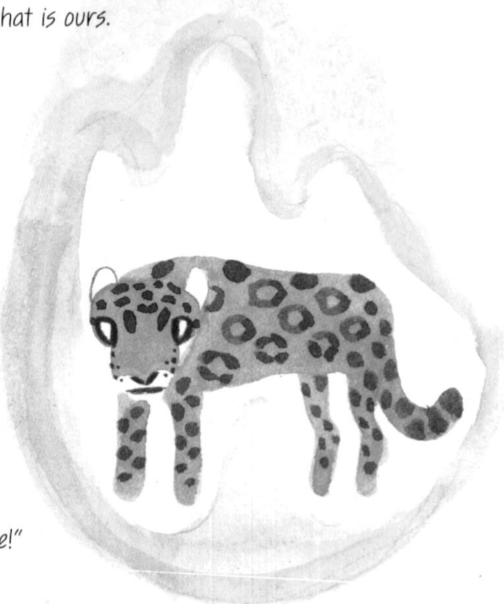

"How?" I said.
"That's impossible!"

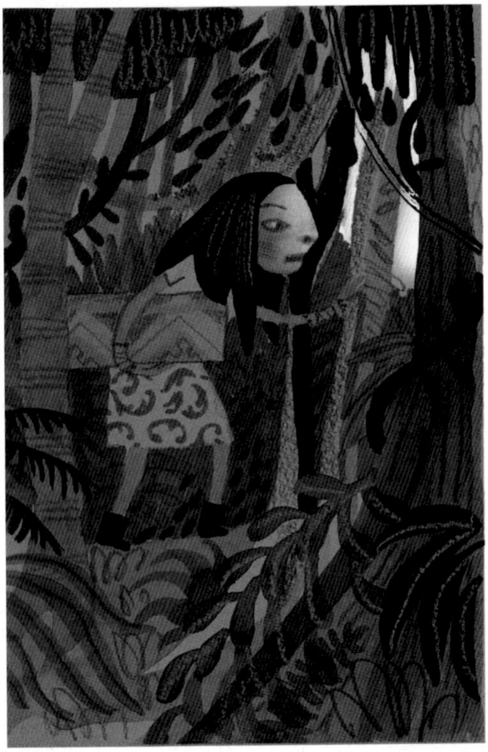

It replied:

"I am the voice within you. At every
moment, you will know what you
must do, where you must go."

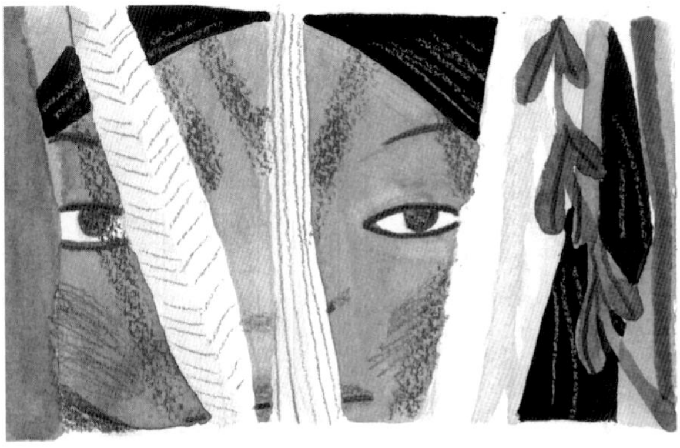

This is as far as my brother got.

A few more steps and I'll be fully visible
to those vicious armed guards.

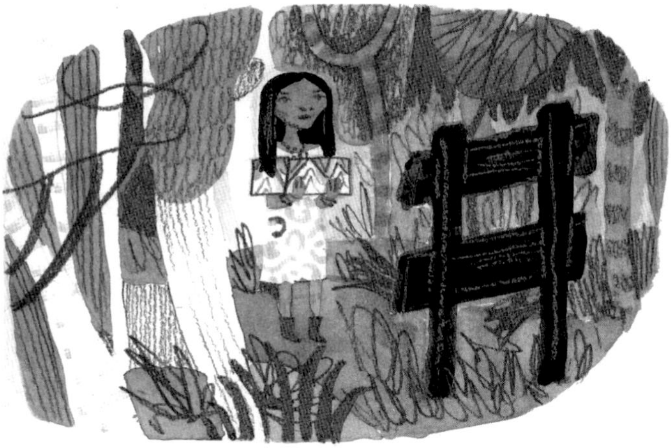

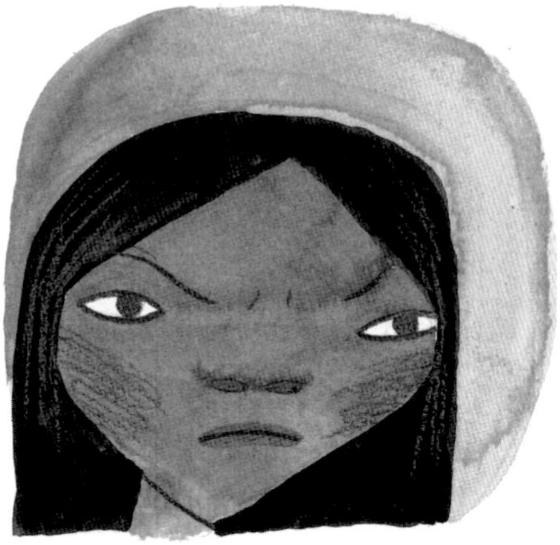

The jaguar pushes me to keep going. I don't know if it's playing a trick on me, but it keeps telling me something I still don't believe to be true:

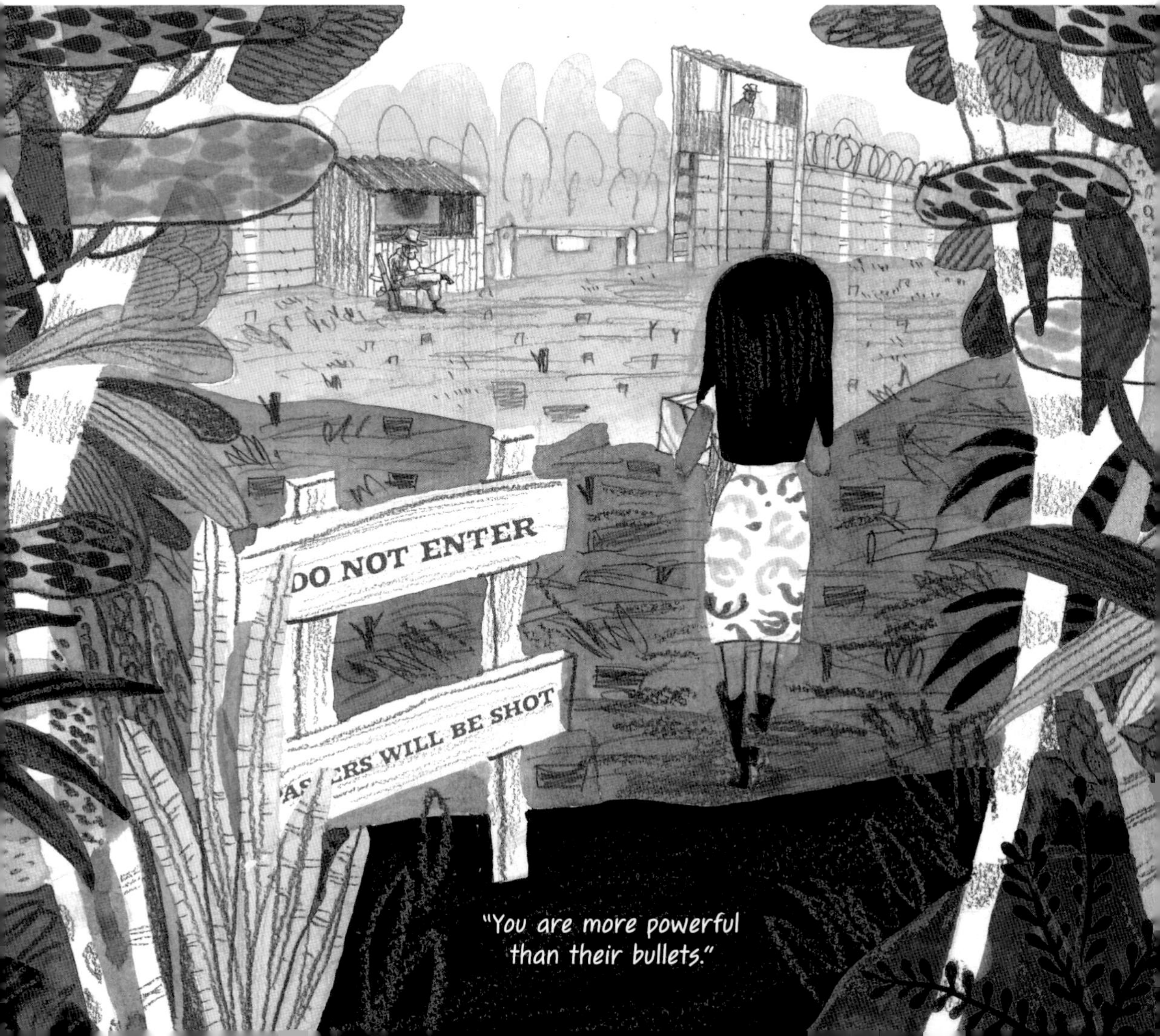
DO NOT ENTER
WILL BE SHOT
"You are more powerful than their bullets."

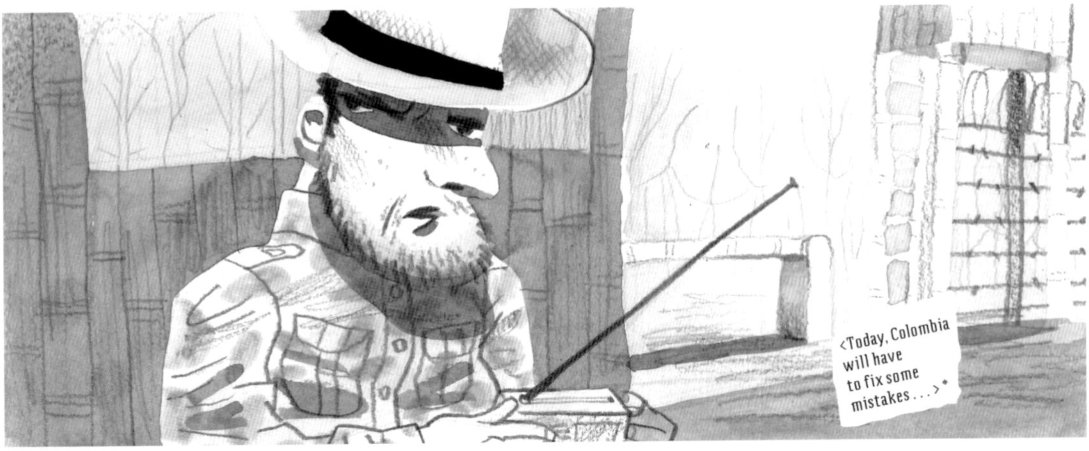
<Today, Colombia will have to fix some mistakes . . .>*

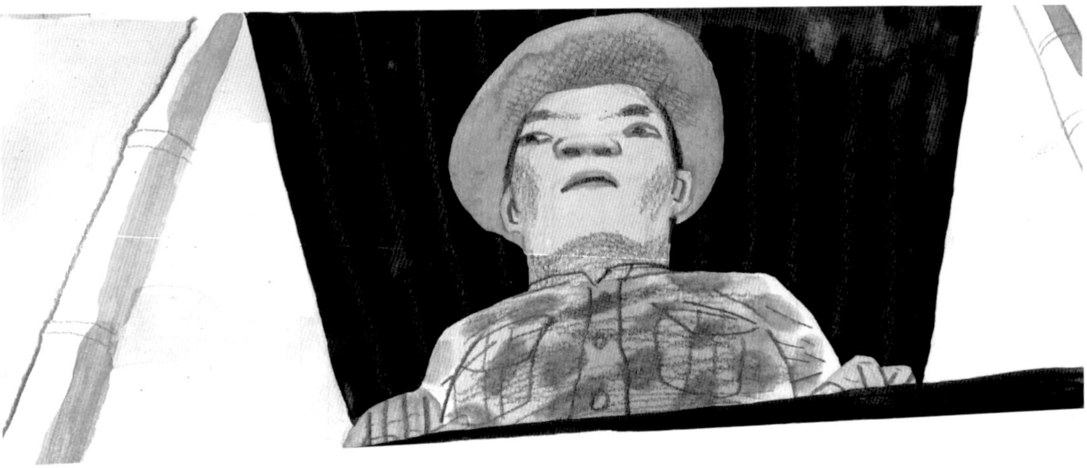

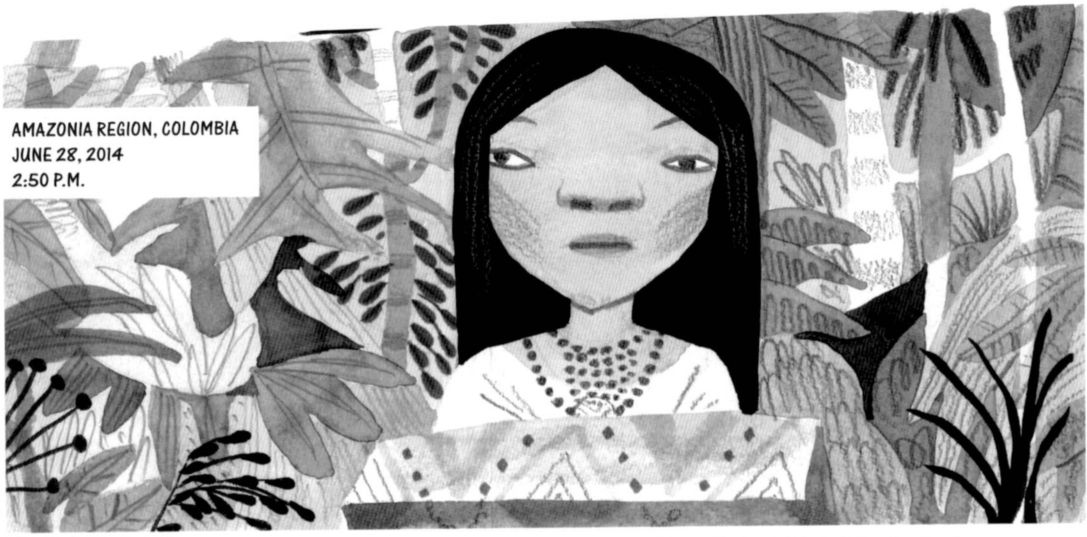
AMAZONIA REGION, COLOMBIA
JUNE 28, 2014
2:50 P.M.

*Dialogue within brackets is spoken in the Spanish language. Dialogue is otherwise spoken in the local dialect of the Quechua language.

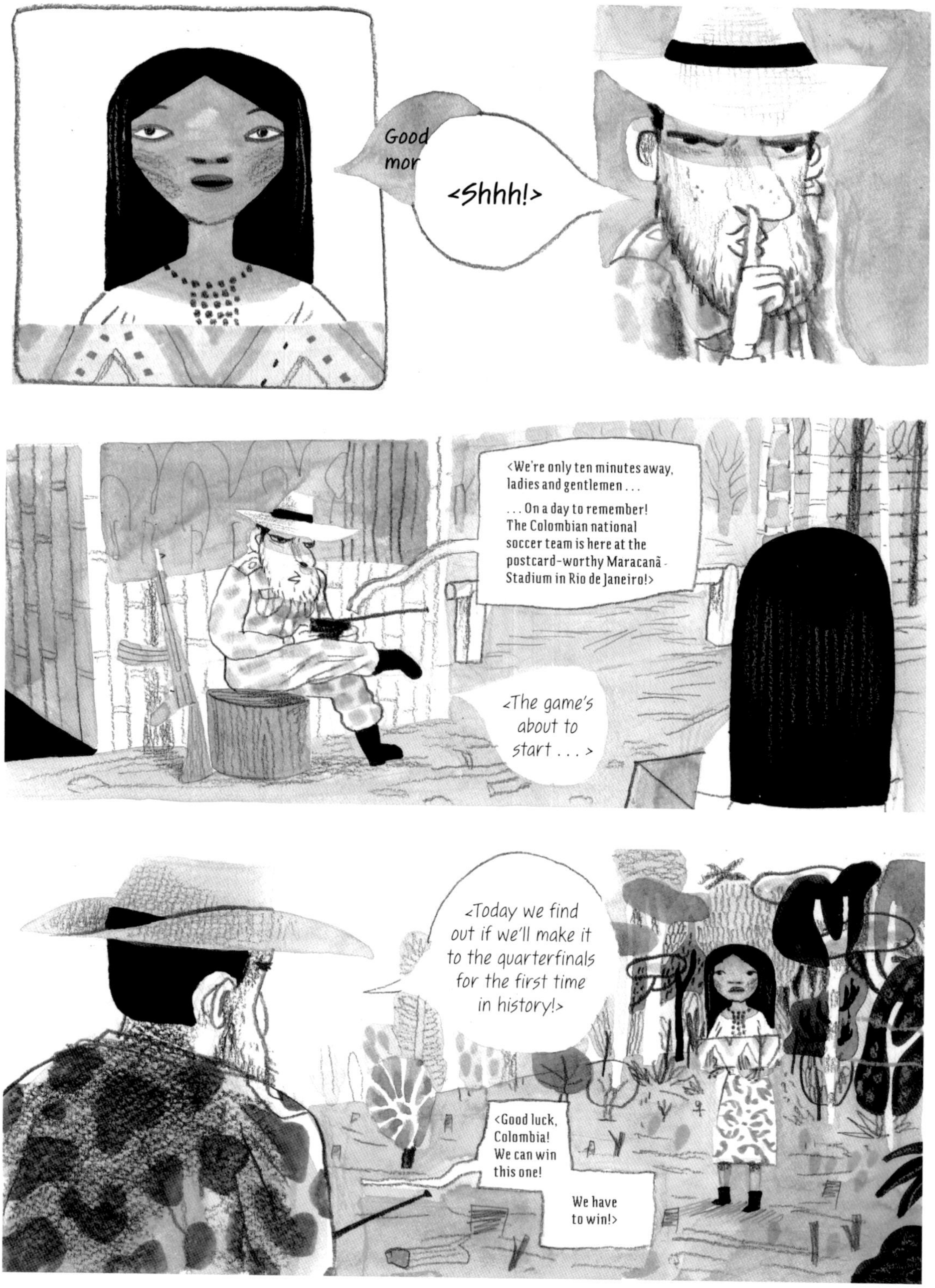
Good mor
<Shhh!>
<We're only ten minutes away, ladies and gentlemen . . .
. . . On a day to remember! The Colombian national soccer team is here at the postcard-worthy Maracanã Stadium in Rio de Janeiro!>
<The game's about to start . . . >
<Today we find out if we'll make it to the quarterfinals for the first time in history!>
<Good luck, Colombia! We can win this one!
We have to win!>

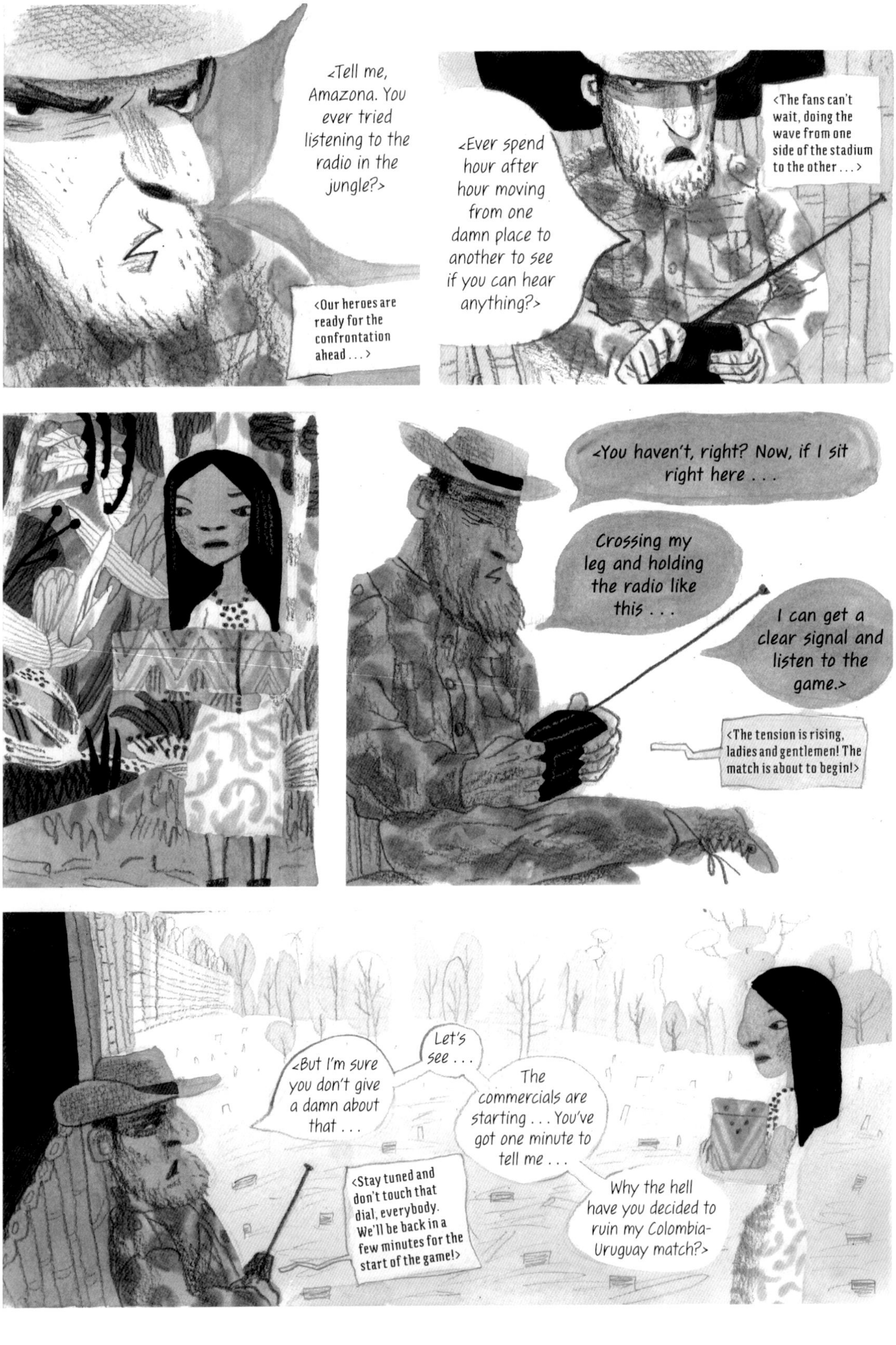
<Tell me, Amazona. You ever tried listening to the radio in the jungle?>
<Our heroes are ready for the confrontation ahead . . . >
<Ever spend hour after hour moving from one damn place to another to see if you can hear anything?>
<The fans can't wait, doing the wave from one side of the stadium to the other . . . >
<You haven't, right? Now, if I sit right here . . .
Crossing my leg and holding the radio like this . . .
I can get a clear signal and listen to the game.>
<The tension is rising, ladies and gentlemen! The match is about to begin!>
<But I'm sure you don't give a damn about that . . .
Let's see . . .
The commercials are starting . . . You've got one minute to tell me . . .
Why the hell have you decided to ruin my Colombia-Uruguay match?>
<Stay tuned and don't touch that dial, everybody. We'll be back in a few minutes for the start of the game!>

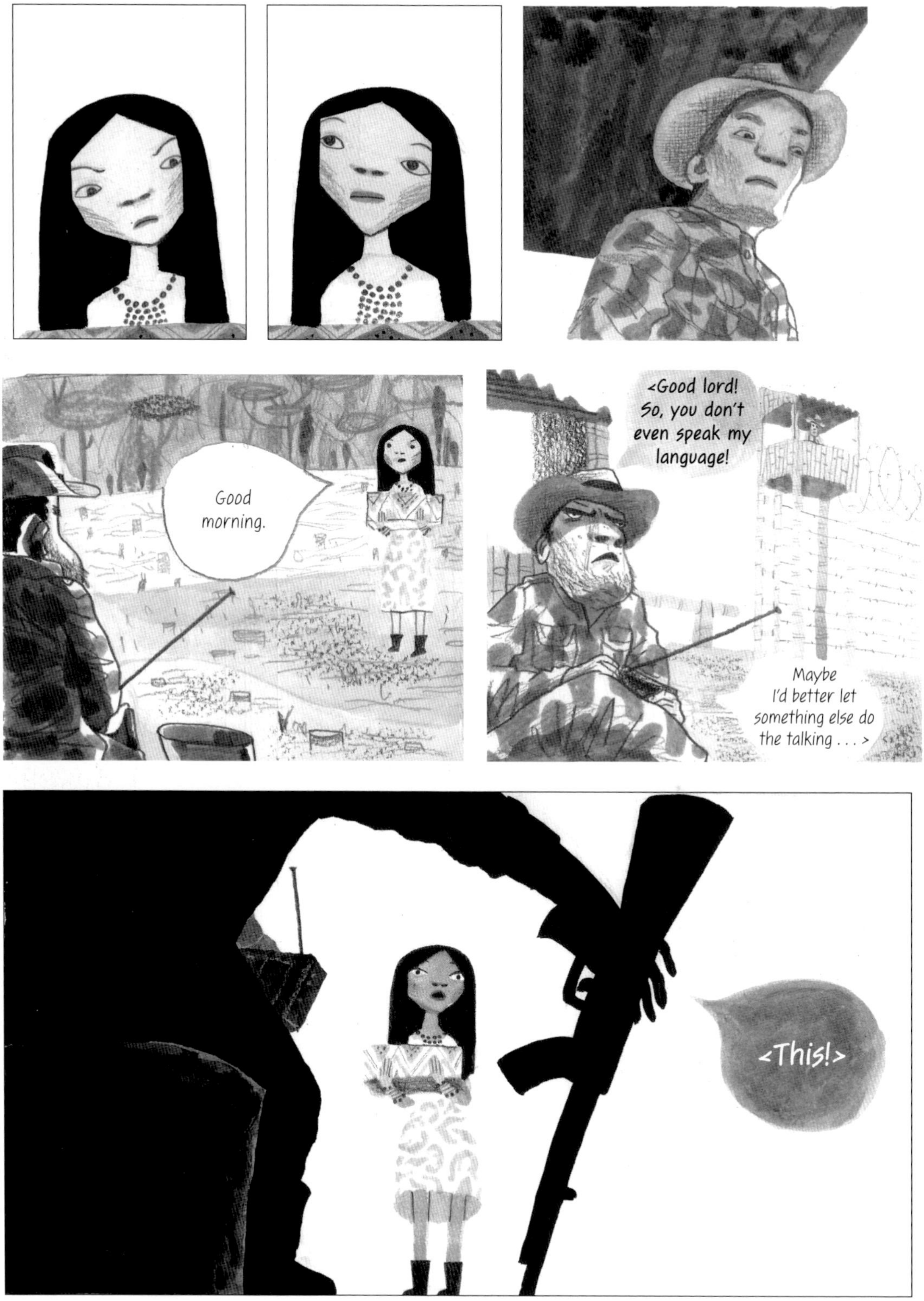
Good morning.
<Good lord! So, you don't even speak my language!
Maybe I'd better let something else do the talking . . . >
<This!>

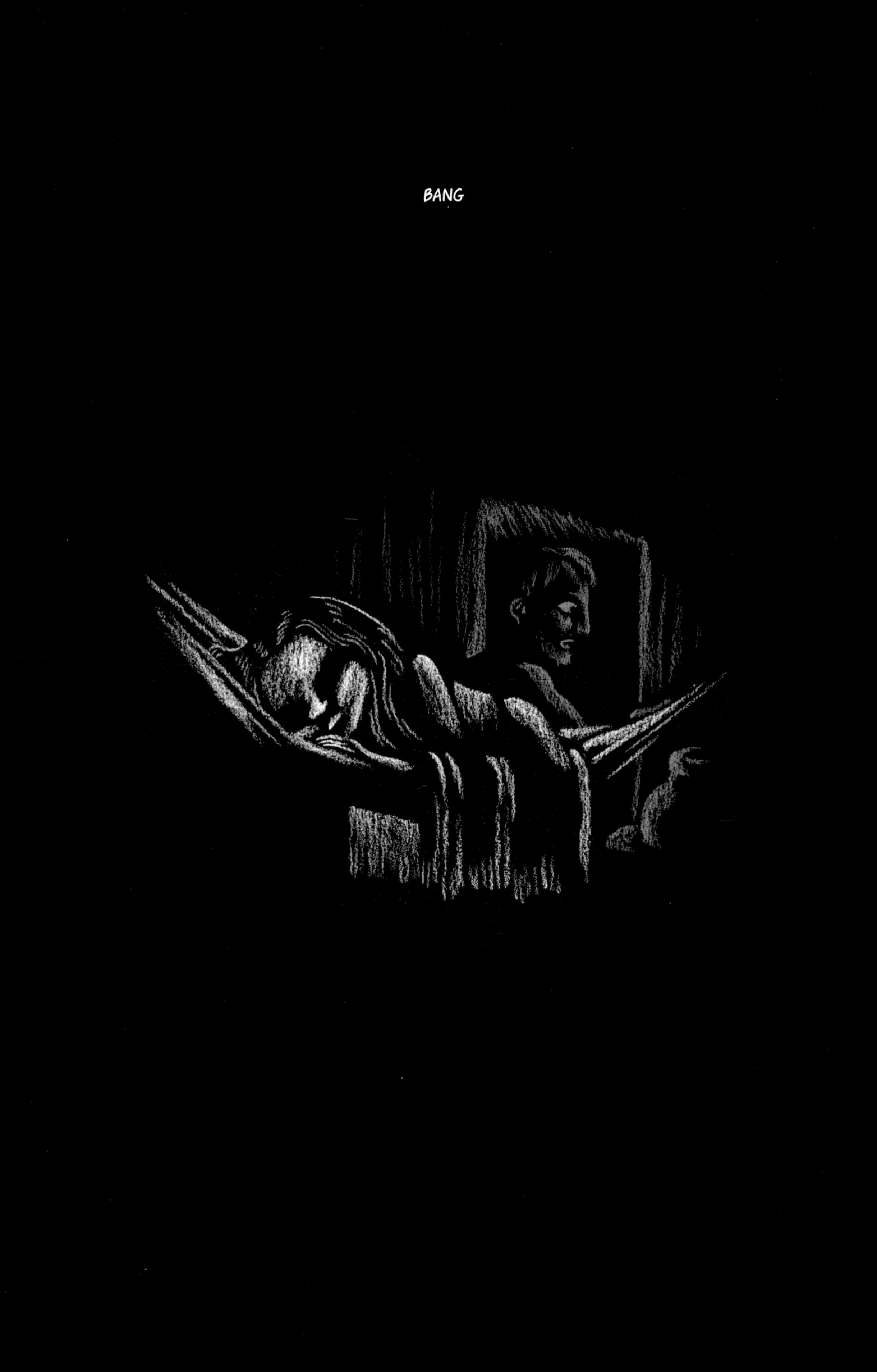
BANG

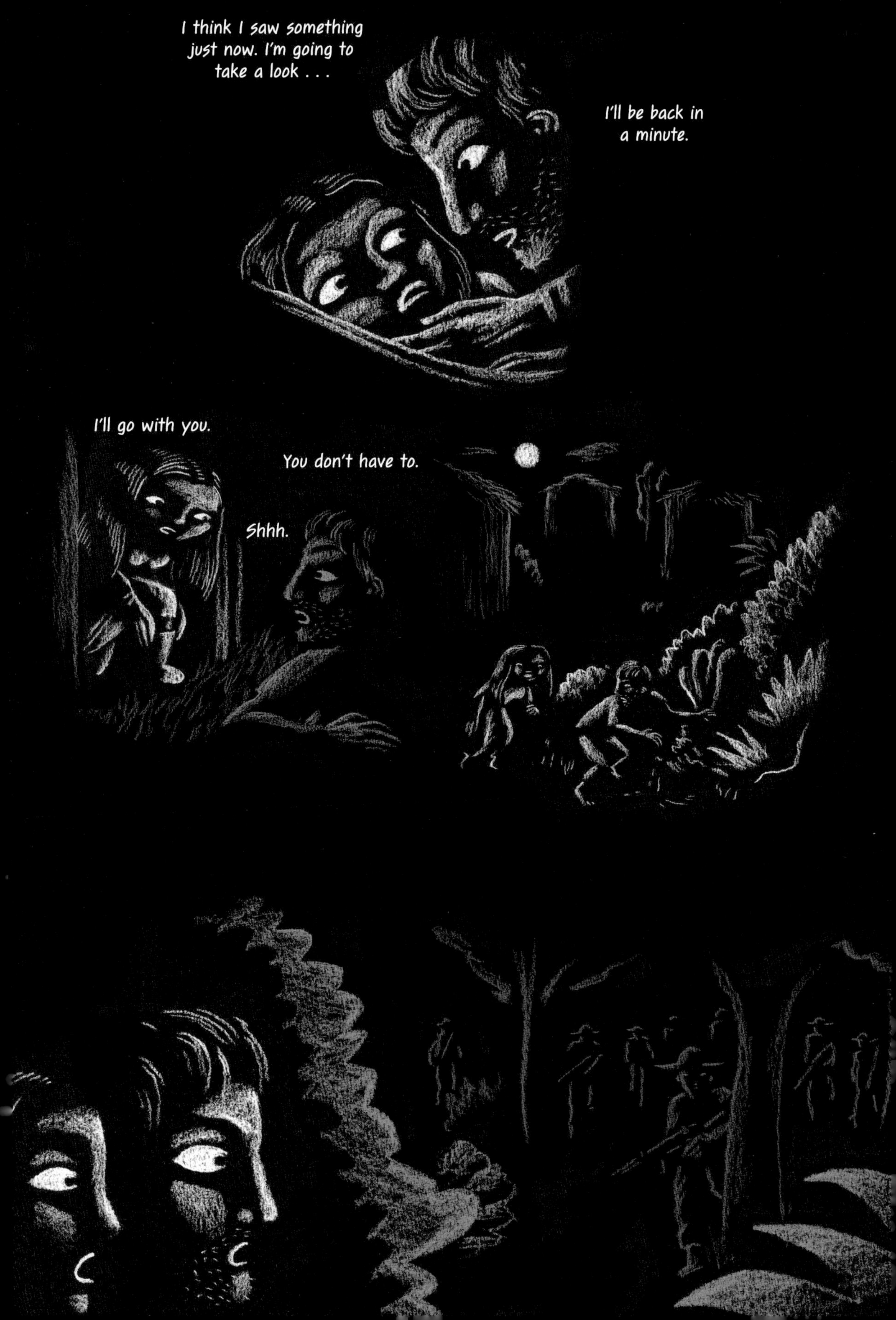
I think I saw something just now. I'm going to take a look . . .
I'll be back in a minute.
I'll go with you.
You don't have to.
Shhh.

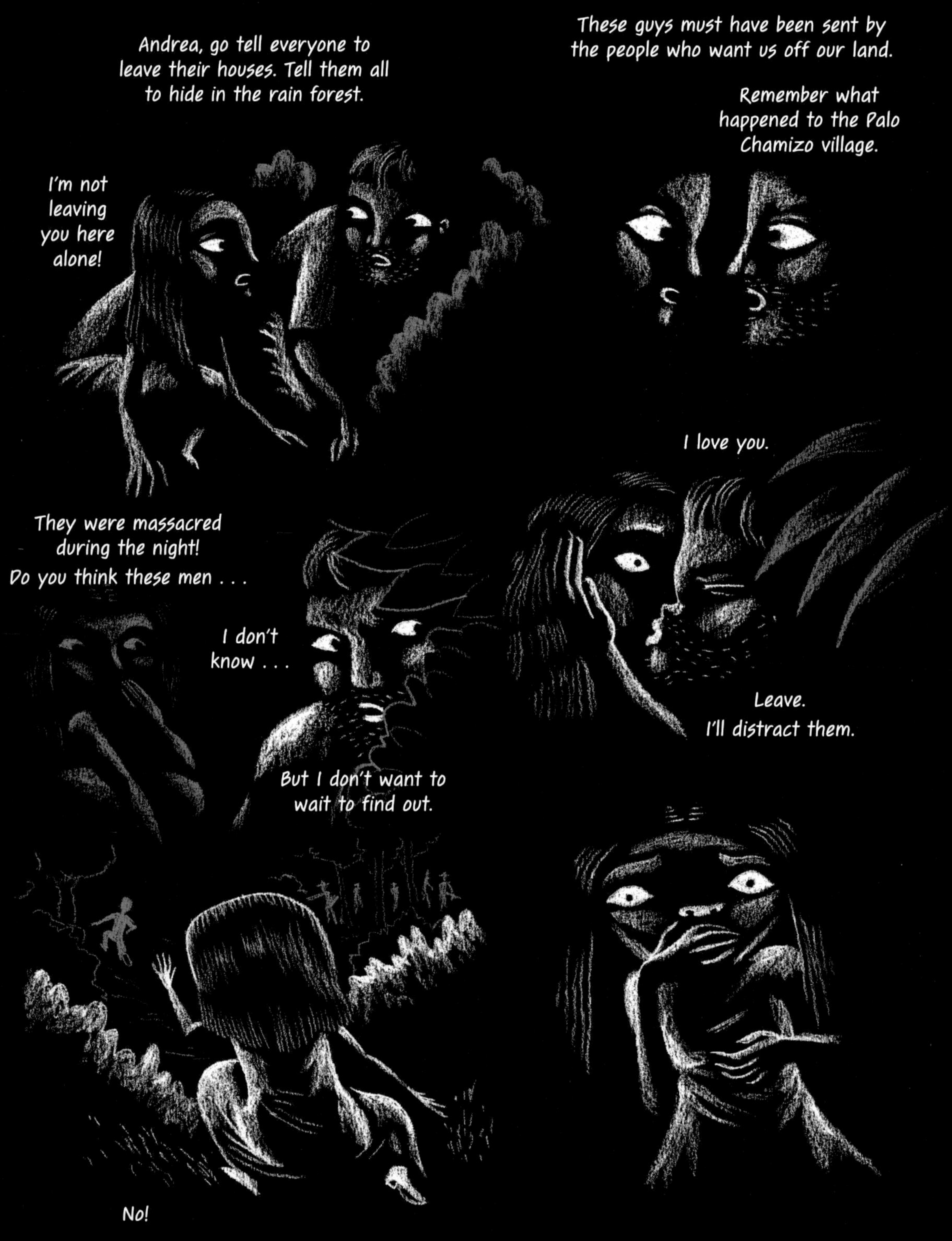

Andrea, go tell everyone to leave their houses. Tell them all to hide in the rain forest.
I'm not leaving you here alone!
These guys must have been sent by the people who want us off our land.
Remember what happened to the Palo Chamizo village.
They were massacred during the night!
Do you think these men . . .
I don't know . . .
But I don't want to wait to find out.
I love you.
Leave.
I'll distract them.
No!

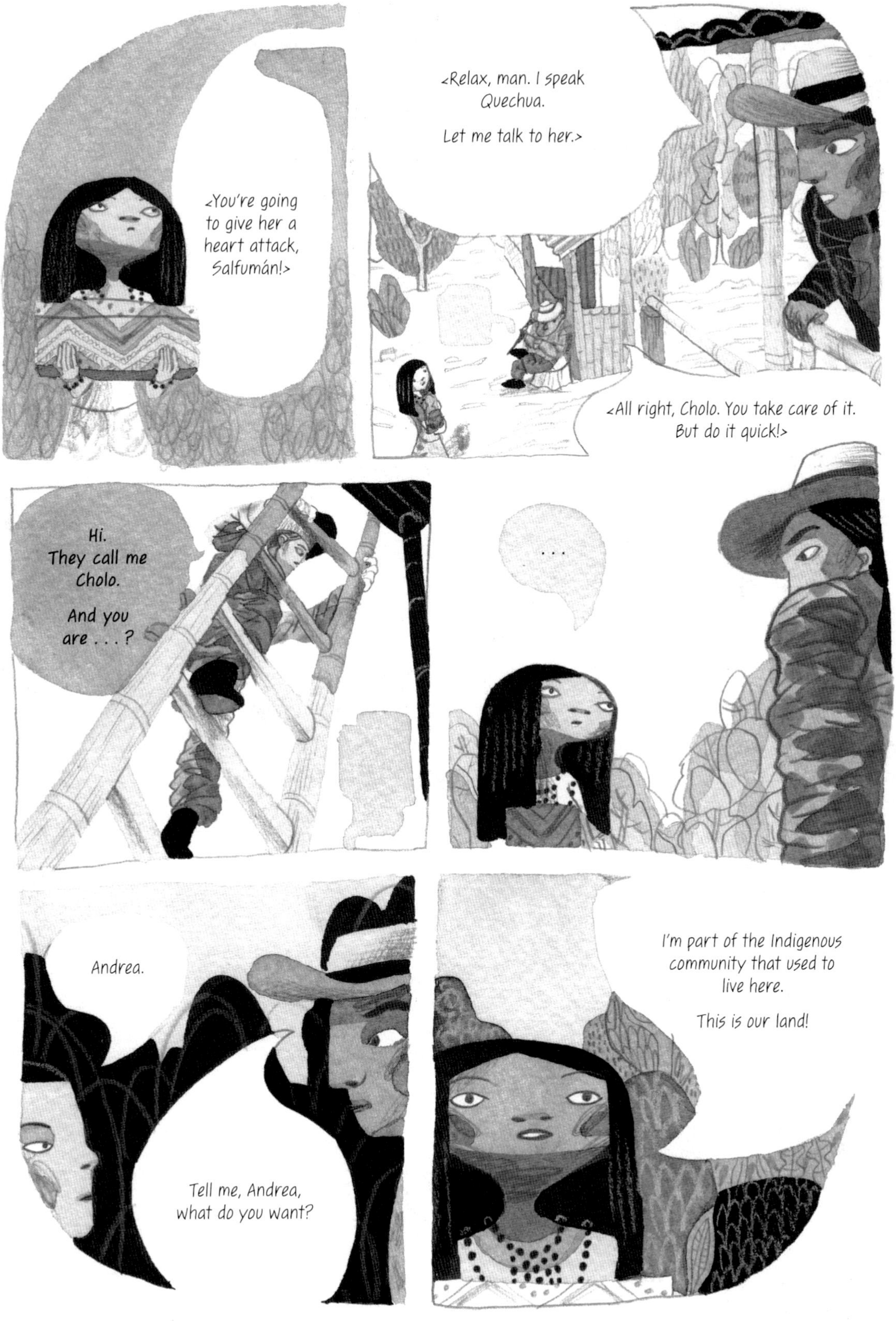
<You're going to give her a heart attack, Salfumán!>
<Relax, man. I speak Quechua.
Let me talk to her.>
<All right, Cholo. You take care of it. But do it quick!>
Hi. They call me Cholo.
And you are . . . ?
. . .
Andrea.
Tell me, Andrea, what do you want?
I'm part of the Indigenous community that used to live here.
This is our land!

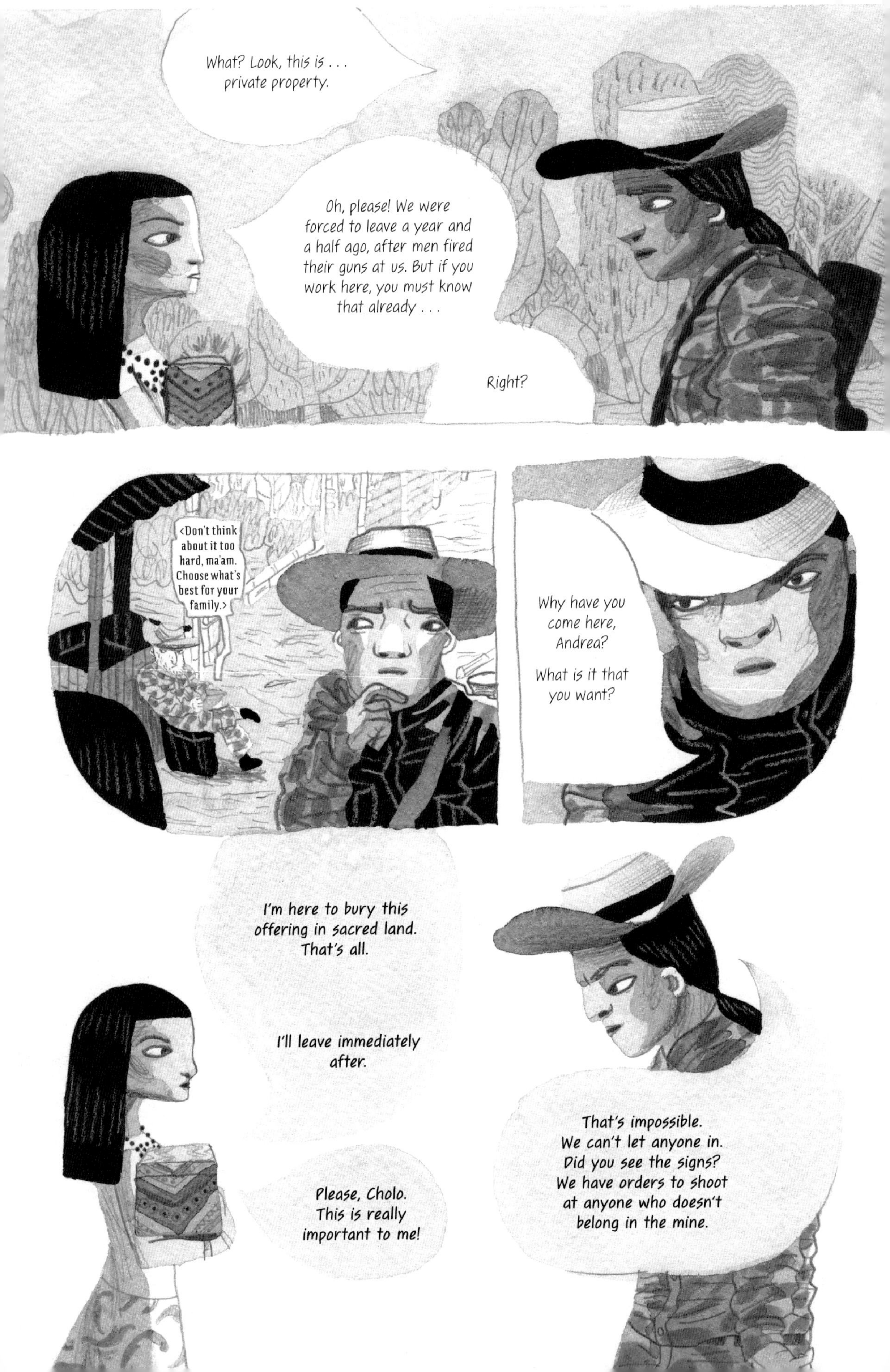
What? Look, this is . . . private property.
Oh, please! We were forced to leave a year and a half ago, after men fired their guns at us. But if you work here, you must know that already . . .
Right?
<Don't think about it too hard, ma'am. Choose what's best for your family.>
Why have you come here, Andrea?
What is it that you want?
I'm here to bury this offering in sacred land. That's all.
I'll leave immediately after.
That's impossible. We can't let anyone in. Did you see the signs? We have orders to shoot at anyone who doesn't belong in the mine.
Please, Cholo. This is really important to me!

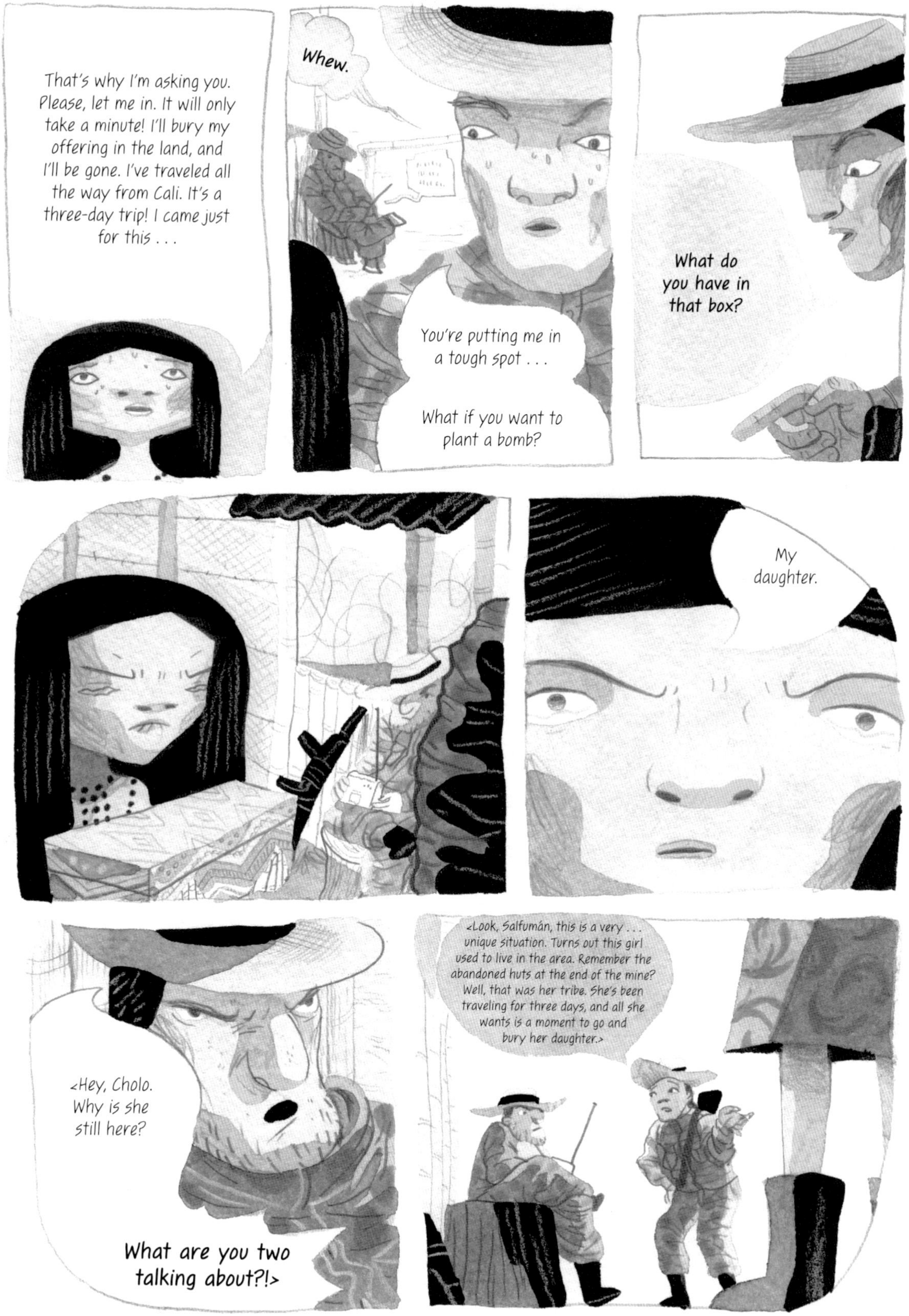
That's why I'm asking you. Please, let me in. It will only take a minute! I'll bury my offering in the land, and I'll be gone. I've traveled all the way from Cali. It's a three-day trip! I came just for this . . .
Whew.
You're putting me in a tough spot . . .
What if you want to plant a bomb?
What do you have in that box?
My daughter.
<Hey, Cholo. Why is she still here?
What are you two talking about?!>
<Look, Salfumán, this is a very . . . unique situation. Turns out this girl used to live in the area. Remember the abandoned huts at the end of the mine? Well, that was her tribe. She's been traveling for three days, and all she wants is a moment to go and bury her daughter.>

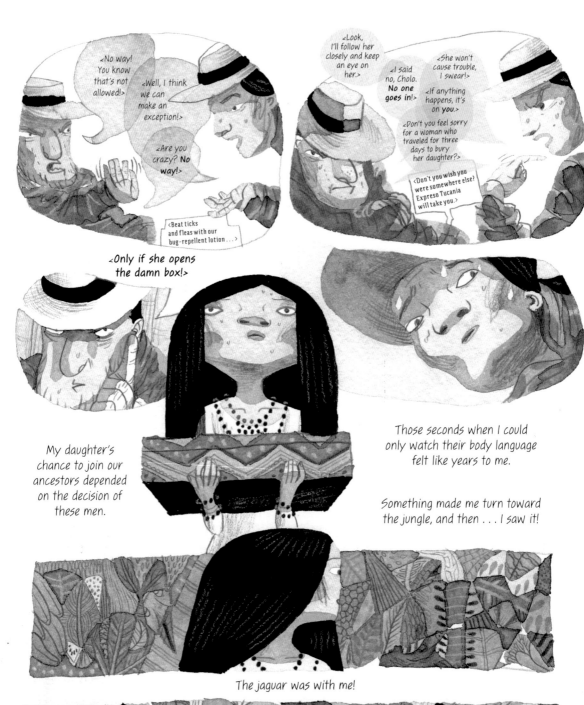

<No way! You know that's not allowed!>
<Well, I think we can make an exception!>
<Are you crazy? **No way!**>
<Beat ticks and fleas with our bug-repellent lotion . . .>
<Look, I'll follow her closely and keep an eye on her.>
<I said no, Cholo. **No one goes in**!>
<She won't cause trouble, I swear!>
<If anything happens, it's on **you**.>
<Don't you feel sorry for a woman who traveled for three days to bury her daughter?>
<Don't you wish you were somewhere else? Expreso Tucania will take you.>
<Only if she opens the damn box!>
My daughter's chance to join our ancestors depended on the decision of these men.
Those seconds when I could only watch their body language felt like years to me.
Something made me turn toward the jungle, and then . . . I saw it!
The jaguar was with me!

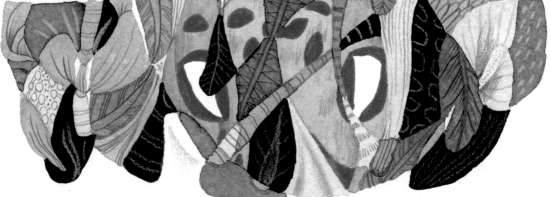

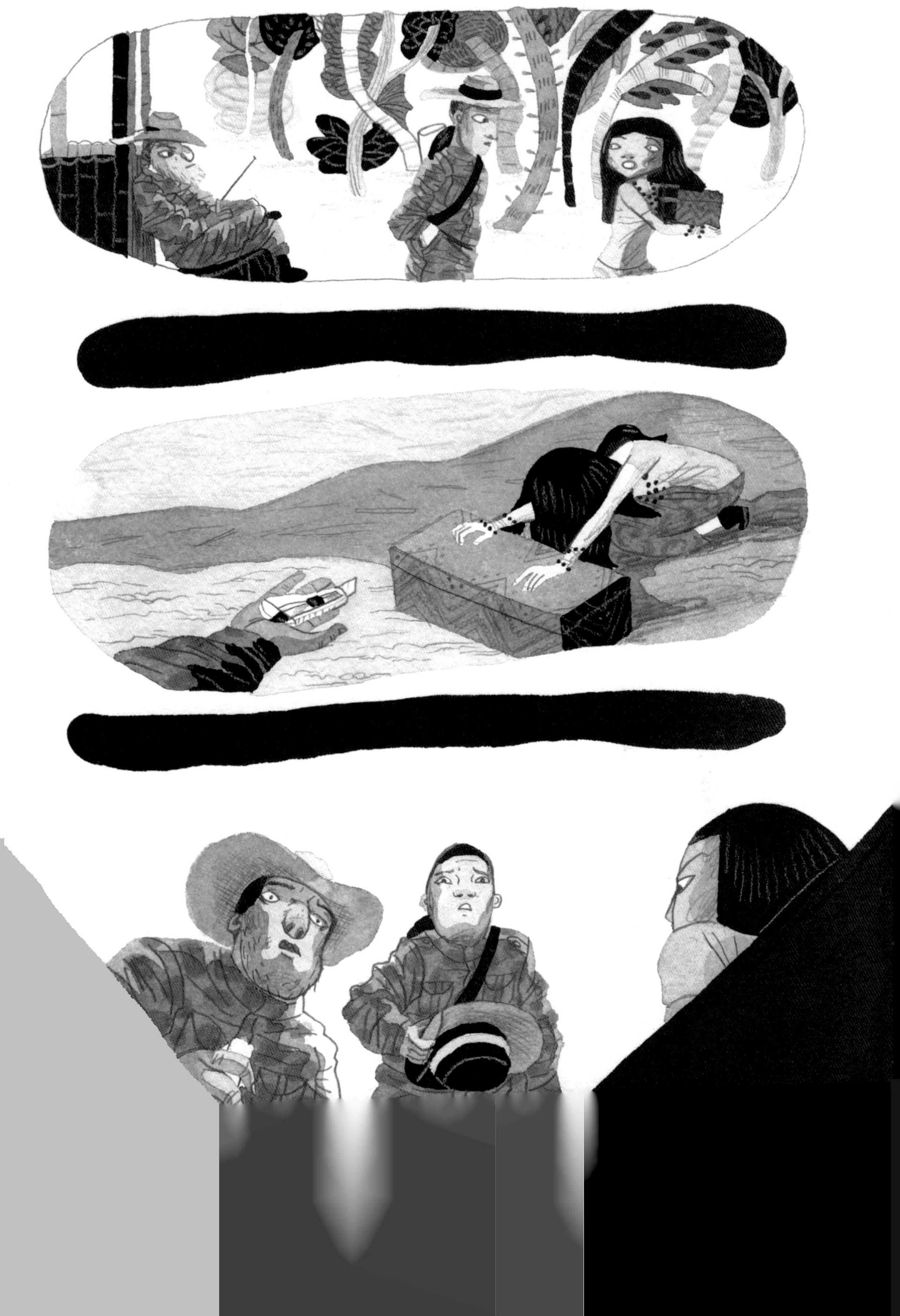

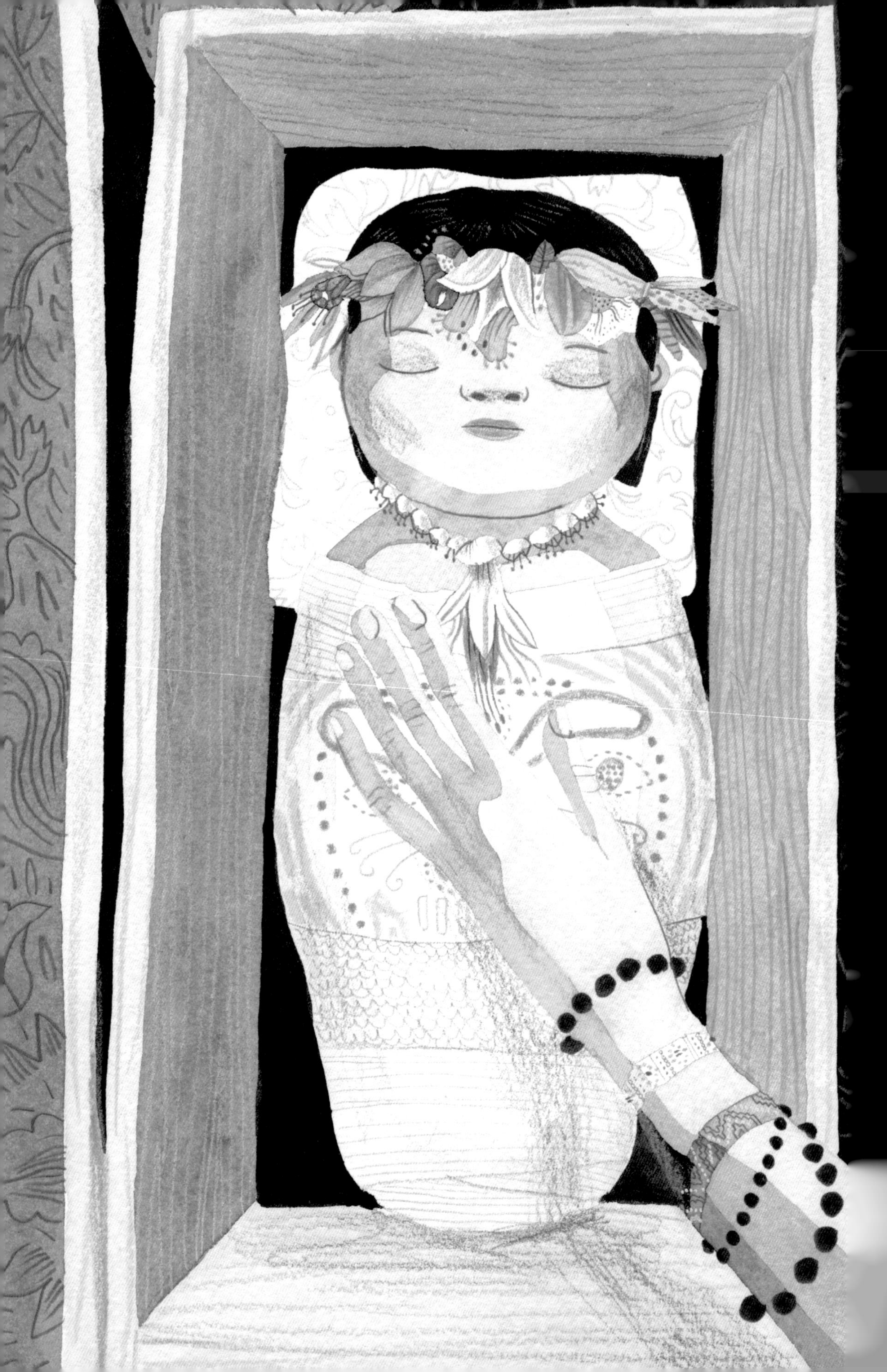

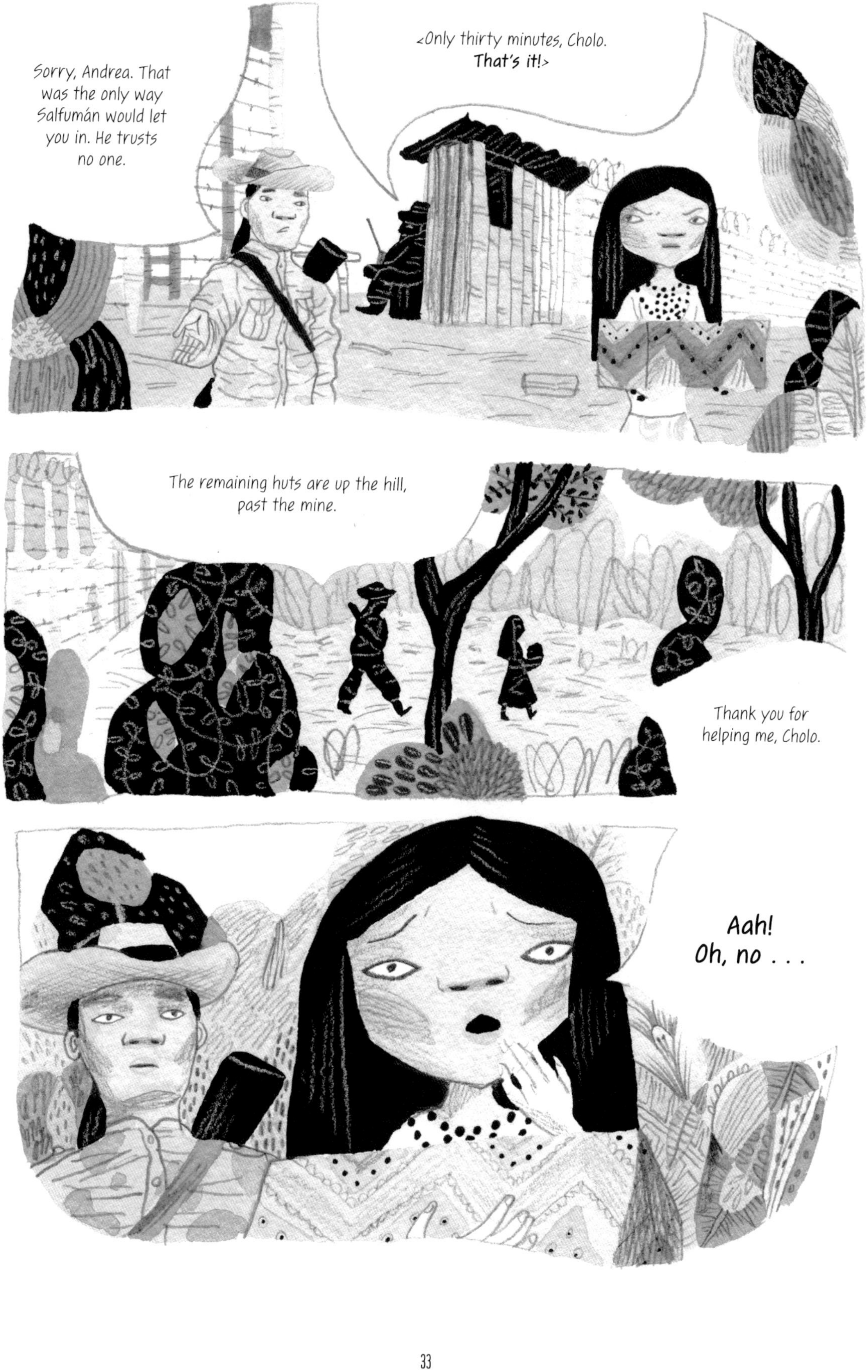
Sorry, Andrea. That was the only way Salfumán would let you in. He trusts no one.
<Only thirty minutes, Cholo. **That's it!**>
The remaining huts are up the hill, past the mine.
Thank you for helping me, Cholo.
Aah! Oh, no . . .

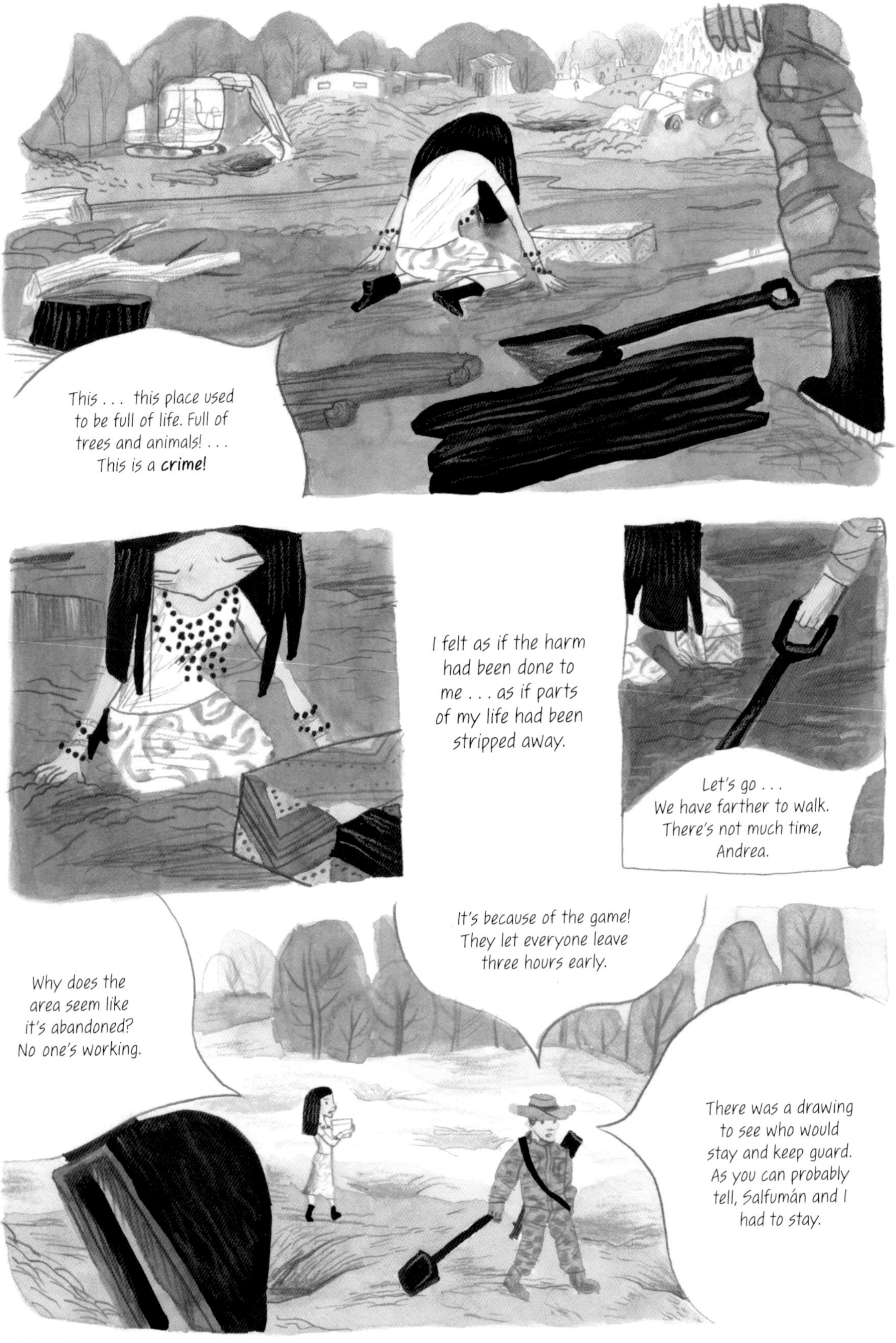
This . . . this place used to be full of life. Full of trees and animals! . . . This is a **crime!**
I felt as if the harm had been done to me . . . as if parts of my life had been stripped away.
Let's go . . . We have farther to walk. There's not much time, Andrea.
Why does the area seem like it's abandoned? No one's working.
It's because of the game! They let everyone leave three hours early.
There was a drawing to see who would stay and keep guard. As you can probably tell, Salfumán and I had to stay.

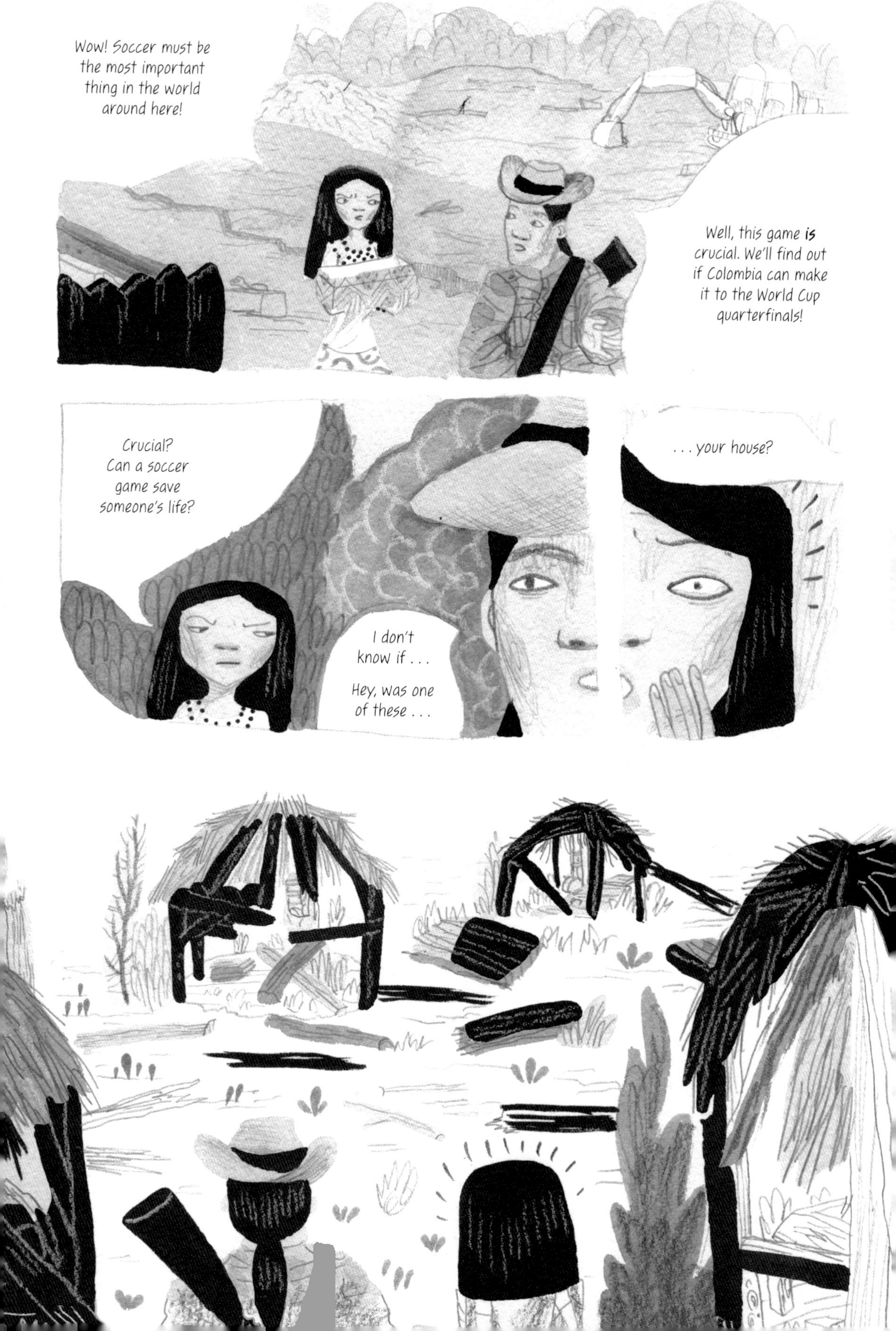

Wow! Soccer must be the most important thing in the world around here!
Well, this game **is** crucial. We'll find out if Colombia can make it to the World Cup quarterfinals!
Crucial? Can a soccer game save someone's life?
I don't know if . . .
Hey, was one of these . . .
. . . your house?

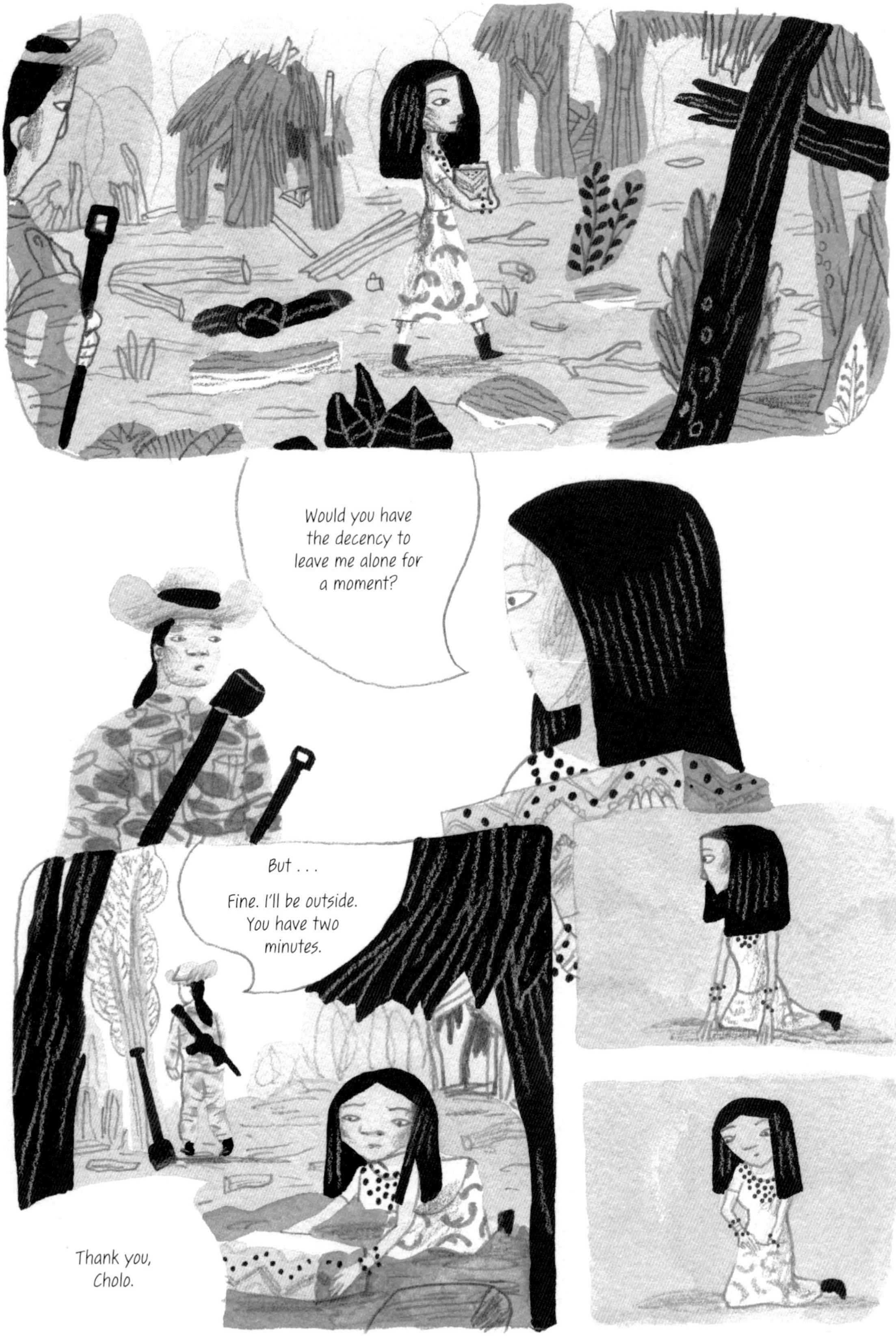
Would you have the decency to leave me alone for a moment?
But . . .
Fine. I'll be outside. You have two minutes.
Thank you, Cholo.

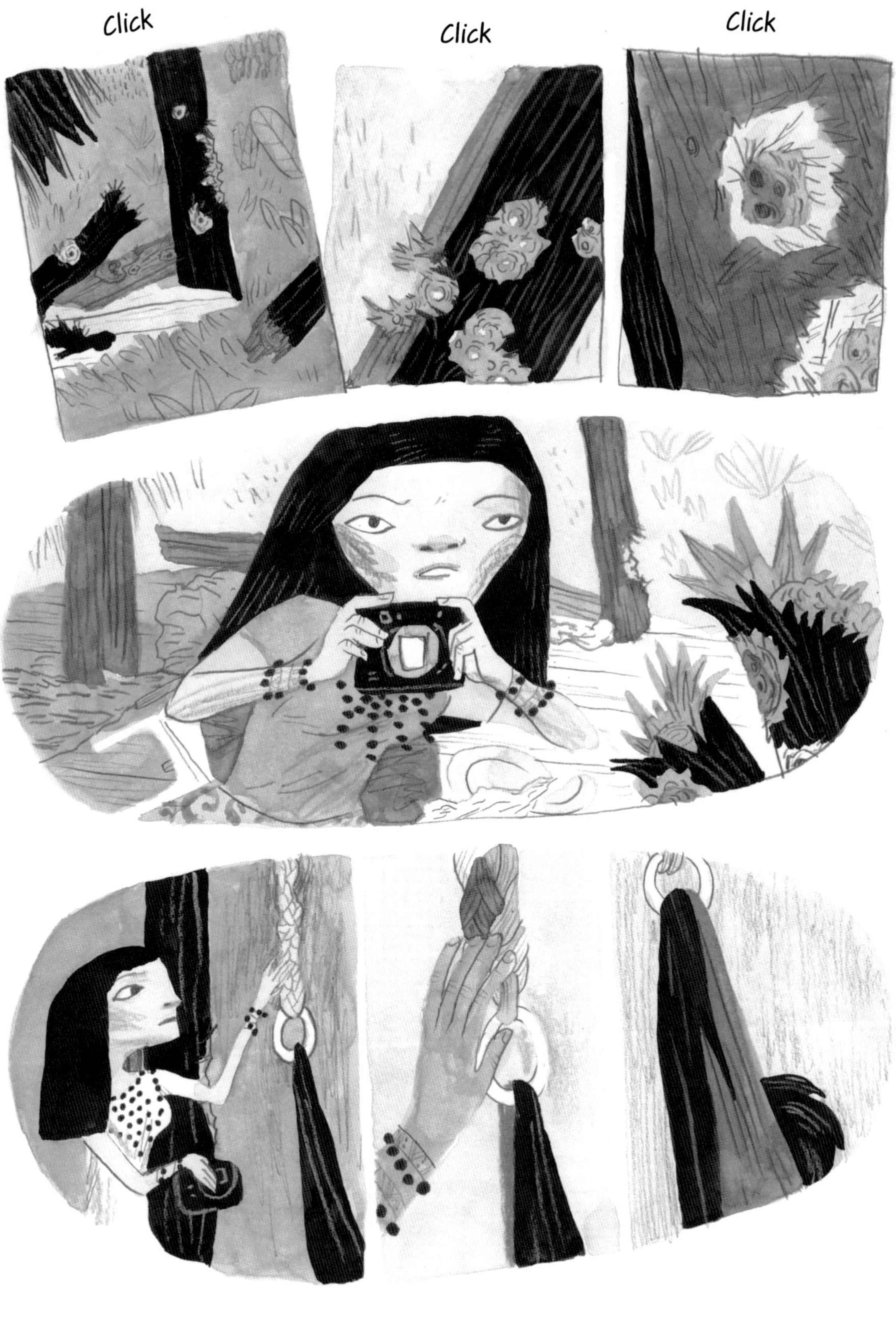
Click
Click
Click

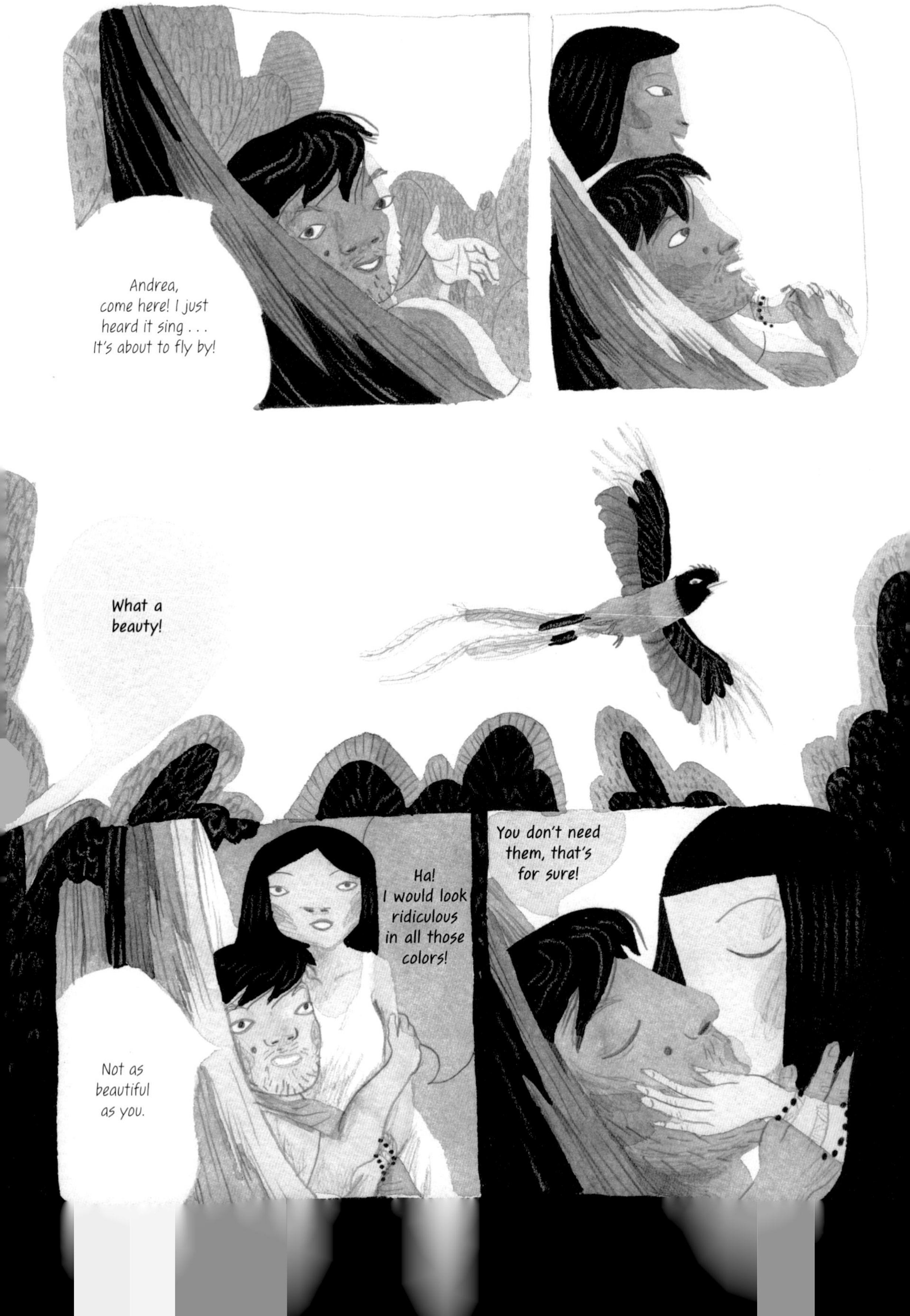
Andrea, come here! I just heard it sing . . . It's about to fly by!
What a beauty!
Not as beautiful as you.
Ha! I would look ridiculous in all those colors!
You don't need them, that's for sure!

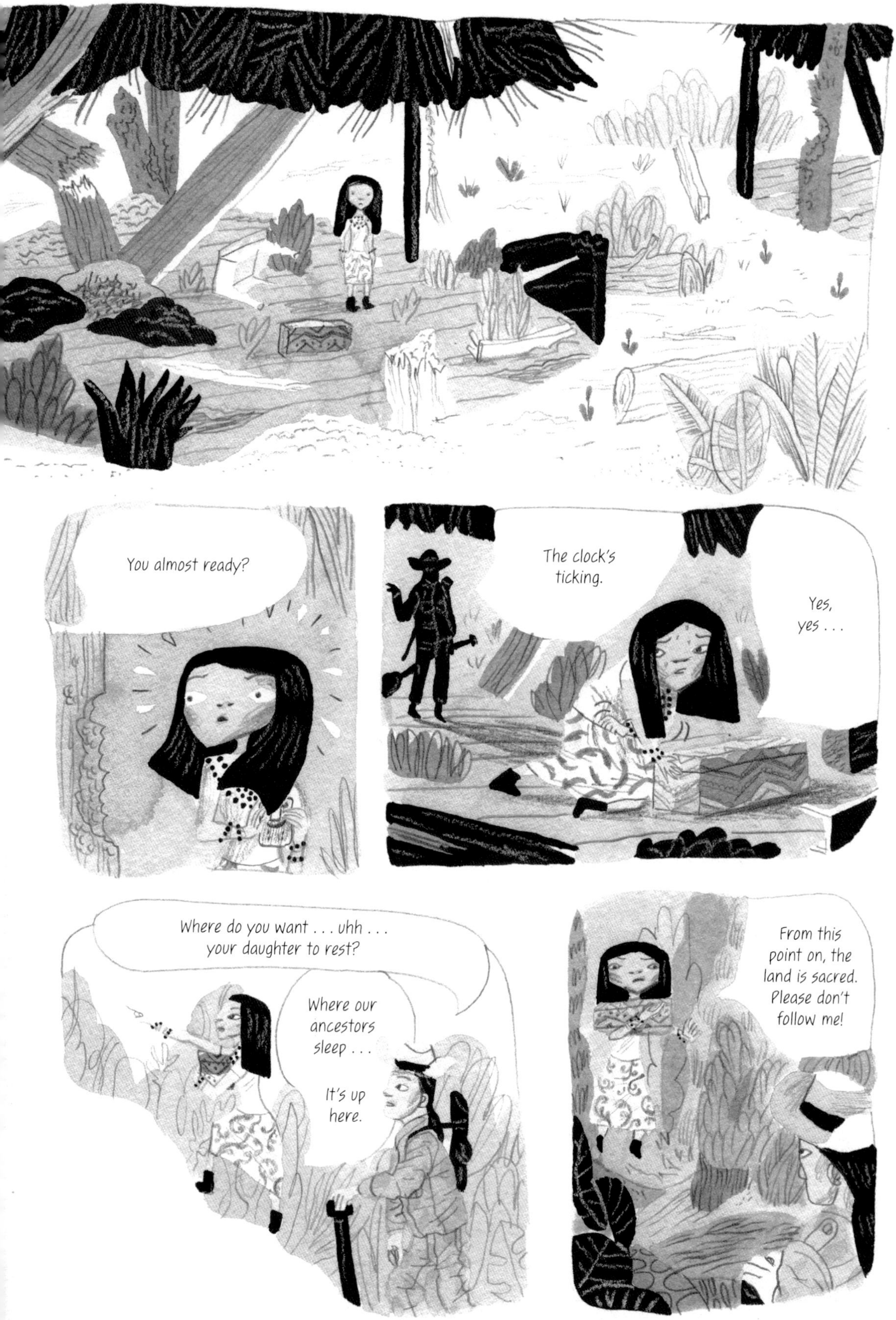

You almost ready?
The clock's ticking.
Yes, yes . . .
Where do you want . . . uhh . . . your daughter to rest?
Where our ancestors sleep . . .
It's up here.
From this point on, the land is sacred. Please don't follow me!

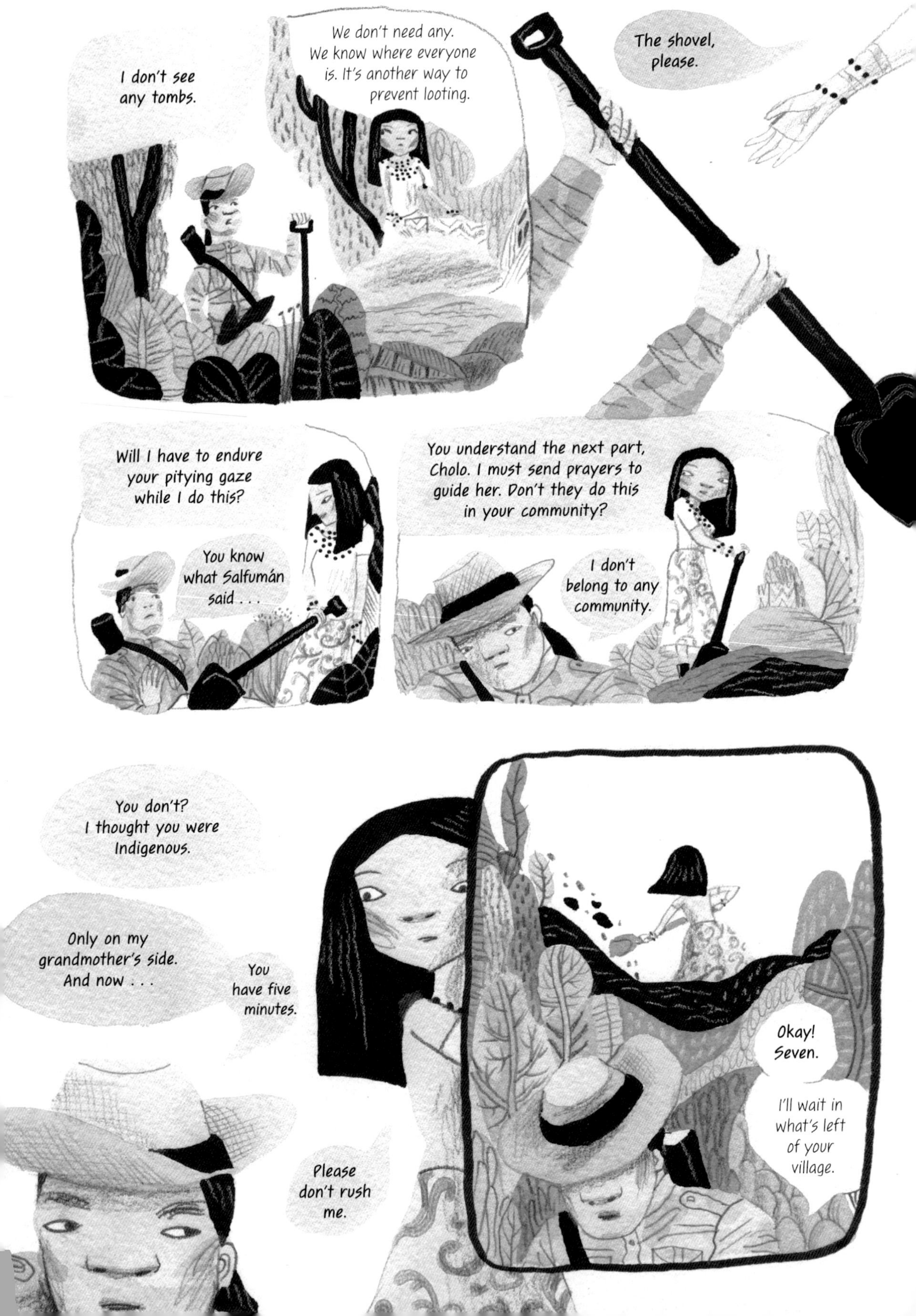
I don't see any tombs.
We don't need any. We know where everyone is. It's another way to prevent looting.
The shovel, please.
Will I have to endure your pitying gaze while I do this?
You know what Salfumán said . . .
You understand the next part, Cholo. I must send prayers to guide her. Don't they do this in your community?
I don't belong to any community.
You don't? I thought you were Indigenous.
Only on my grandmother's side. And now . . .
You have five minutes.
Please don't rush me.
Okay! Seven.
I'll wait in what's left of your village.

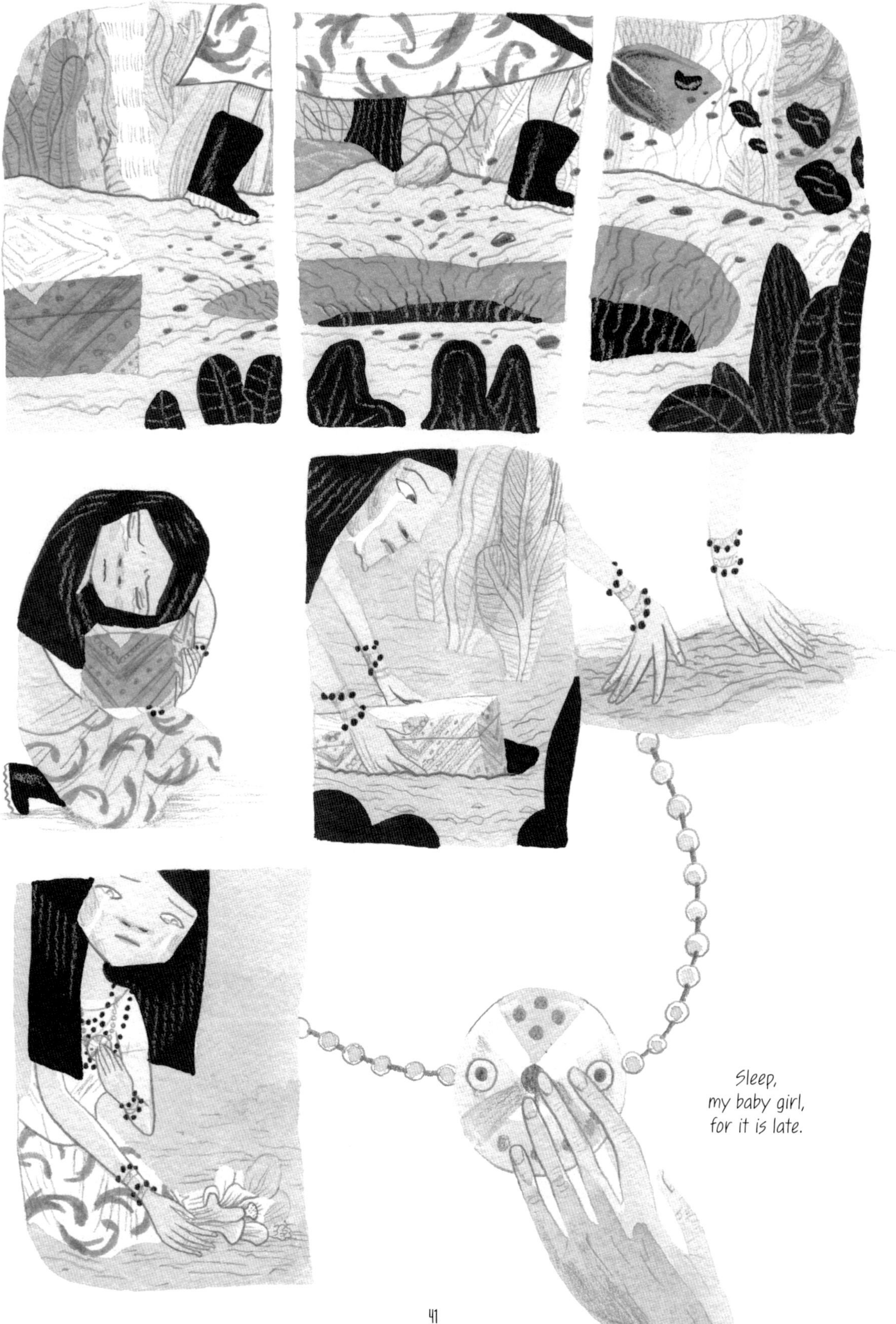
Sleep,
my baby girl,
for it is late.

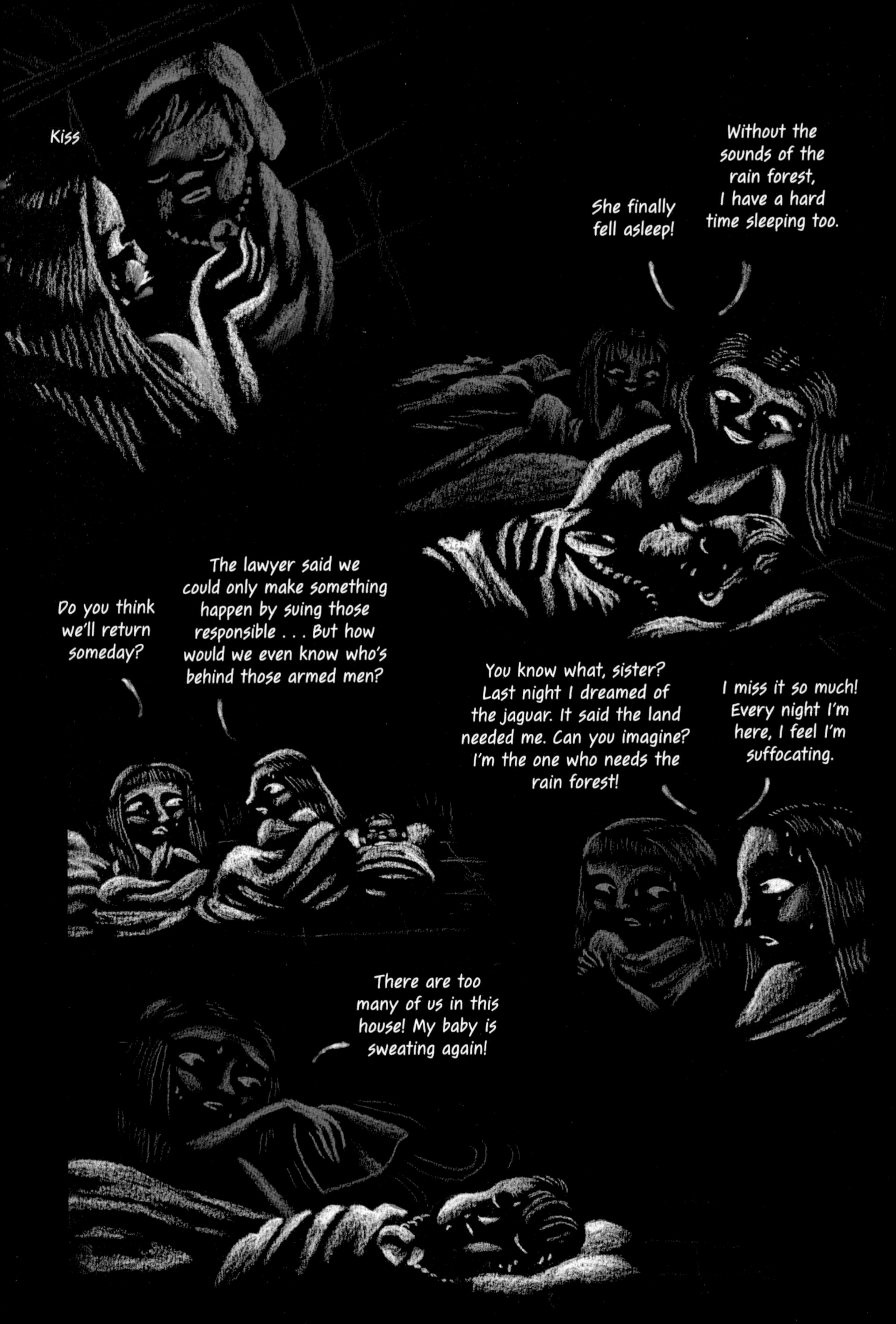
Kiss
She finally fell asleep!
Without the sounds of the rain forest, I have a hard time sleeping too.
Do you think we'll return someday?
The lawyer said we could only make something happen by suing those responsible . . . But how would we even know who's behind those armed men?
You know what, sister? Last night I dreamed of the jaguar. It said the land needed me. Can you imagine? I'm the one who needs the rain forest!
I miss it so much! Every night I'm here, I feel I'm suffocating.
There are too many of us in this house! My baby is sweating again!

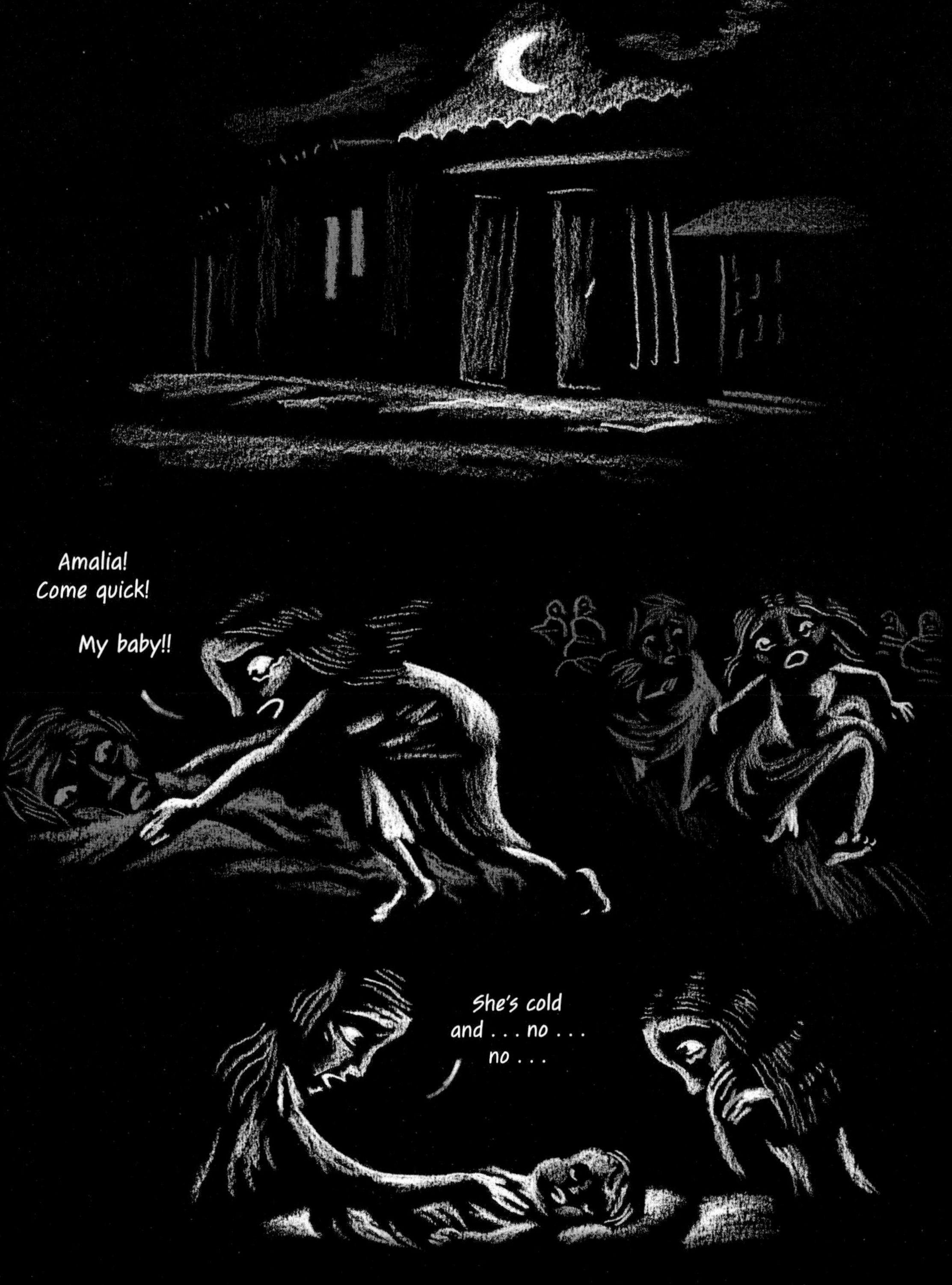
Amalia! Come quick!
My baby!!
She's cold and . . . no . . . no . . .

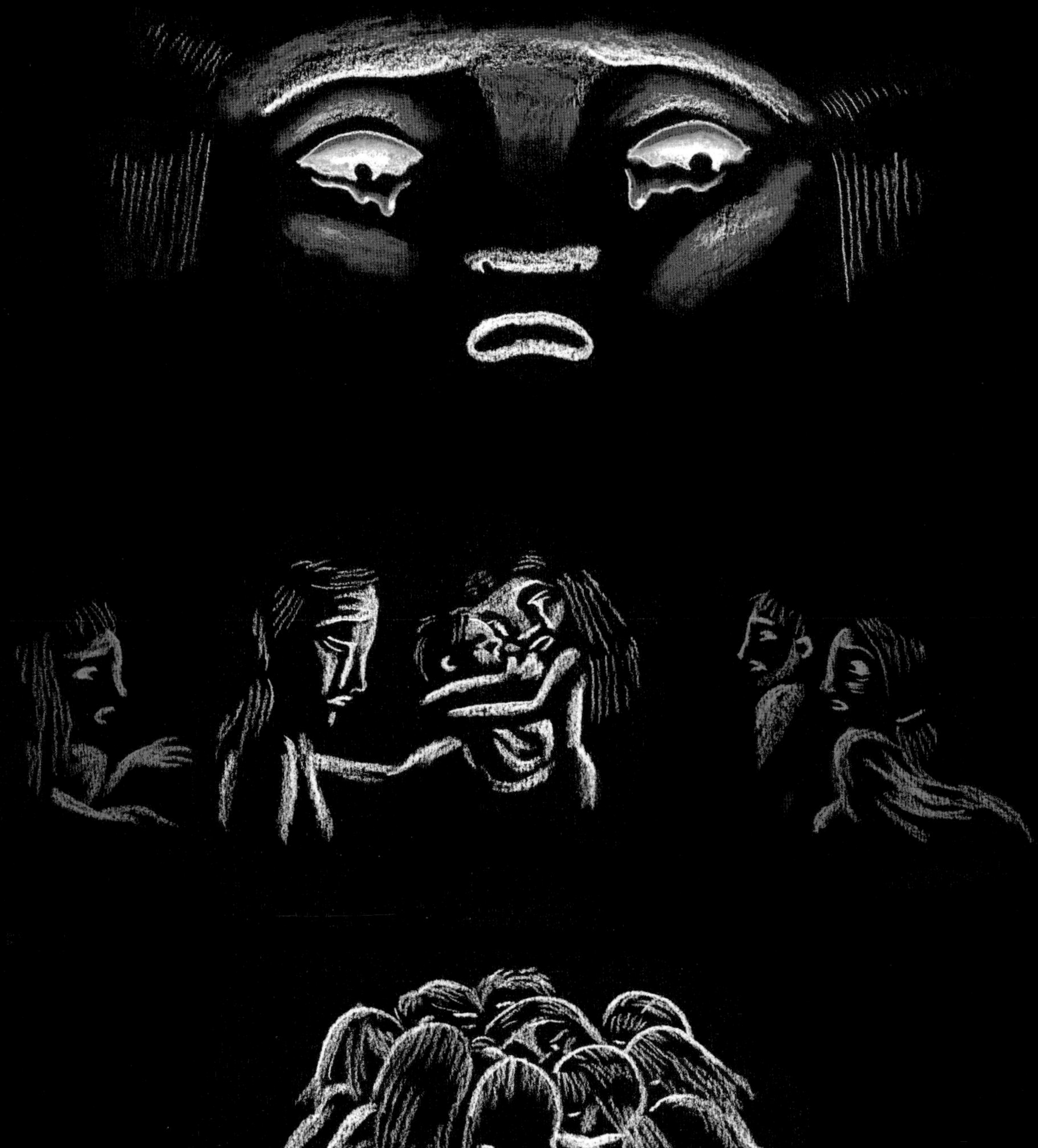

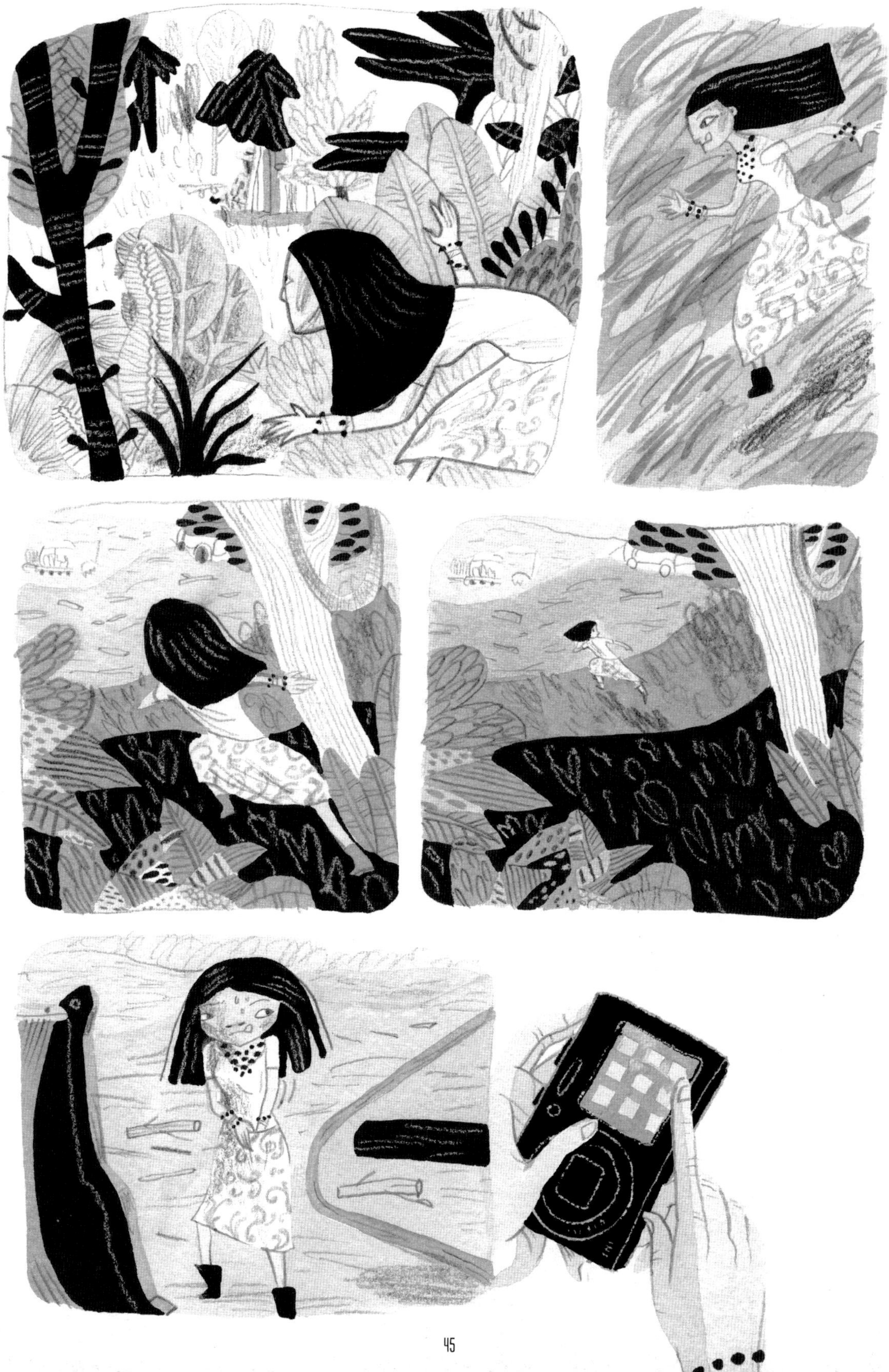

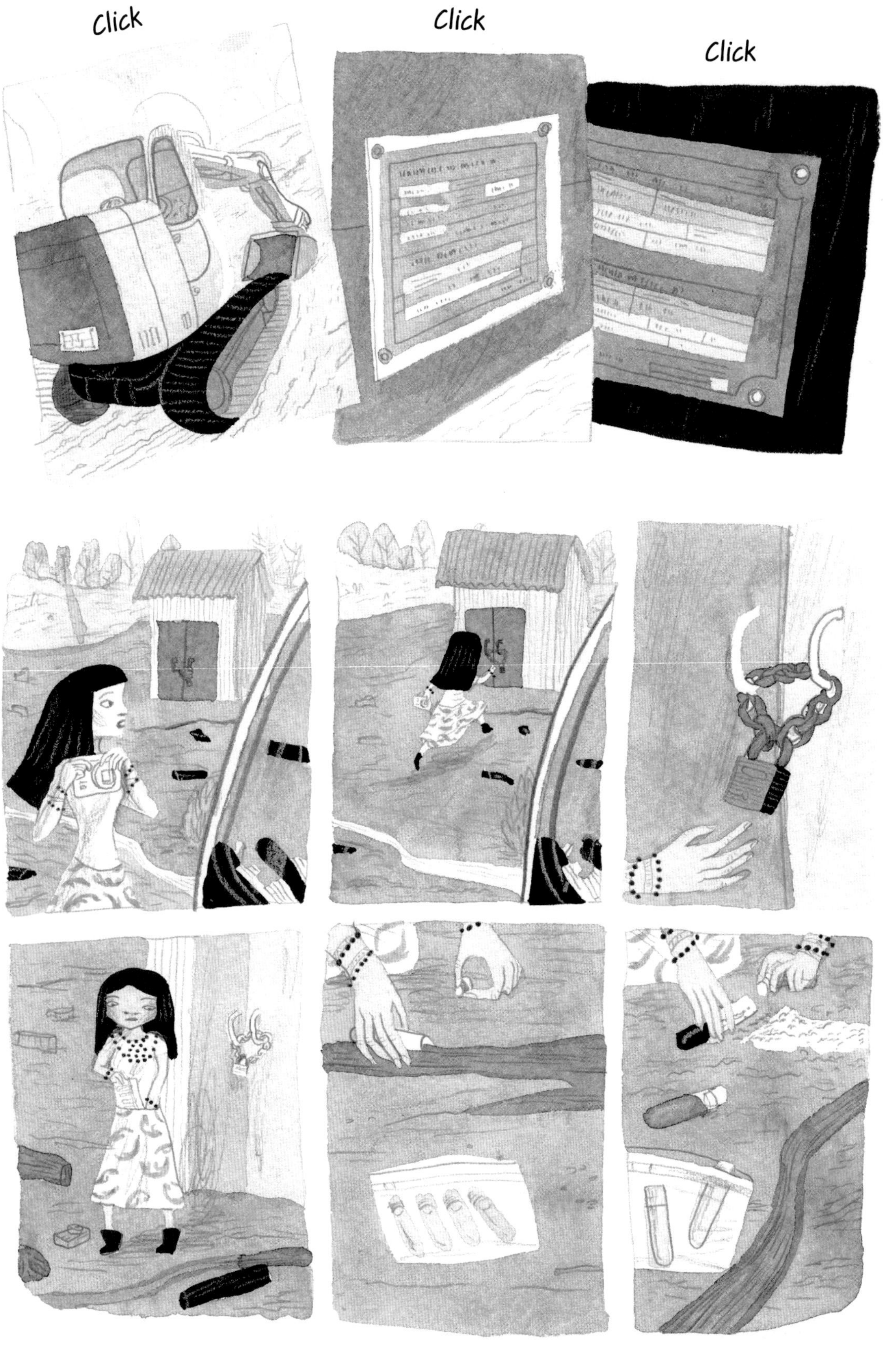
Click
Click
Click

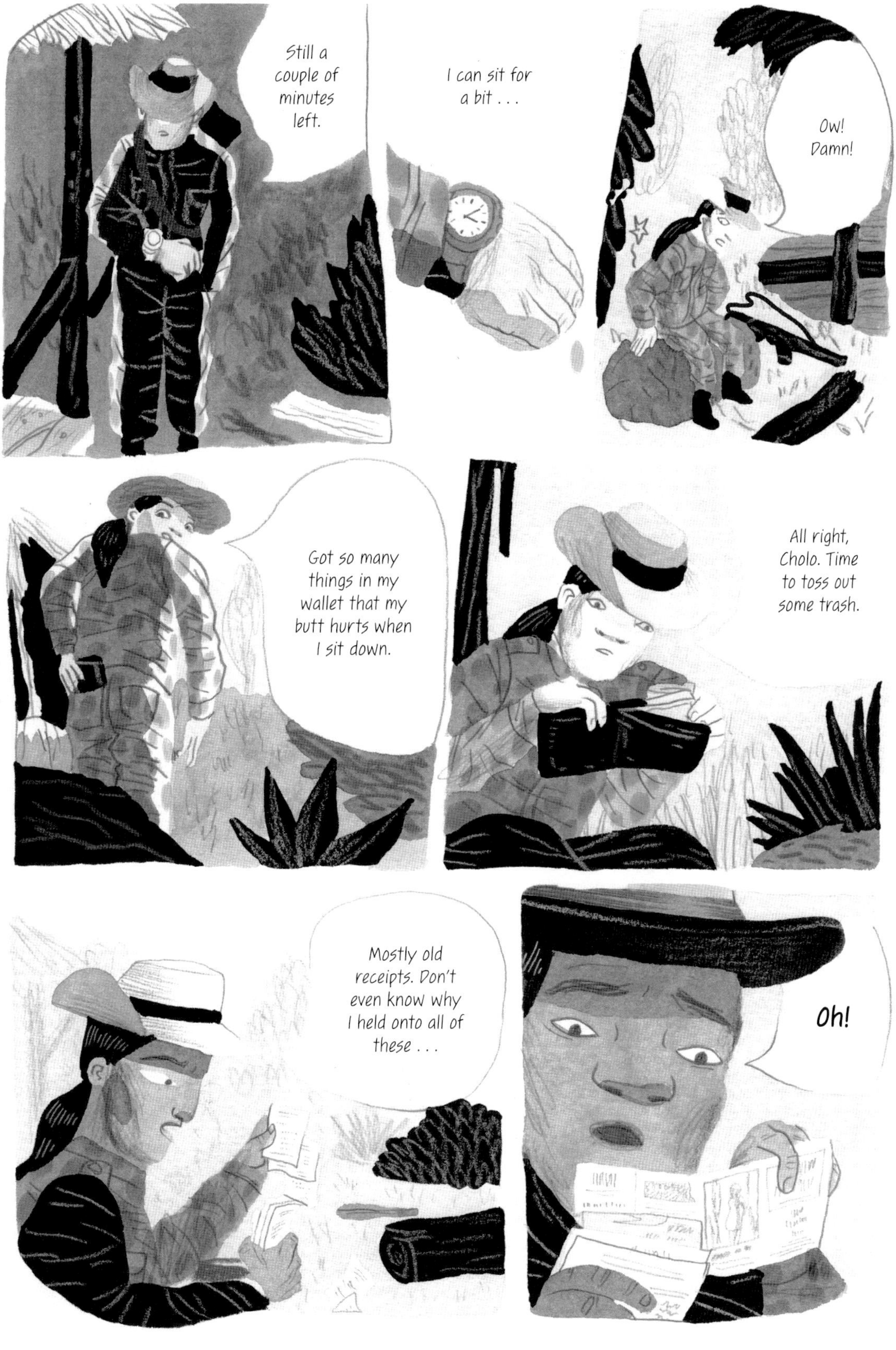
Still a couple of minutes left.
I can sit for a bit . . .
Ow! Damn!
Got so many things in my wallet that my butt hurts when I sit down.
All right, Cholo. Time to toss out some trash.
Mostly old receipts. Don't even know why I held onto all of these . . .
Oh!

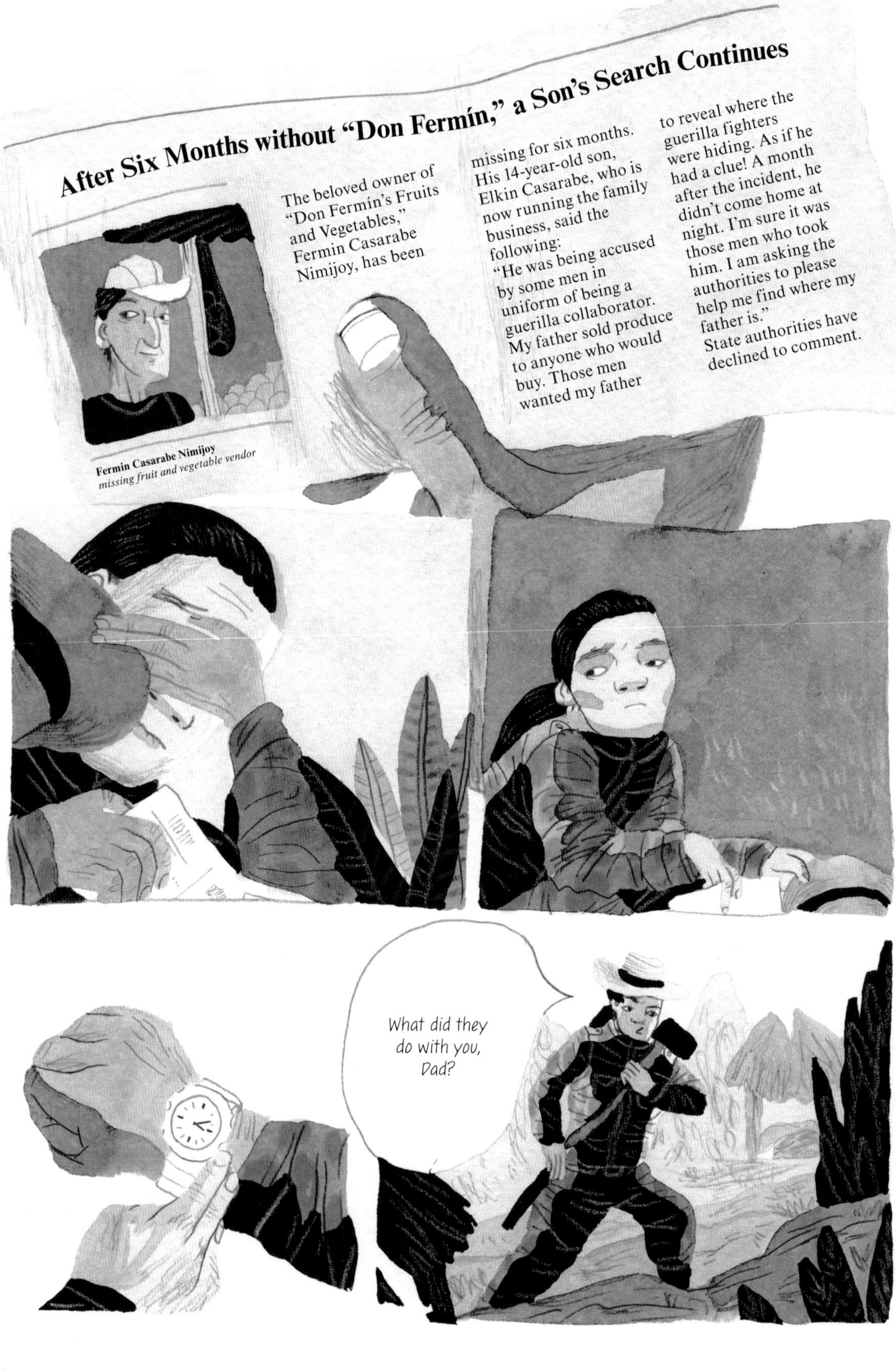
After Six Months without "Don Fermín," a Son's Search Continues
The beloved owner of "Don Fermín's Fruits and Vegetables," Fermin Casarabe Nimijoy, has been missing for six months. His 14-year-old son, Elkin Casarabe, who is now running the family business, said the following:
"He was being accused by some men in uniform of being a guerilla collaborator. My father sold produce to anyone who would buy. Those men wanted my father to reveal where the guerilla fighters were hiding. As if he had a clue! A month after the incident, he didn't come home at night. I'm sure it was those men who took him. I am asking the authorities to please help me find where my father is."
State authorities have declined to comment.
Fermin Casarabe Nimijoy
missing fruit and vegetable vendor
What did they do with you, Dad?

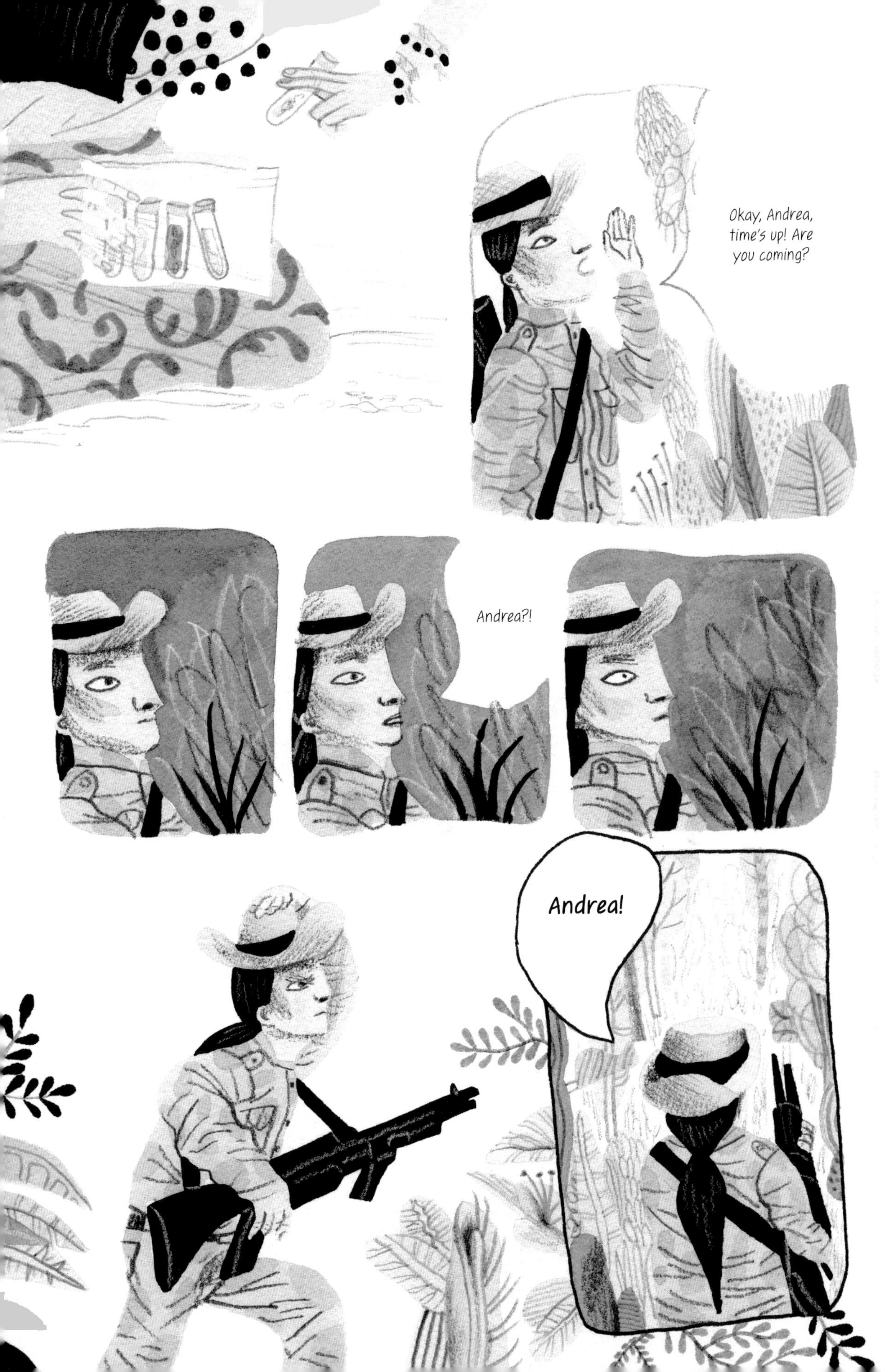
Okay, Andrea, time's up! Are you coming?
Andrea?!
Andrea!

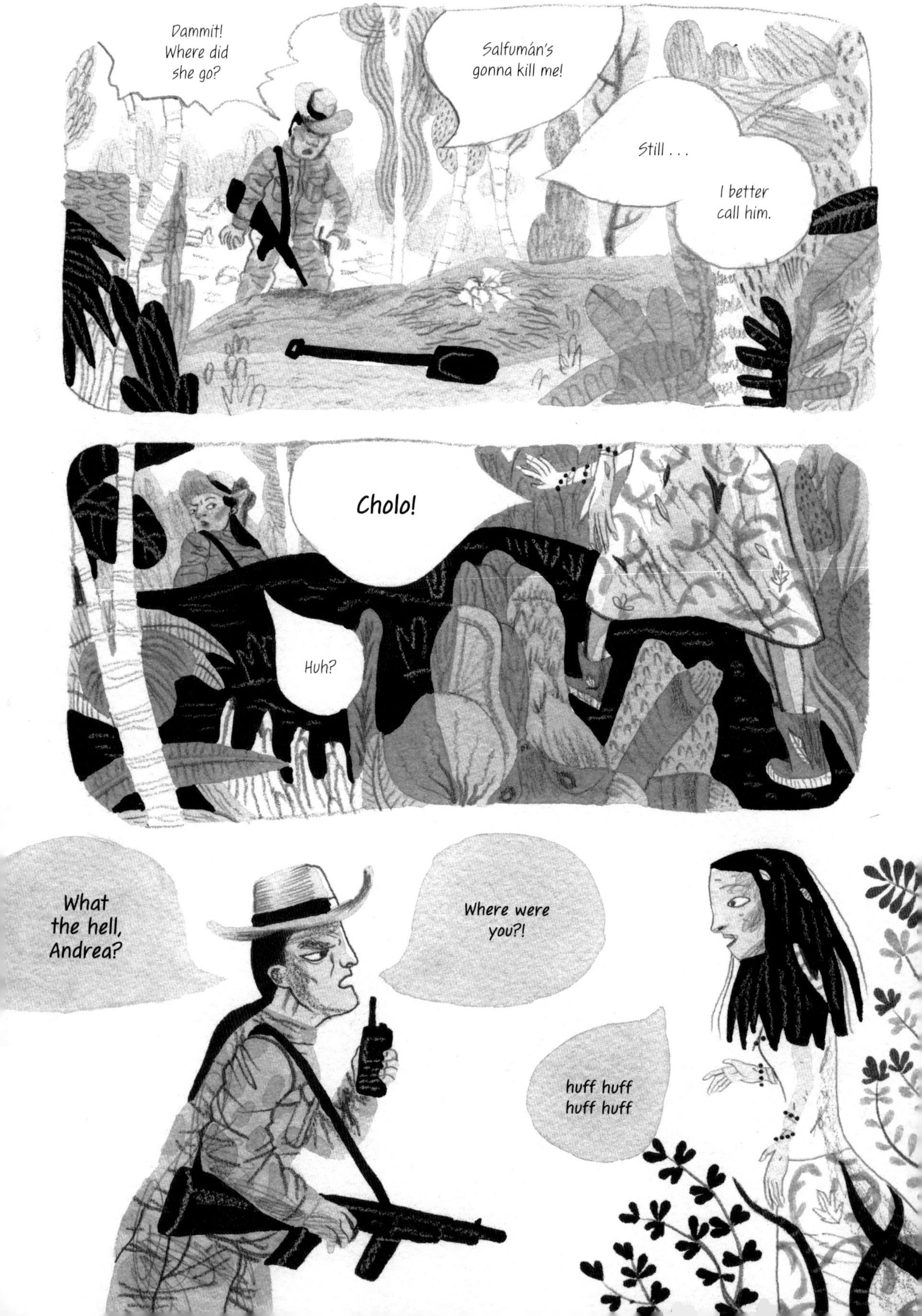
Dammit! Where did she go?
Salfumán's gonna kill me!
Still . . .
I better call him.
Cholo!
Huh?
What the hell, Andrea?
Where were you?!
huff huff huff huff

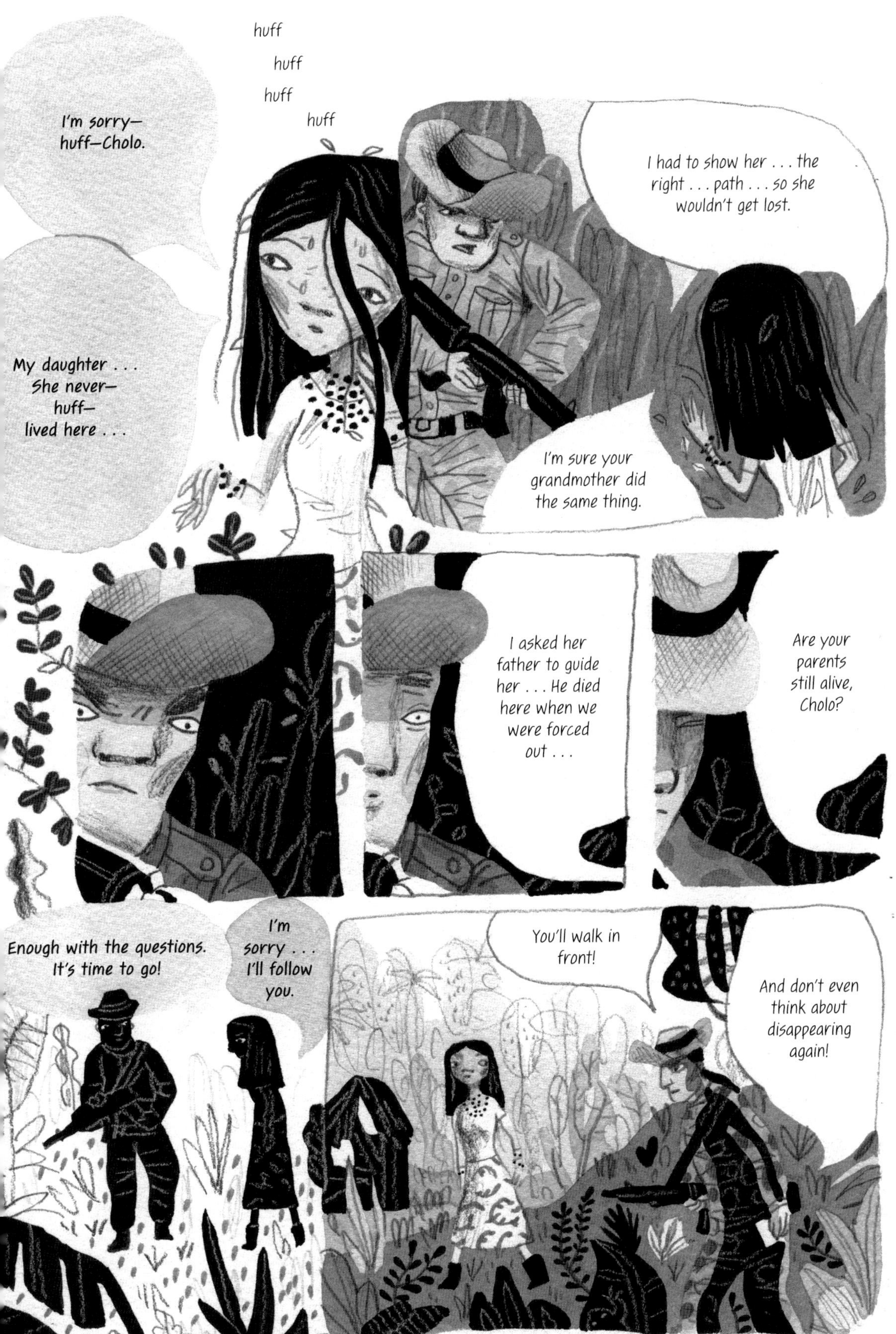
huff
huff
huff
huff
I'm sorry—huff—Cholo.
I had to show her . . . the right . . . path . . . so she wouldn't get lost.
My daughter . . . She never—huff—lived here . . .
I'm sure your grandmother did the same thing.
I asked her father to guide her . . . He died here when we were forced out . . .
Are your parents still alive, Cholo?
Enough with the questions. It's time to go!
I'm sorry . . . I'll follow you.
You'll walk in front!
And don't even think about disappearing again!

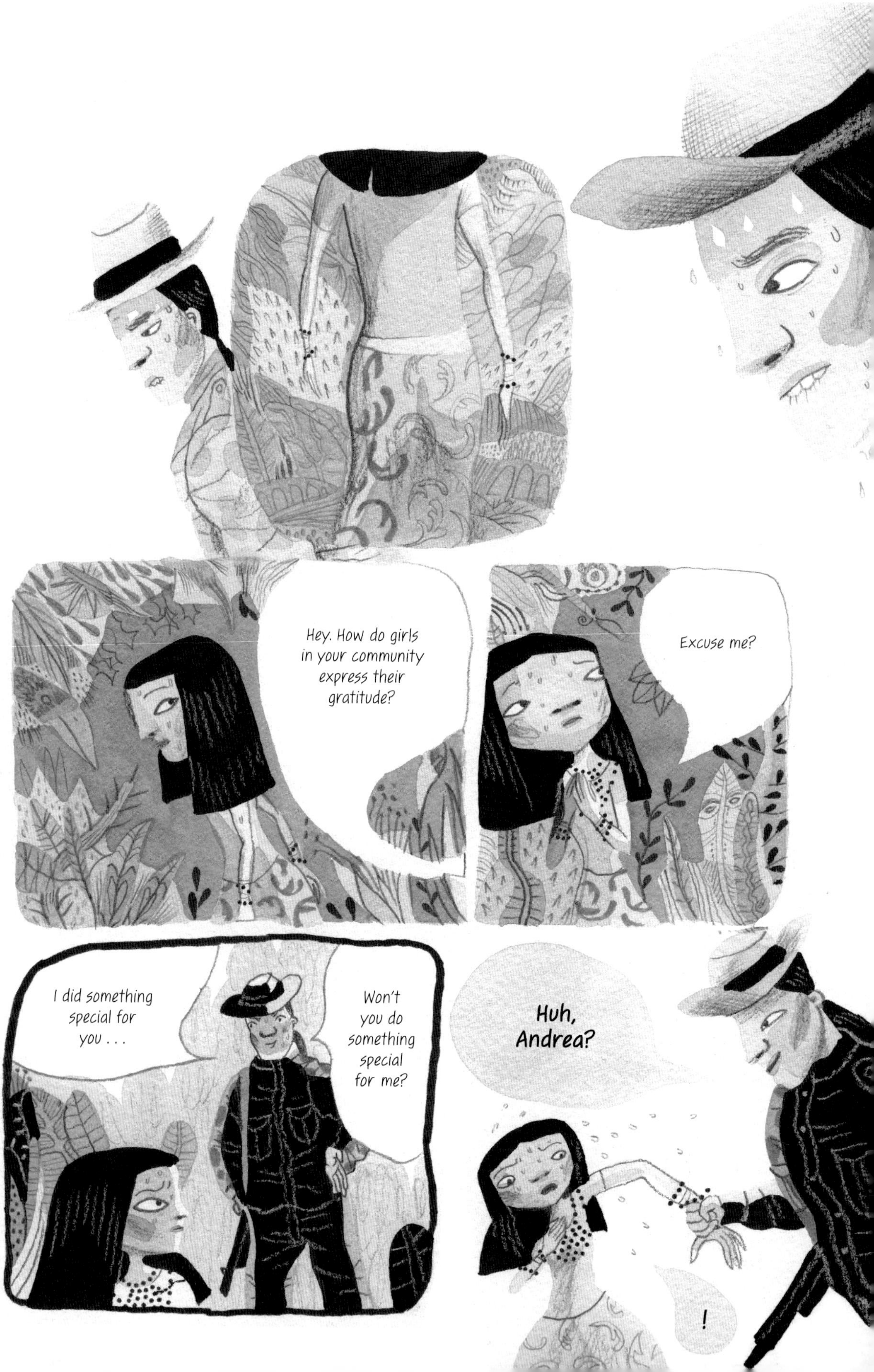

Hey. How do girls in your community express their gratitude?
Excuse me?
I did something special for you . . .
Won't you do something special for me?
Huh, Andrea?
!

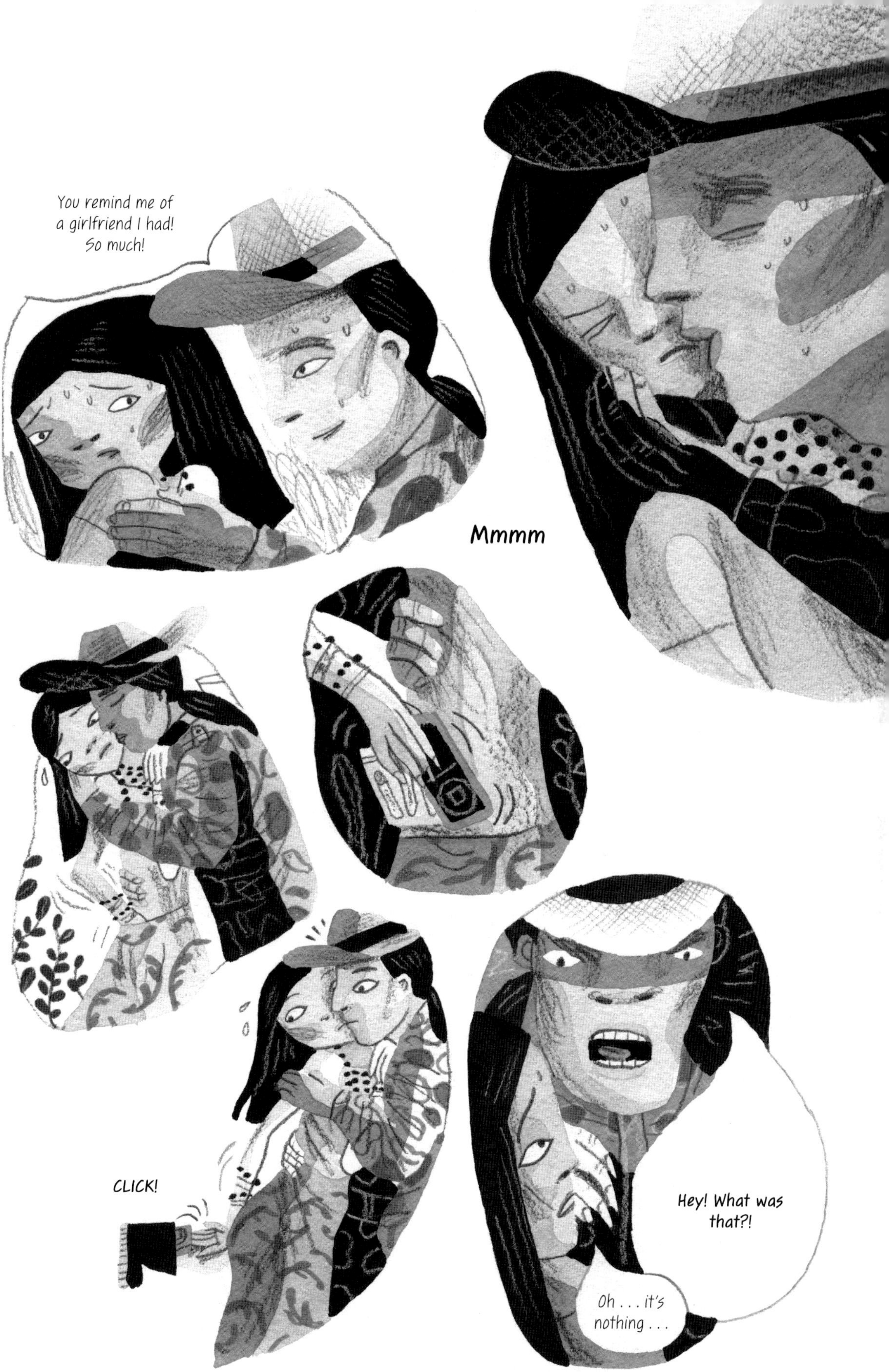
You remind me of a girlfriend I had! So much!
Mmmm
CLICK!
Hey! What was that?!
Oh . . . it's nothing . . .

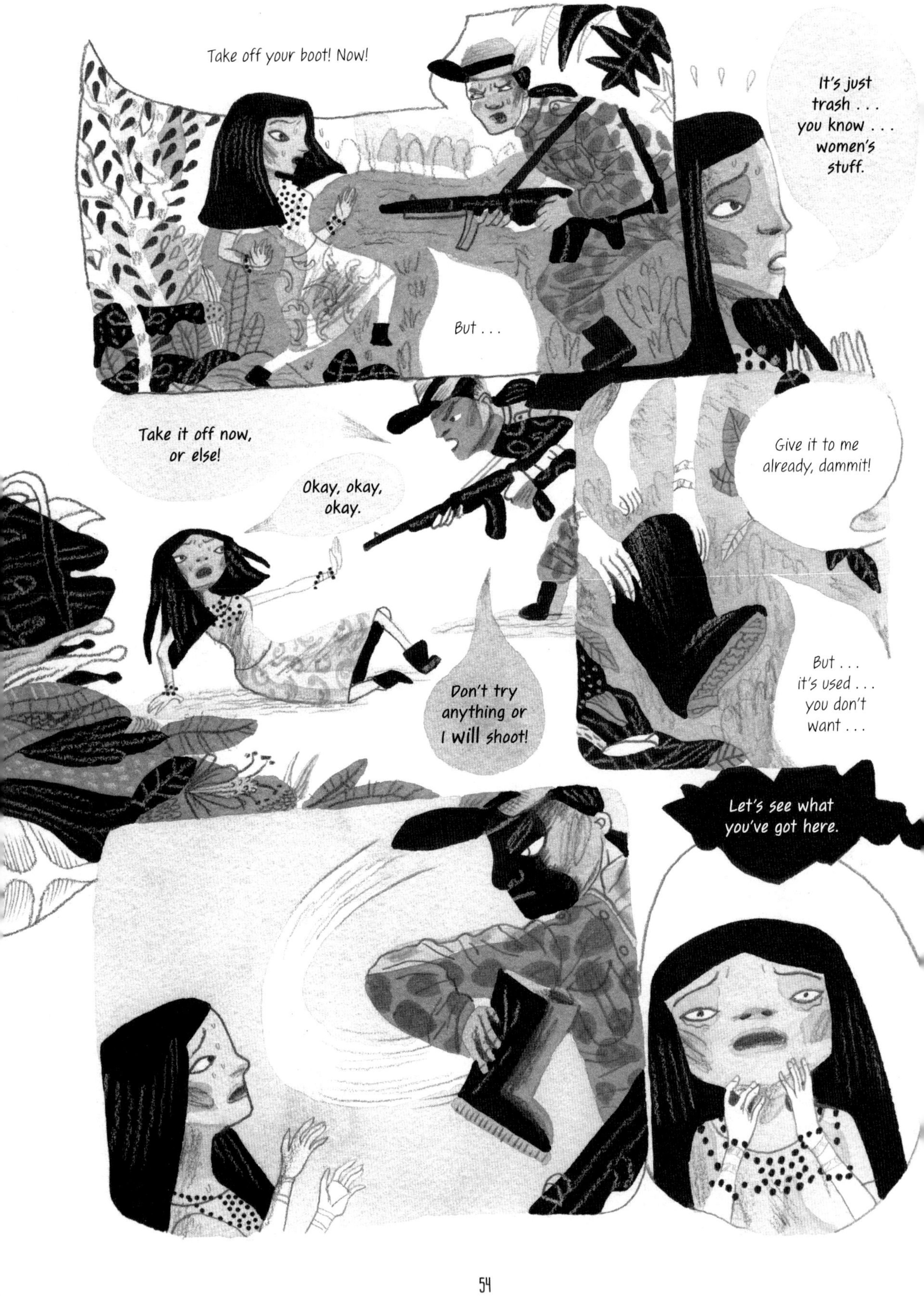

Take off your boot! Now!
It's just trash . . . you know . . . women's stuff.
But . . .
Take it off now, or else!
Okay, okay, okay.
Don't try anything or I will shoot!
Give it to me already, dammit!
But . . . it's used . . . you don't want . . .
Let's see what you've got here.

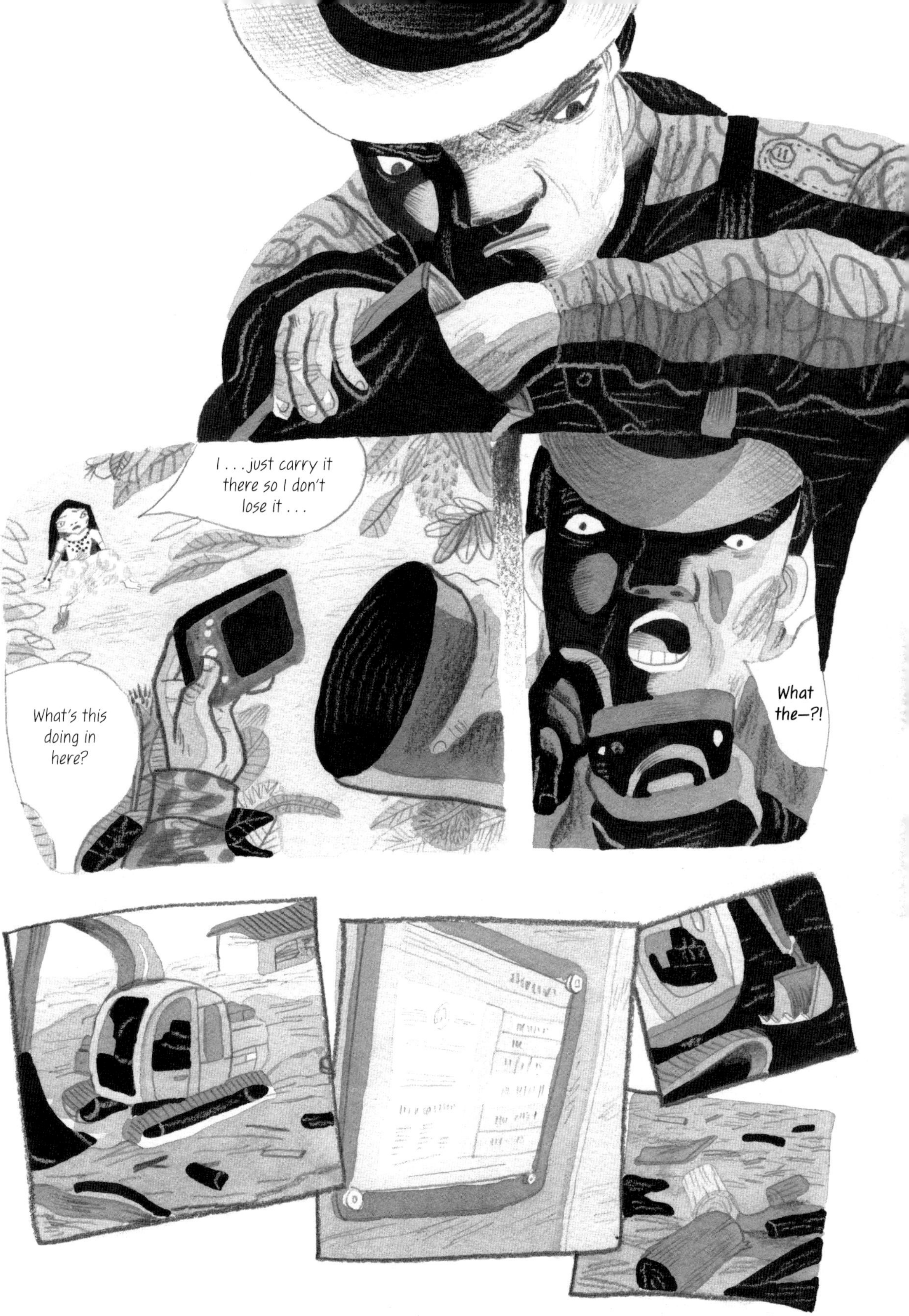
I . . . just carry it there so I don't lose it . . .
What's this doing in here?
What the—?!

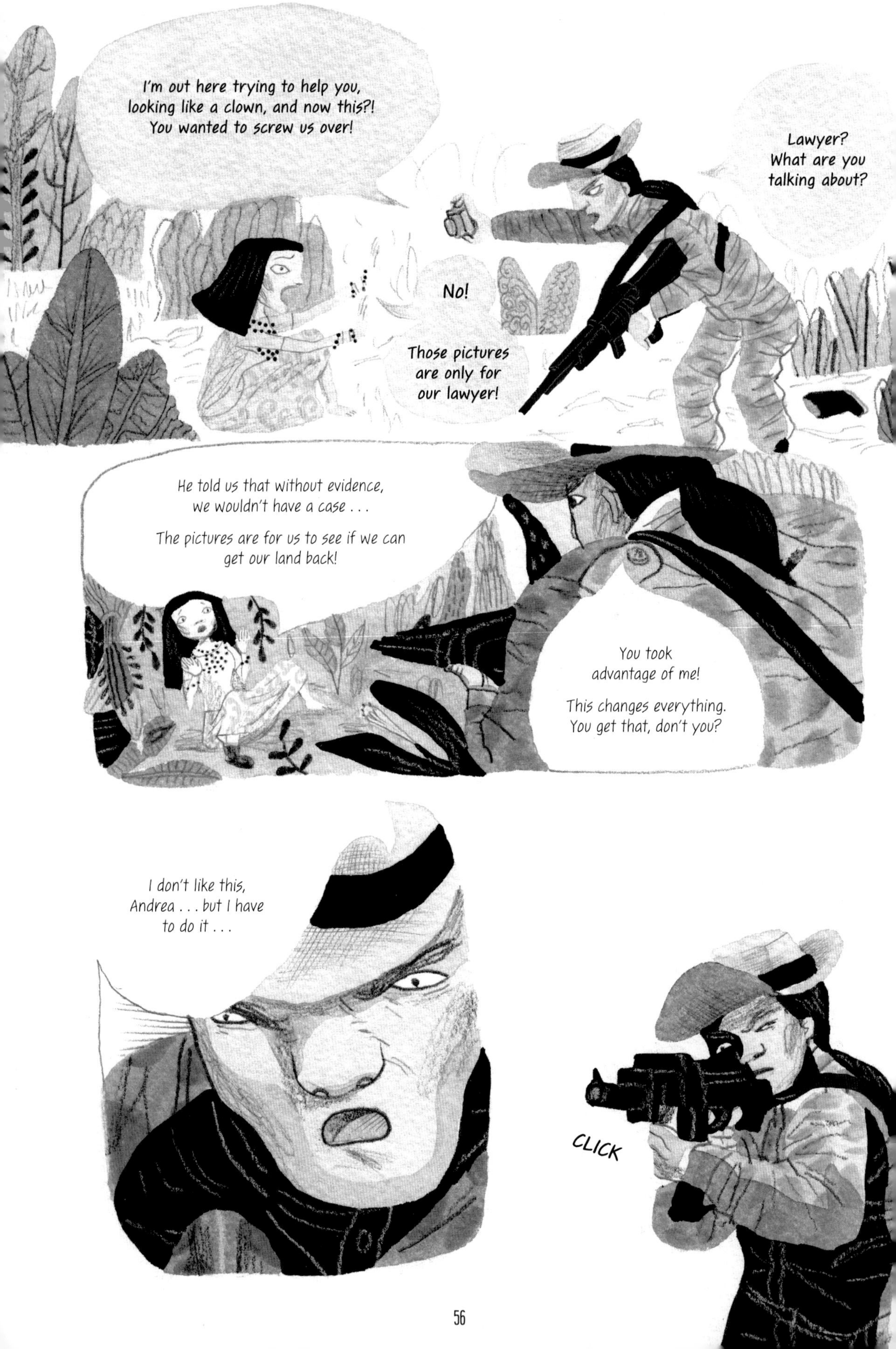
I'm out here trying to help you, looking like a clown, and now this?! You wanted to screw us over!
No!
Those pictures are only for our lawyer!
Lawyer? What are you talking about?
He told us that without evidence, we wouldn't have a case . . .
The pictures are for us to see if we can get our land back!
You took advantage of me!
This changes everything. You get that, don't you?
I don't like this, Andrea . . . but I have to do it . . .
CLICK

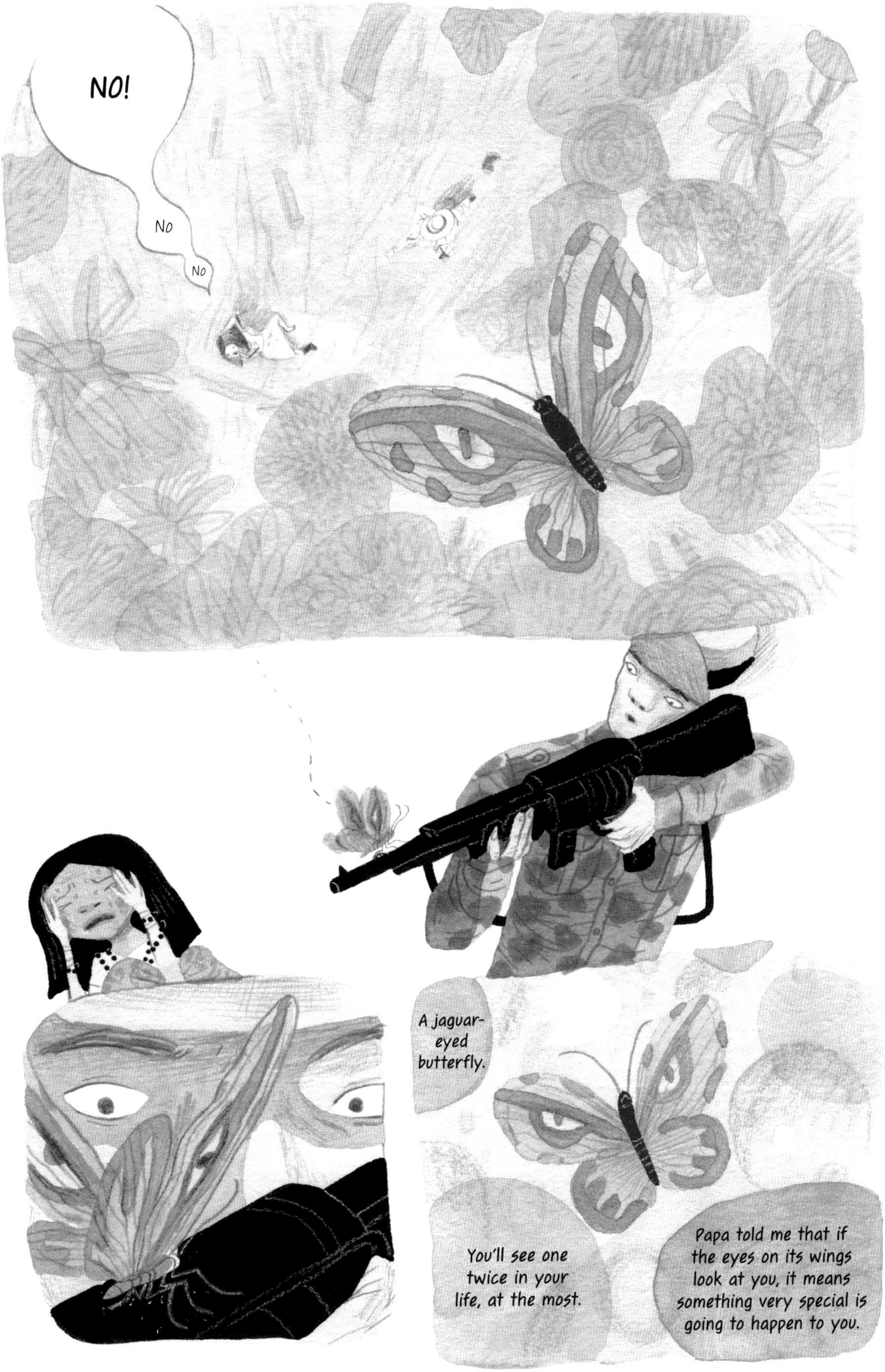
NO!
No
No
A jaguar-eyed butterfly.
You'll see one twice in your life, at the most.
Papa told me that if the eyes on its wings look at you, it means something very special is going to happen to you.

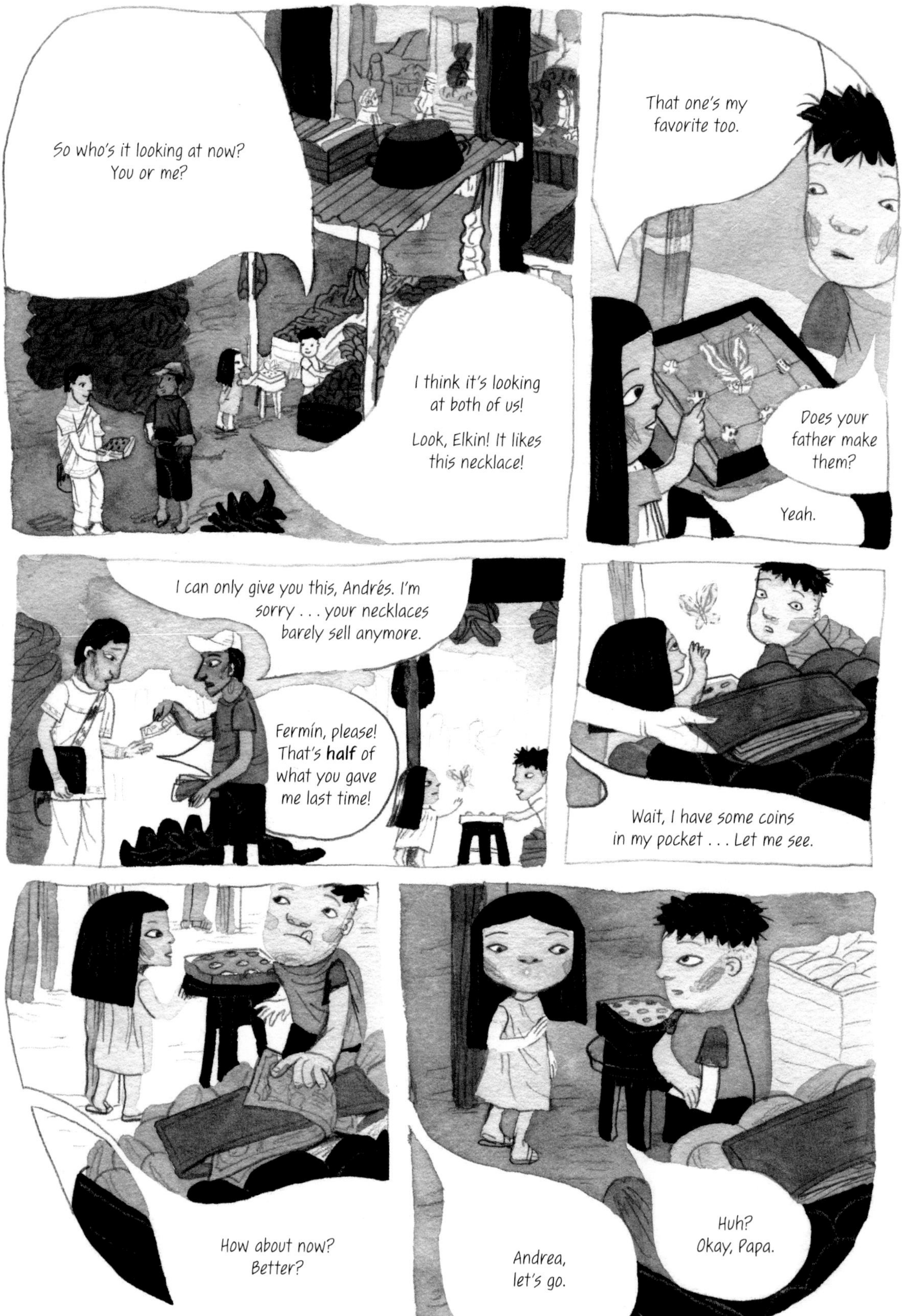
So who's it looking at now? You or me?
I think it's looking at both of us!
Look, Elkin! It likes this necklace!
That one's my favorite too.
Does your father make them?
Yeah.
I can only give you this, Andrés. I'm sorry . . . your necklaces barely sell anymore.
Fermín, please! That's **half** of what you gave me last time!
Wait, I have some coins in my pocket . . . Let me see.
How about now? Better?
Andrea, let's go.
Huh? Okay, Papa.

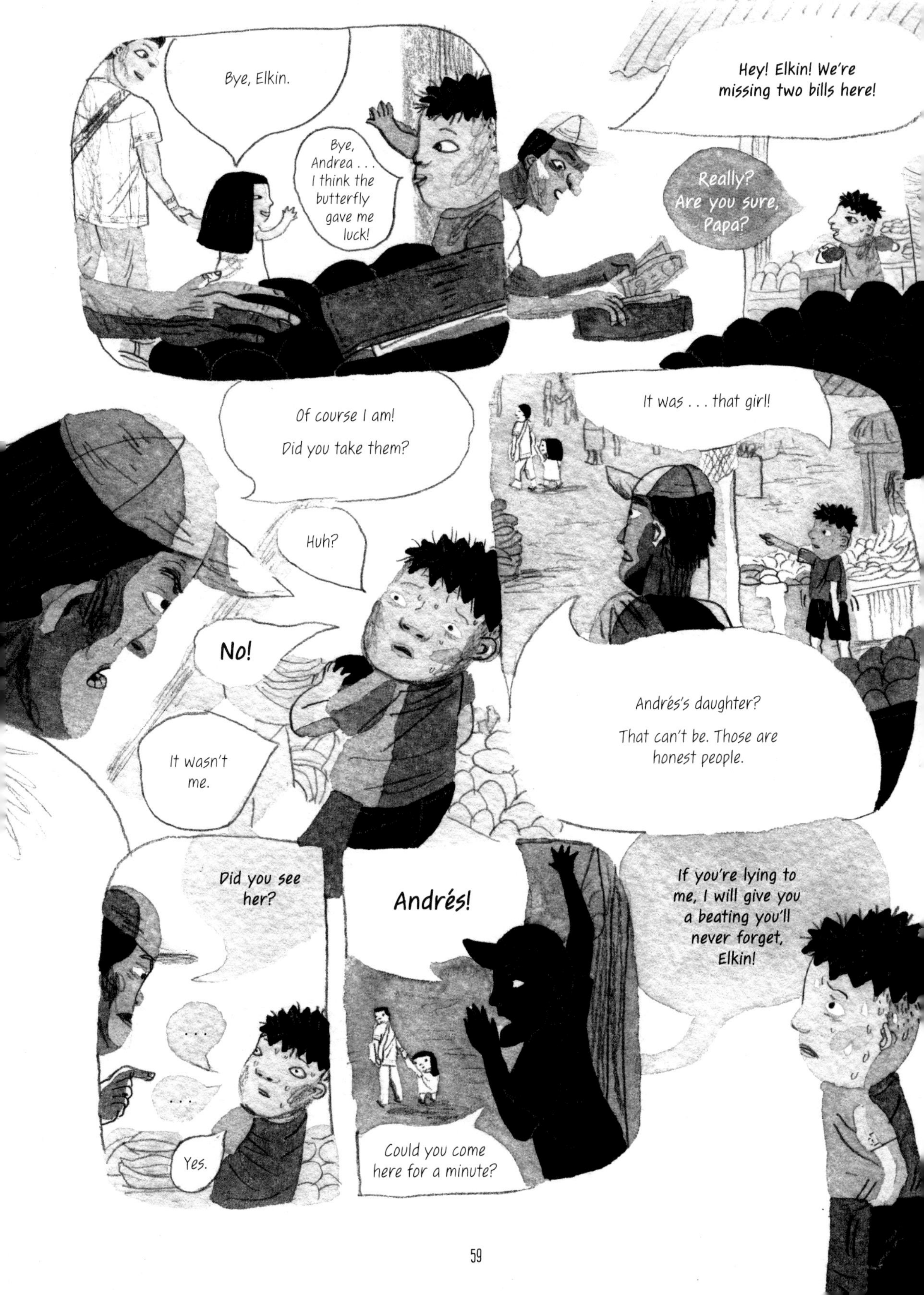
Bye, Elkin.
Bye, Andrea . . . I think the butterfly gave me luck!
Hey! Elkin! We're missing two bills here!
Really? Are you sure, Papa?
Of course I am!
Did you take them?
Huh?
No!
It wasn't me.
It was . . . that girl!
Andrés's daughter?
That can't be. Those are honest people.
Did you see her?
. . .
. . .
Yes.
Andrés!
Could you come here for a minute?
If you're lying to me, I will give you a beating you'll never forget, Elkin!

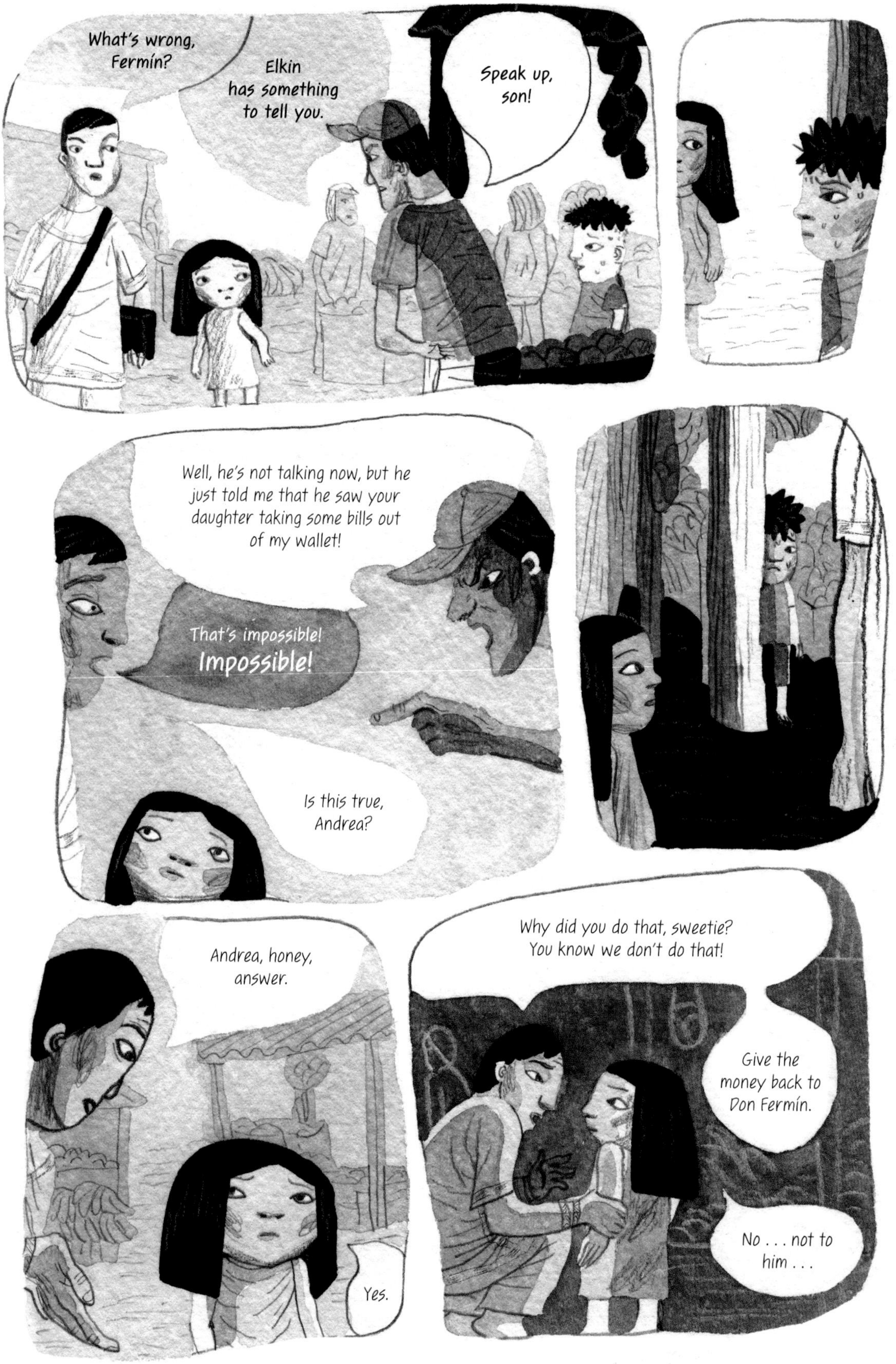

What's wrong, Fermín?
Elkin has something to tell you.
Speak up, son!
Well, he's not talking now, but he just told me that he saw your daughter taking some bills out of my wallet!
That's impossible! Impossible!
Is this true, Andrea?
Andrea, honey, answer.
Yes.
Why did you do that, sweetie? You know we don't do that!
Give the money back to Don Fermín.
No . . . not to him . . .

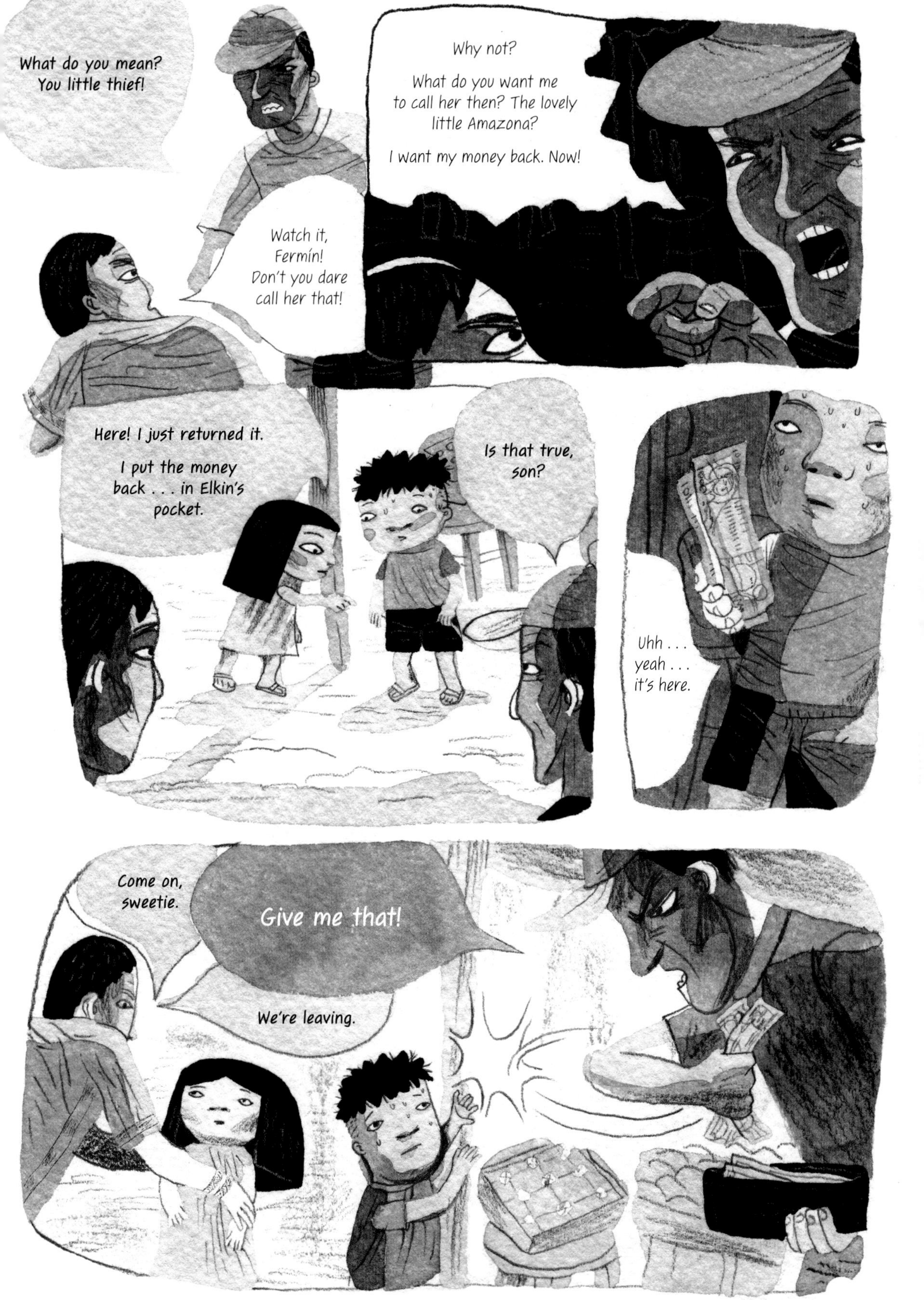
What do you mean? You little thief!
Why not?
What do you want me to call her then? The lovely little Amazona?
I want my money back. Now!
Watch it, Fermín! Don't you dare call her that!
Here! I just returned it.
I put the money back . . . in Elkin's pocket.
Is that true, son?
Uhh . . . yeah . . . it's here.
Come on, sweetie.
Give me that!
We're leaving.

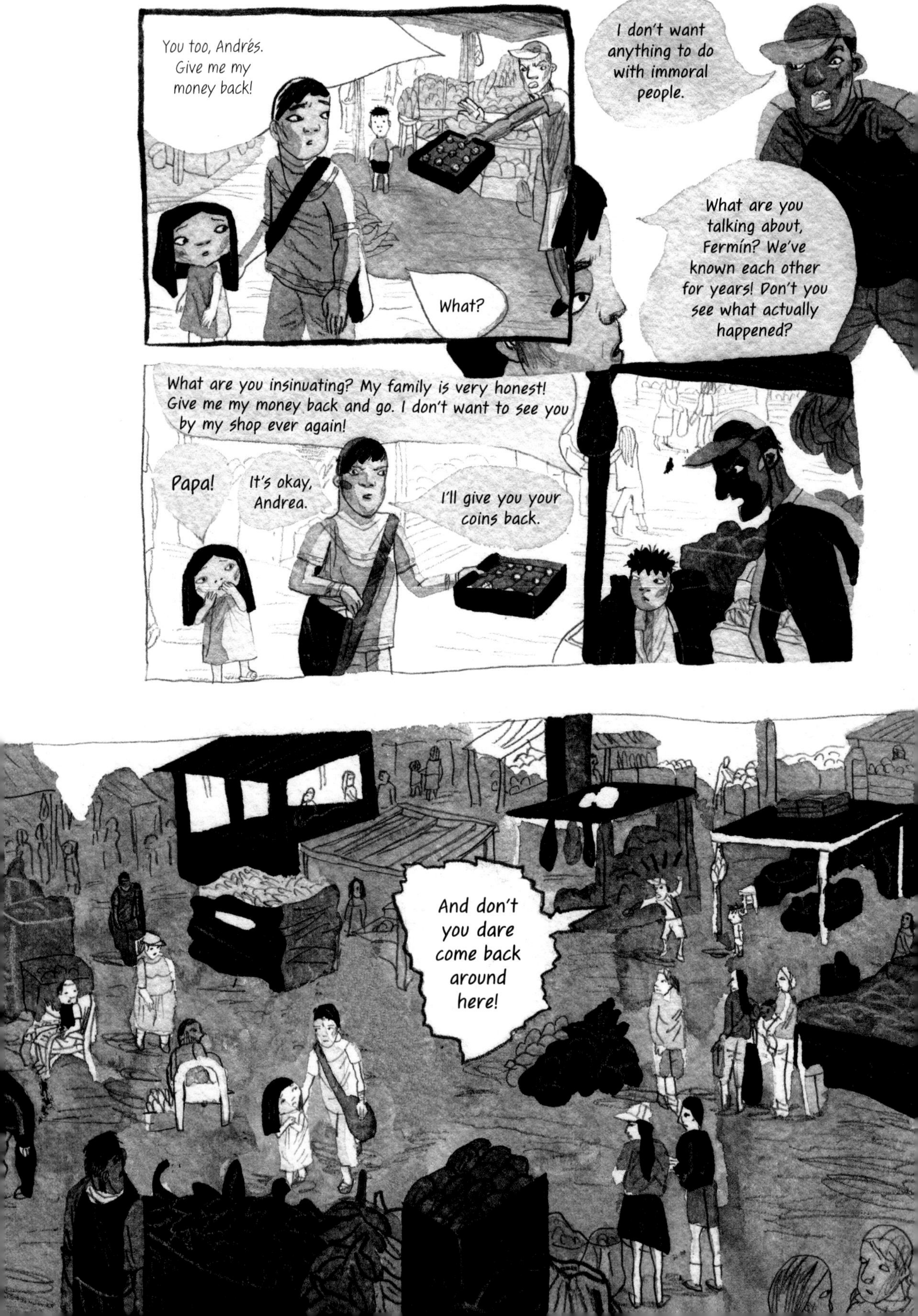
You too, Andrés. Give me my money back!
What?
I don't want anything to do with immoral people.
What are you talking about, Fermín? We've known each other for years! Don't you see what actually happened?
What are you insinuating? My family is very honest! Give me my money back and go. I don't want to see you by my shop ever again!
Papa!
It's okay, Andrea.
I'll give you your coins back.
And don't you dare come back around here!

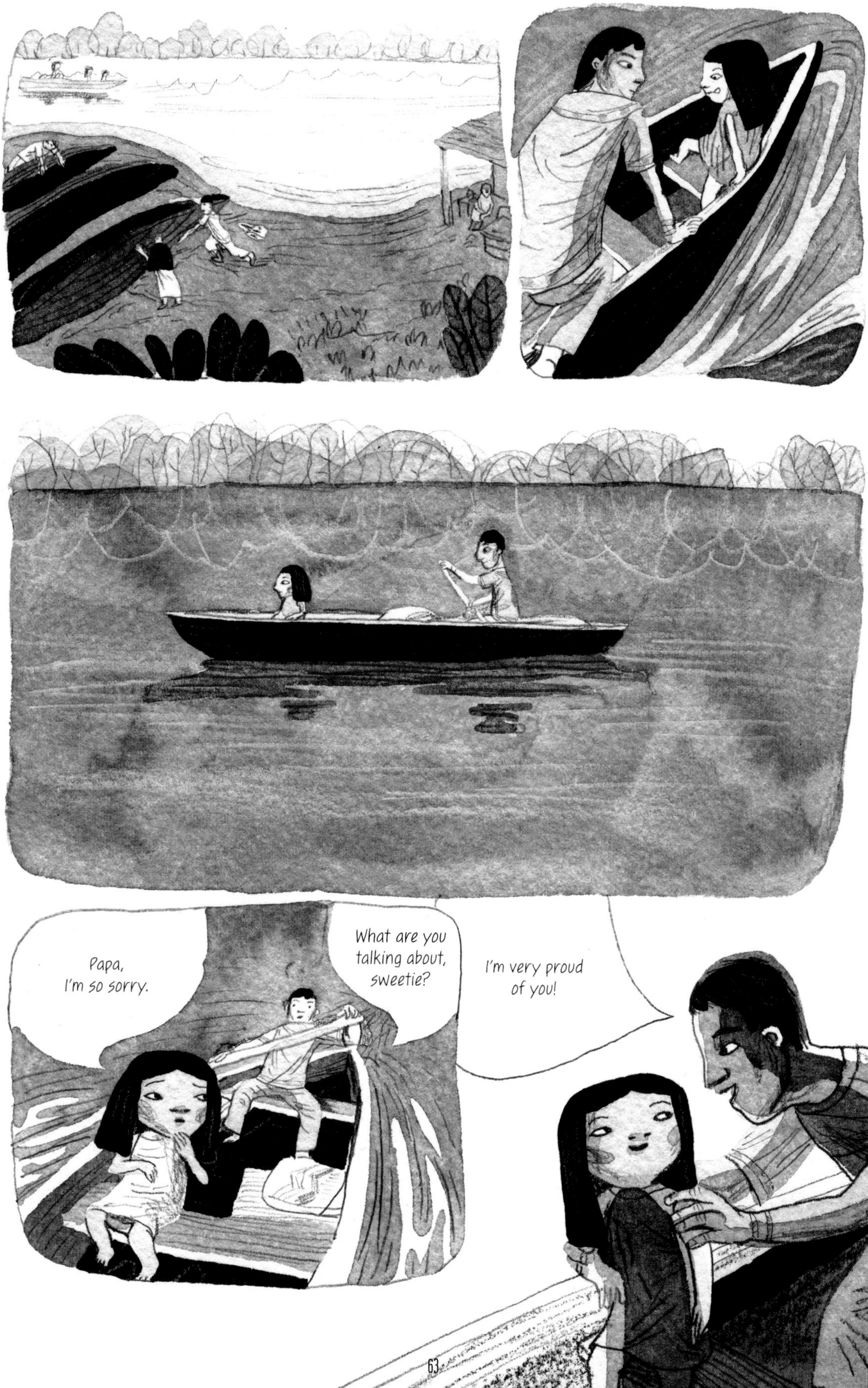

Papa, I'm so sorry.
What are you talking about, sweetie?
I'm very proud of you!

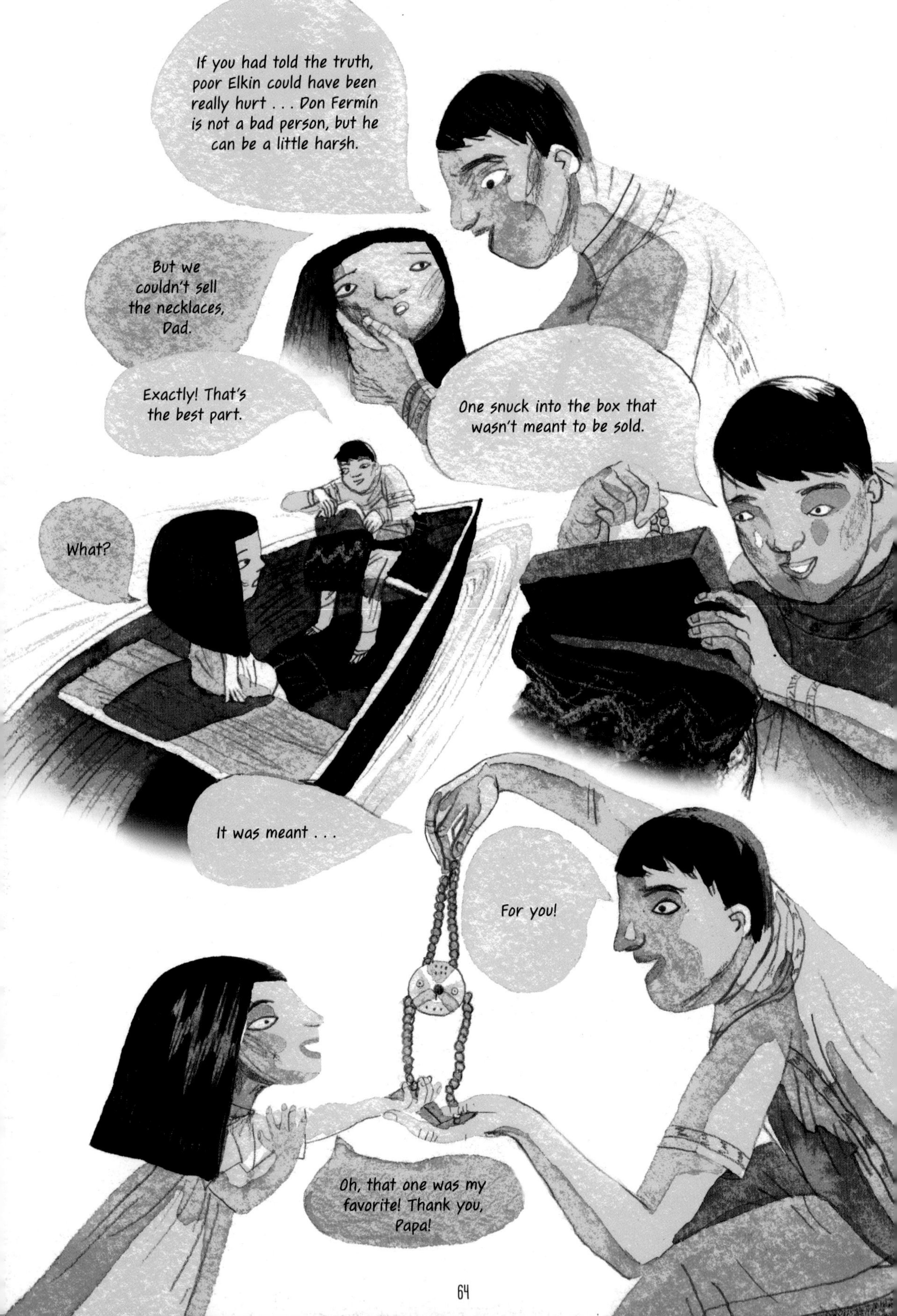
If you had told the truth, poor Elkin could have been really hurt . . . Don Fermín is not a bad person, but he can be a little harsh.
But we couldn't sell the necklaces, Dad.
Exactly! That's the best part.
One snuck into the box that wasn't meant to be sold.
What?
It was meant . . .
For you!
Oh, that one was my favorite! Thank you, Papa!

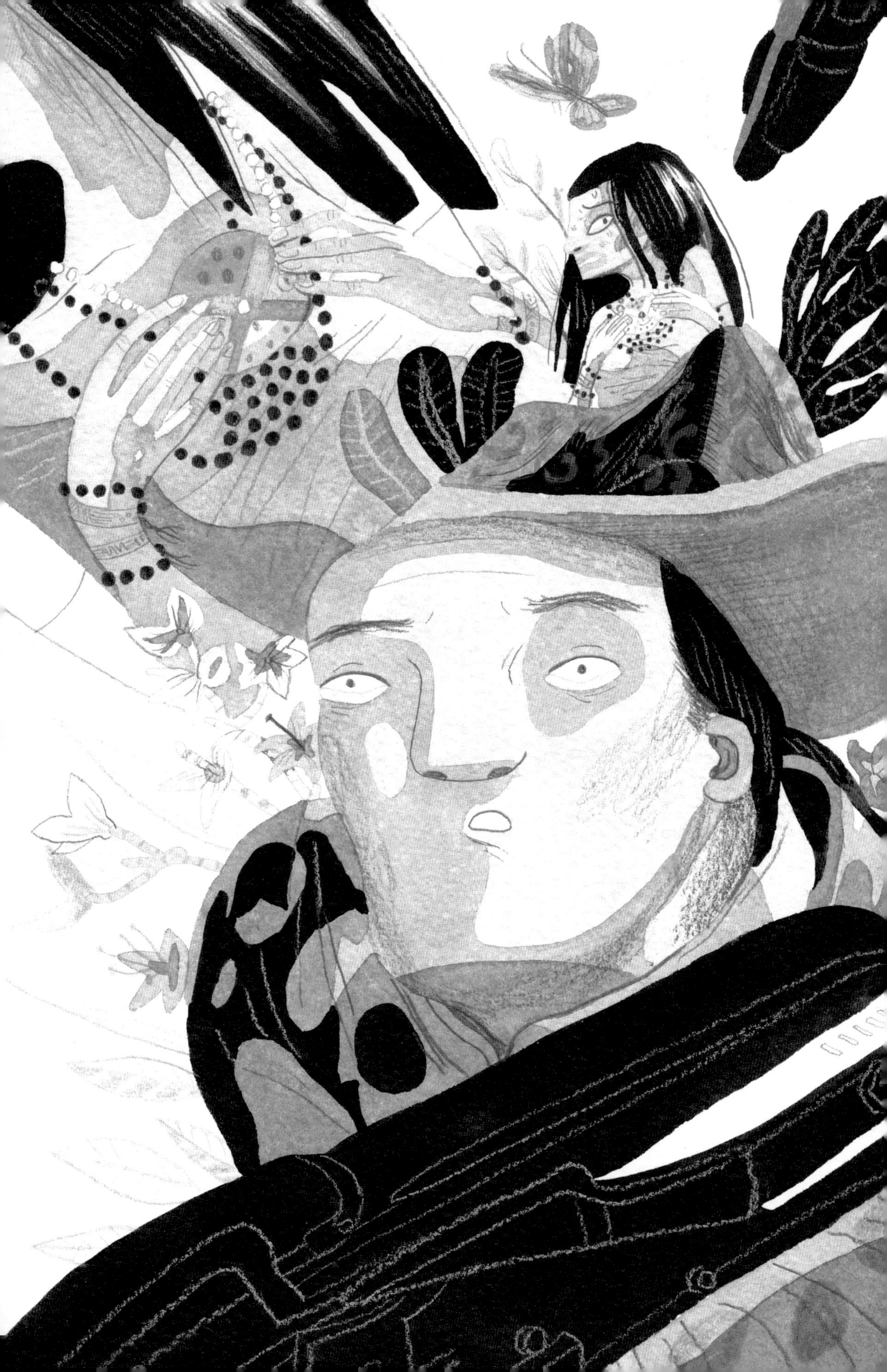

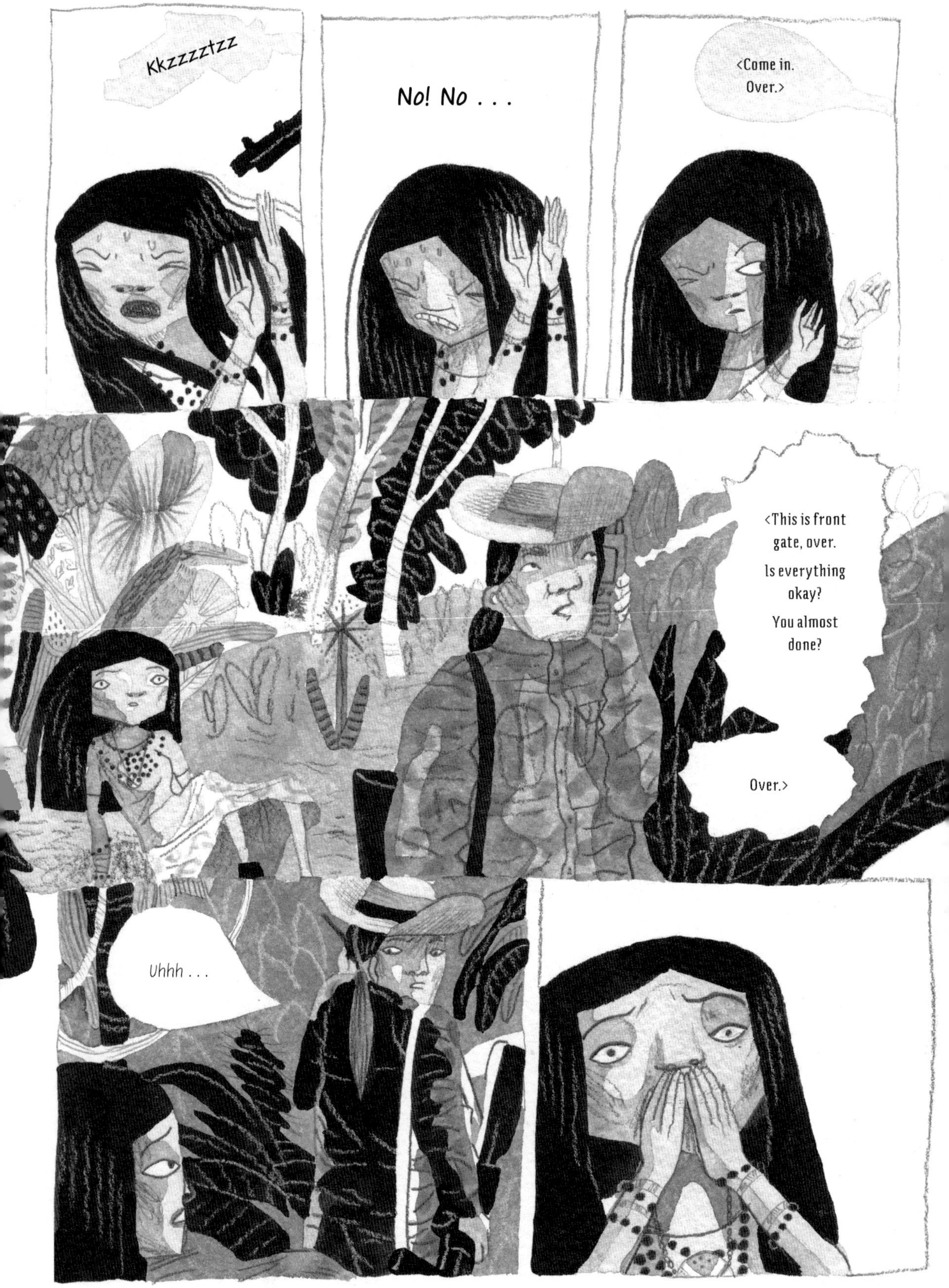
Kkzzzztzz
No! No . . .
<Come in. Over.>
<This is front gate, over. Is everything okay? You almost done?
Over.>
Uhhh . . .

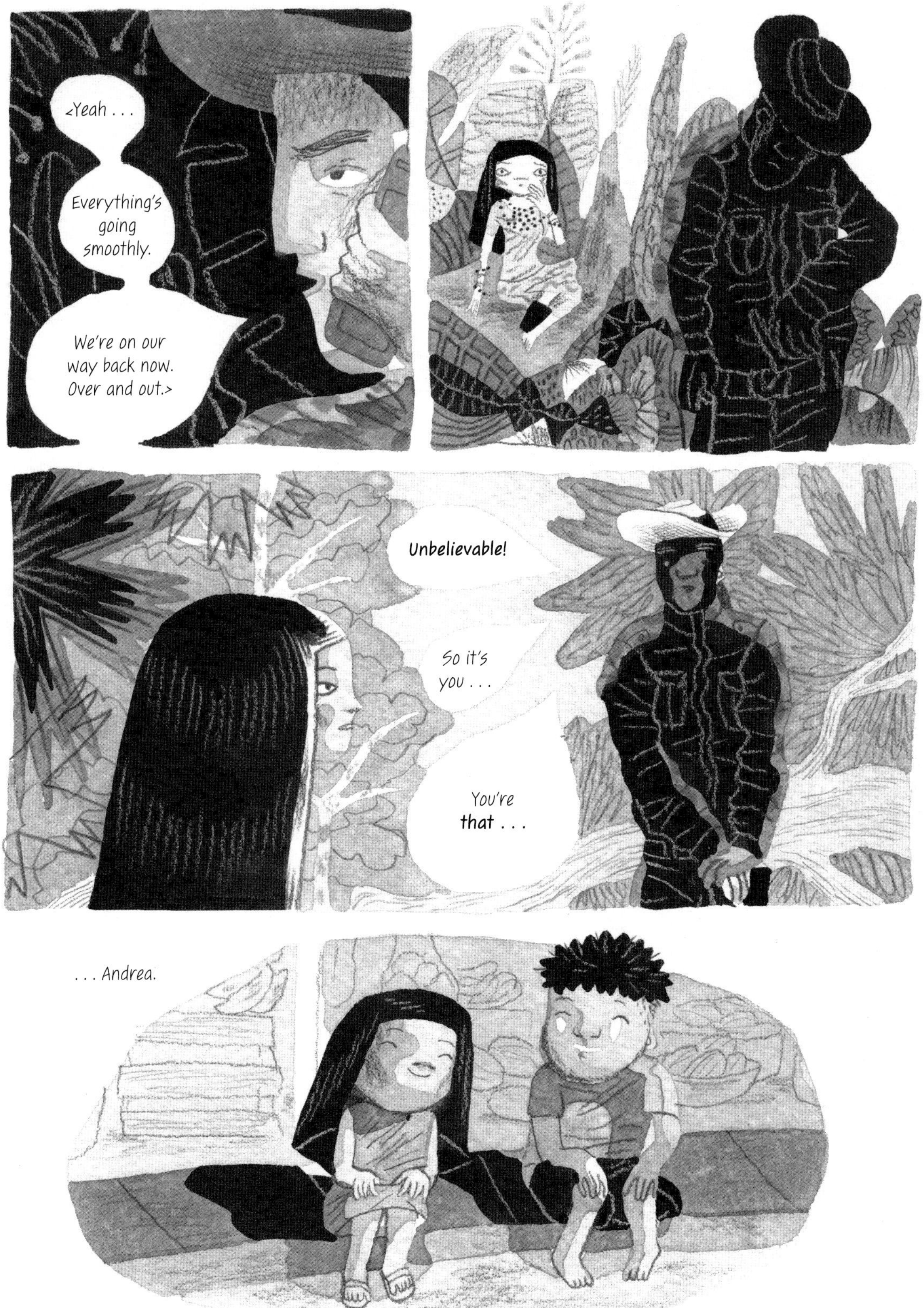
<Yeah . . .
Everything's going smoothly.
We're on our way back now. Over and out.>
Unbelievable!
So it's you . . .
You're **that** . . .
. . . Andrea.

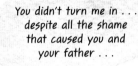I took advantage of
your goodwill.

You didn't turn me in . . .
despite all the shame
that caused you and
your father . . .

I never
thanked you.

Instead, you almost
killed me twice.

Twice?

You weren't part of that
group a year ago? The one
that shot at us in the middle
of the night and kicked us
off our land?

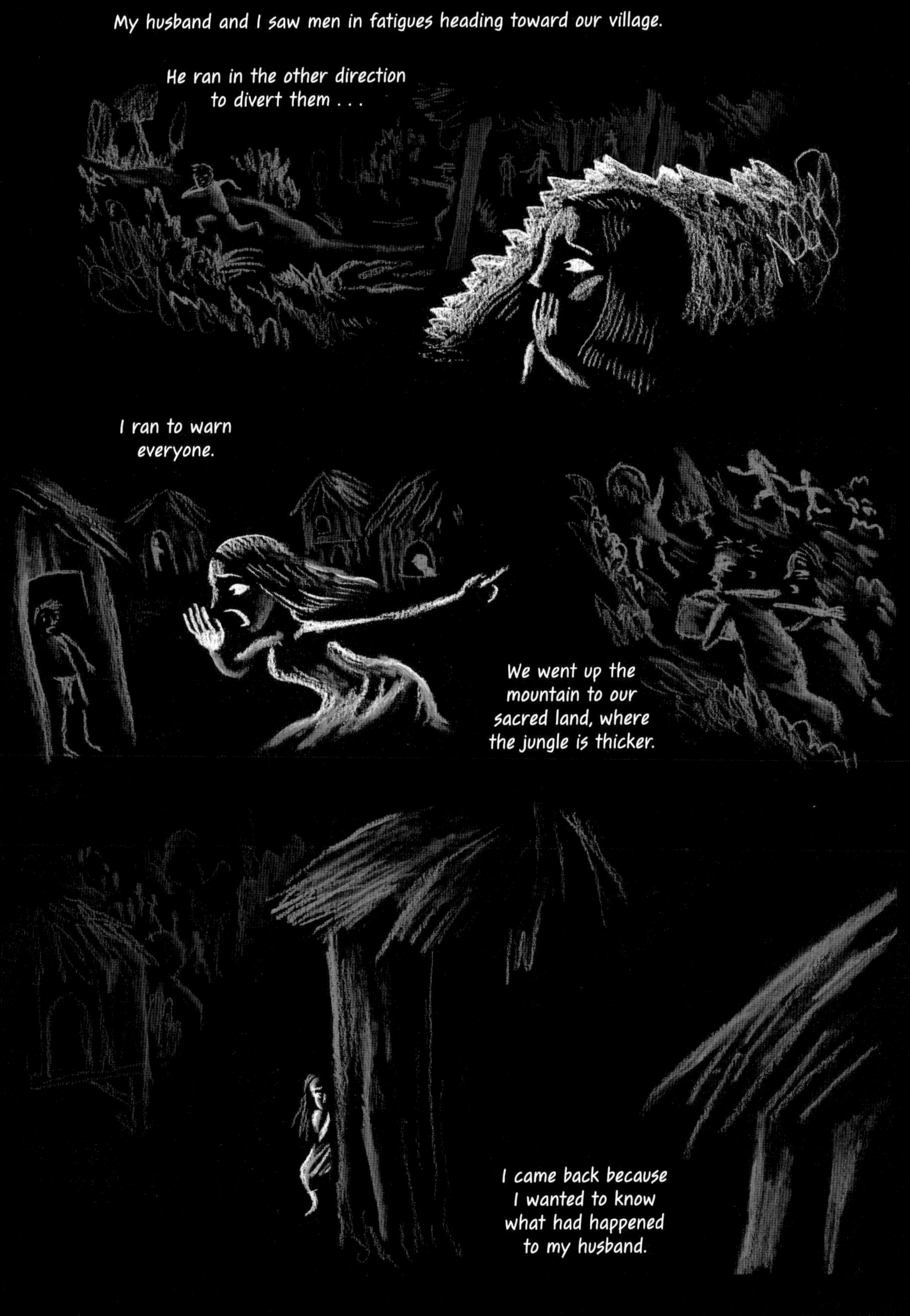
My husband and I saw men in fatigues heading toward our village.
He ran in the other direction to divert them . . .
I ran to warn everyone.
We went up the mountain to our sacred land, where the jungle is thicker.
I came back because I wanted to know what had happened to my husband.

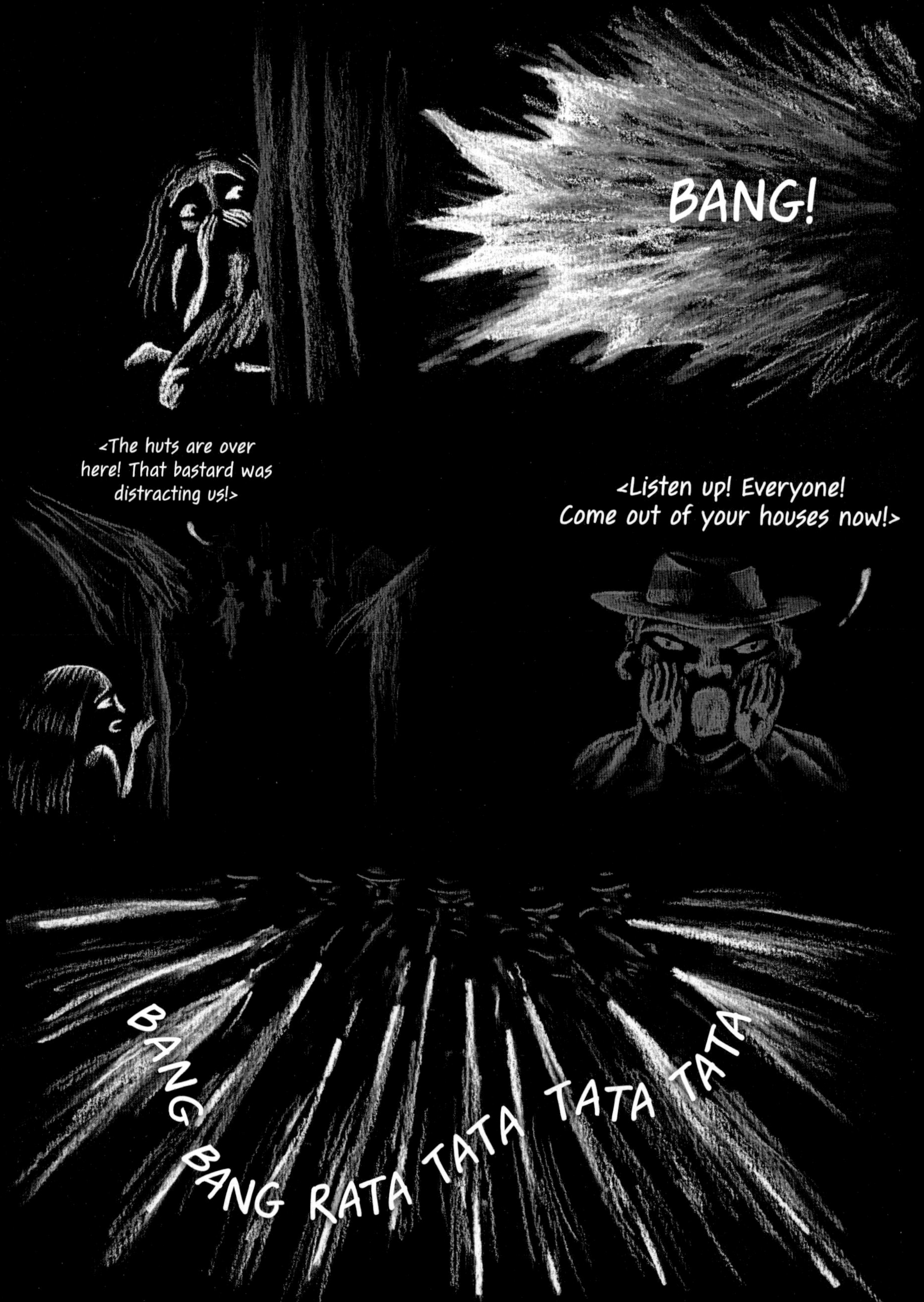
BANG!
<The huts are over here! That bastard was distracting us!>
<Listen up! Everyone! Come out of your houses now!>
BANG BANG RATA TATA TATA TATA

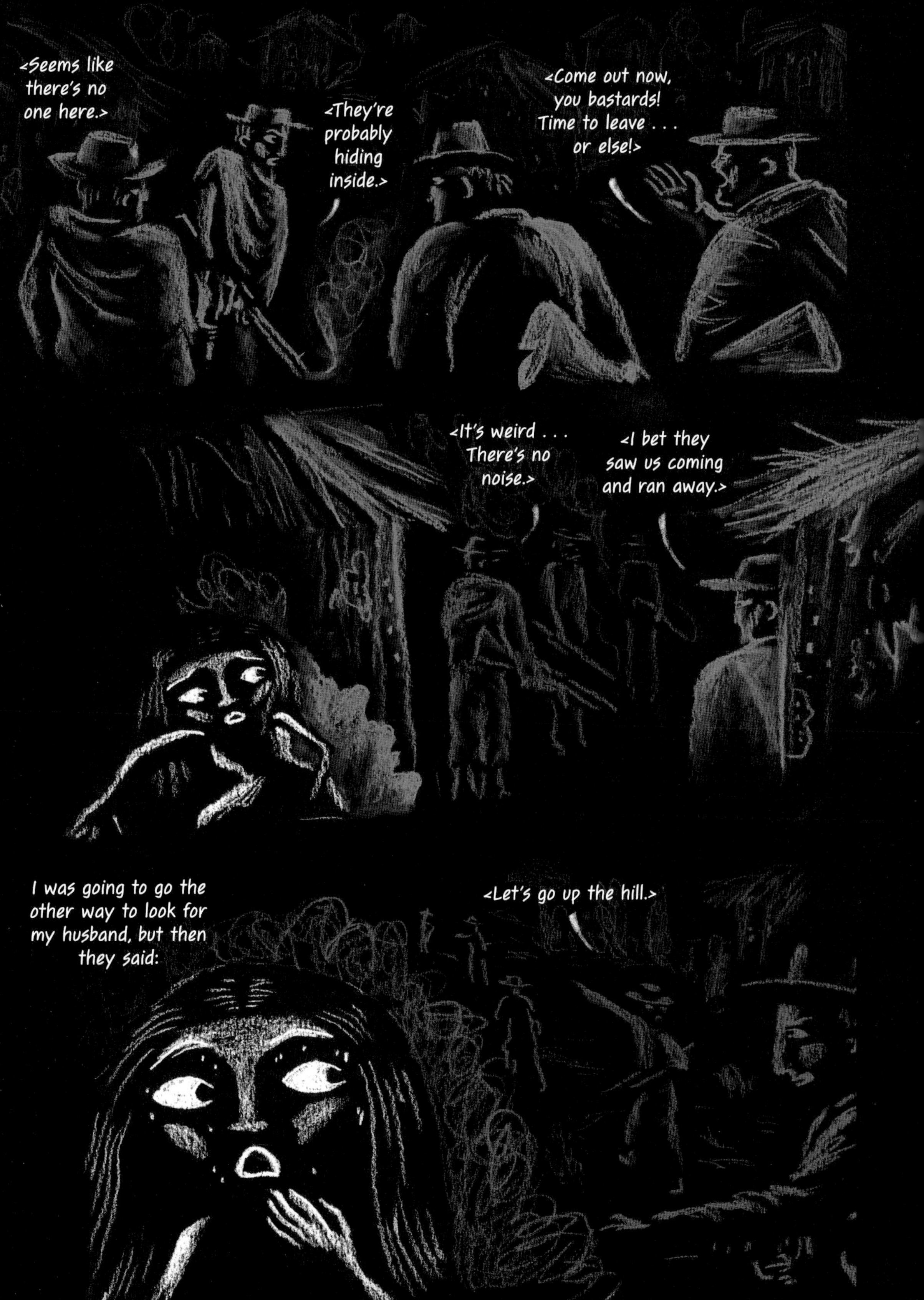
<Seems like there's no one here.>
<They're probably hiding inside.>
<Come out now, you bastards! Time to leave . . . or else!>
<It's weird . . . There's no noise.>
<I bet they saw us coming and ran away.>
I was going to go the other way to look for my husband, but then they said:
<Let's go up the hill.>

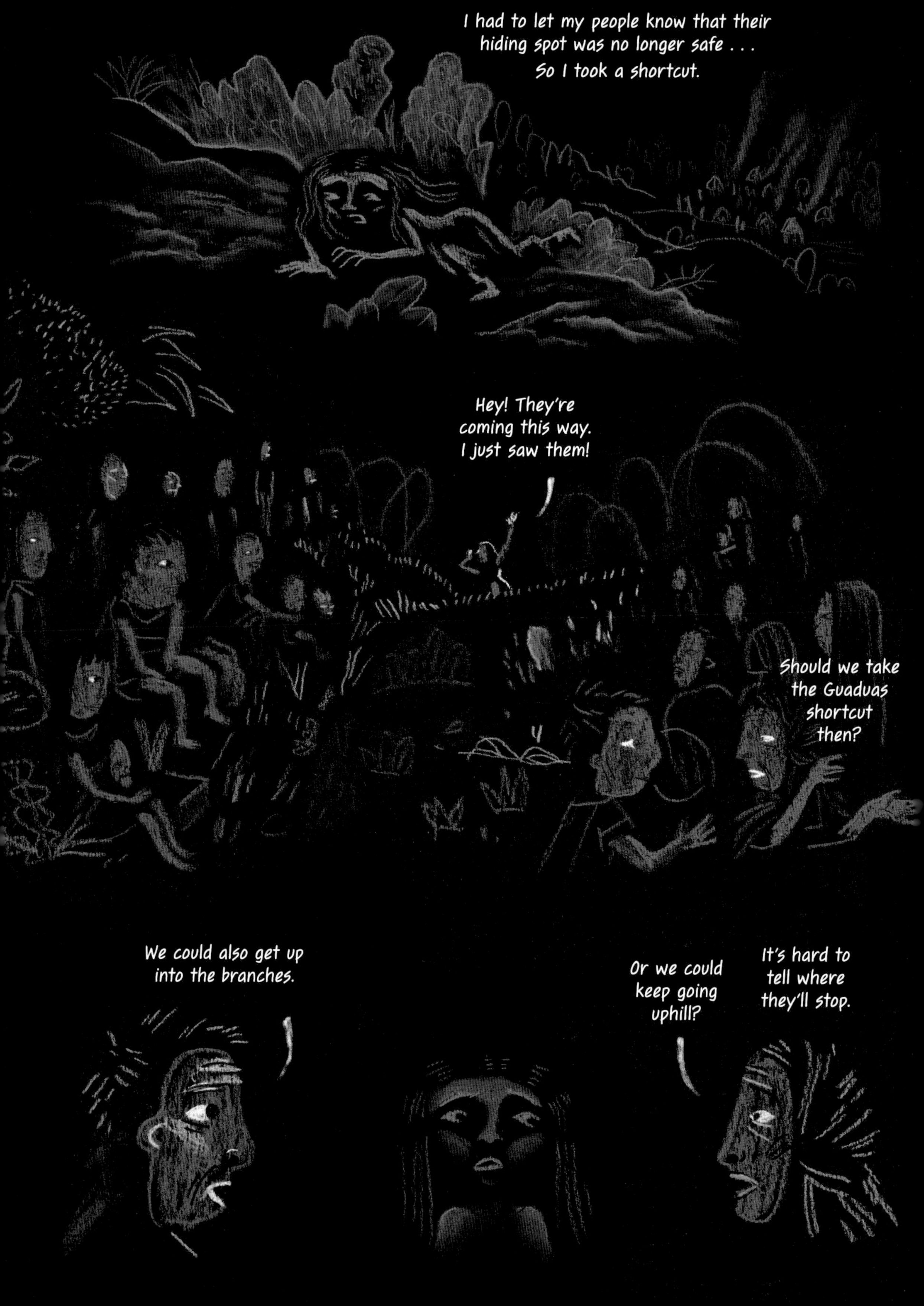
I had to let my people know that their hiding spot was no longer safe . . .
So I took a shortcut.
Hey! They're coming this way. I just saw them!
Should we take the Guaduas shortcut then?
We could also get up into the branches.
Or we could keep going uphill?
It's hard to tell where they'll stop.

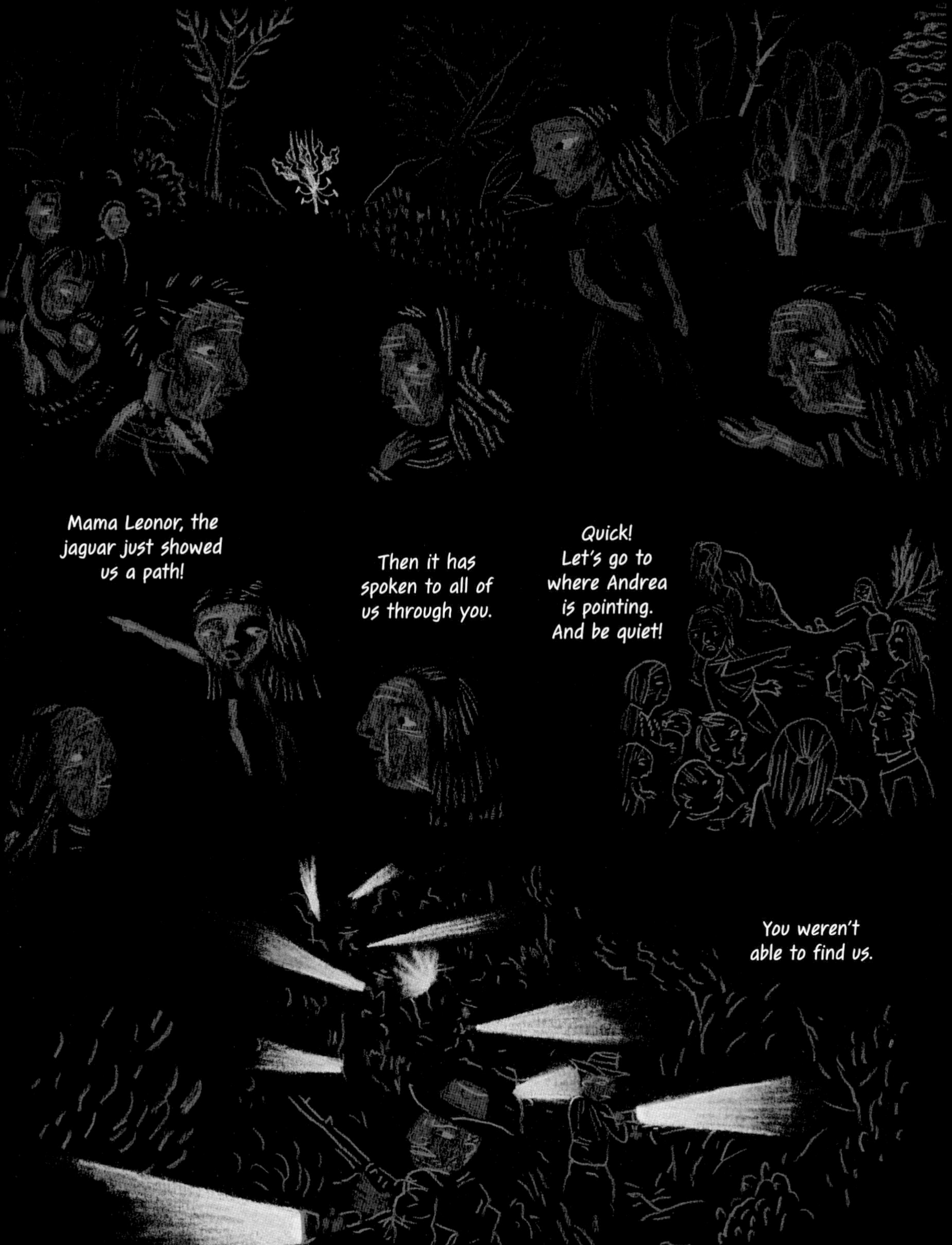
Mama Leonor, the jaguar just showed us a path!
Then it has spoken to all of us through you.
Quick! Let's go to where Andrea is pointing. And be quiet!
You weren't able to find us.

We walked the whole night without taking a break. No one spoke. We moved forward without stopping.

When the sun came out, we were still deep in the rain forest.

Finally, we reached a nearby village with lots of pretty doors . . . which happened to be shut.

We tried to talk to the people, but the only ones who answered were the dogs.

Exhausted, we spent the next night in a soccer field . . . In the dark, it looked as if the field was full of dead bodies.

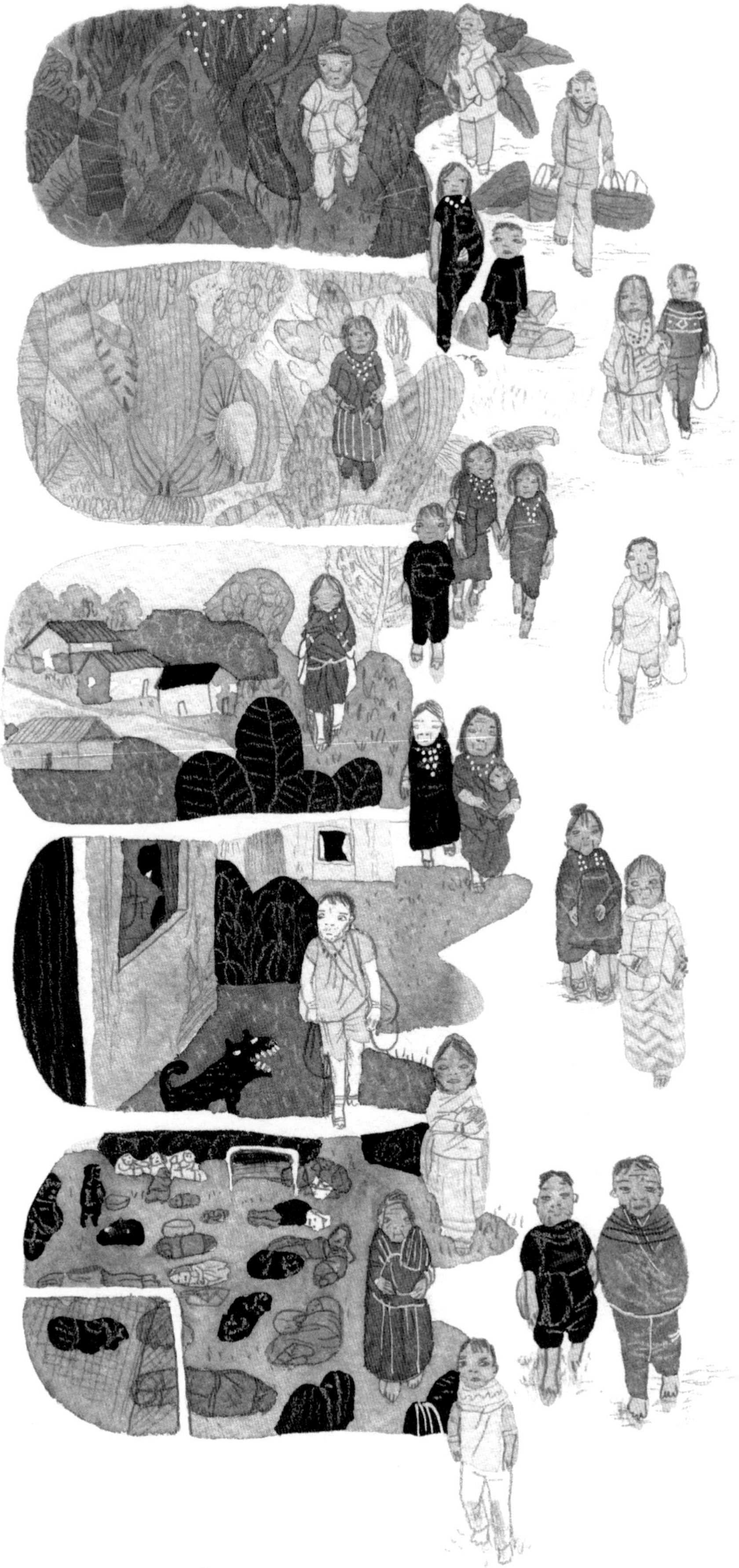

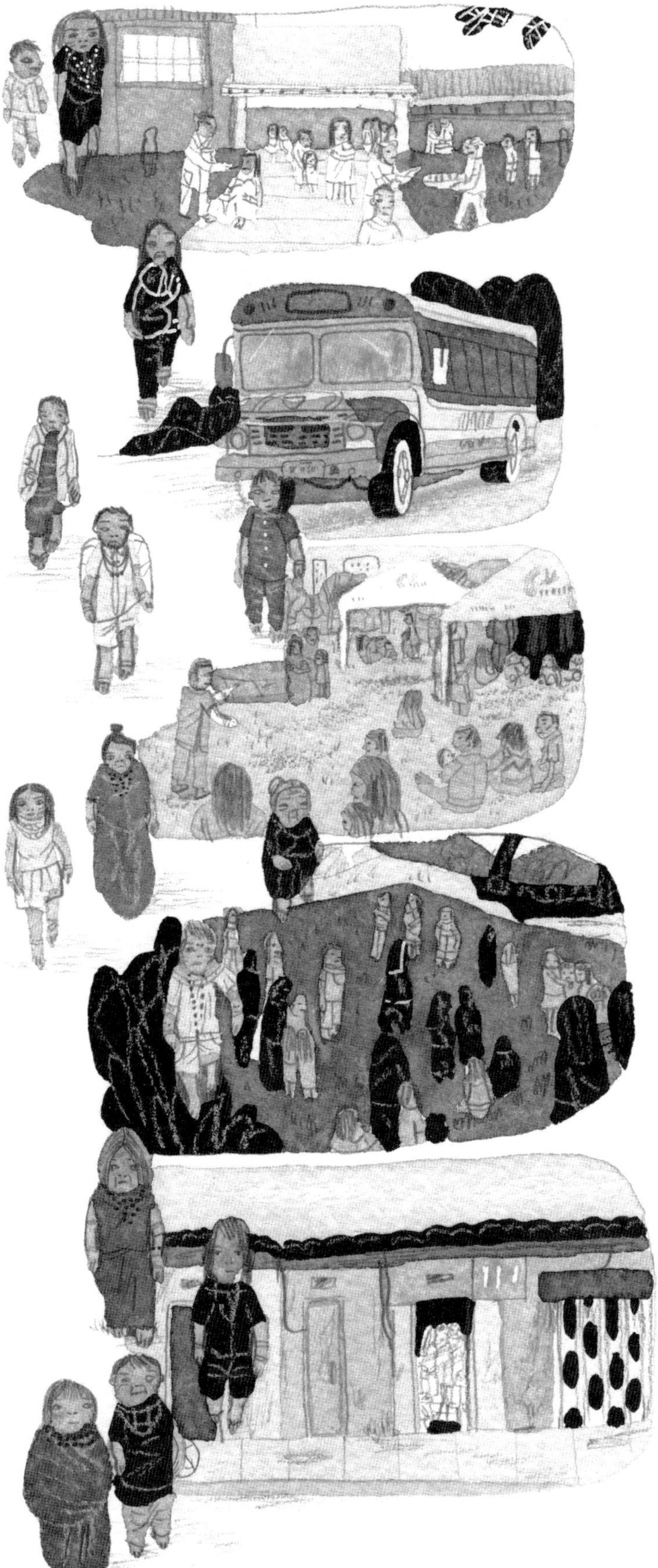

The next day, we arrived in Puerto Asís, where we found medical attention and food . . . The local hospital got in contact with an organization in Cali that said it could help us.

For two days, we zigzagged along a highway that made everyone sick.

When we arrived in Cali, it turned out that another Indigenous community—from Cauca, also displaced—had already taken the spots reserved for us. Instead, we were put up in temporary tents on a public park.

Local authorities relocated us to the outskirts of town while they prepared an empty house for us . . .

The house is in an area with a lot of crime. It's not safe, so we have to take turns guarding the place. It's not hospitable at all . . . But we make do in the few square feet we have. Still—we can't stay there. At night, it's hard to breathe. There's no good airflow, and there are too many of us. My daughter died from a lack of oxygen.

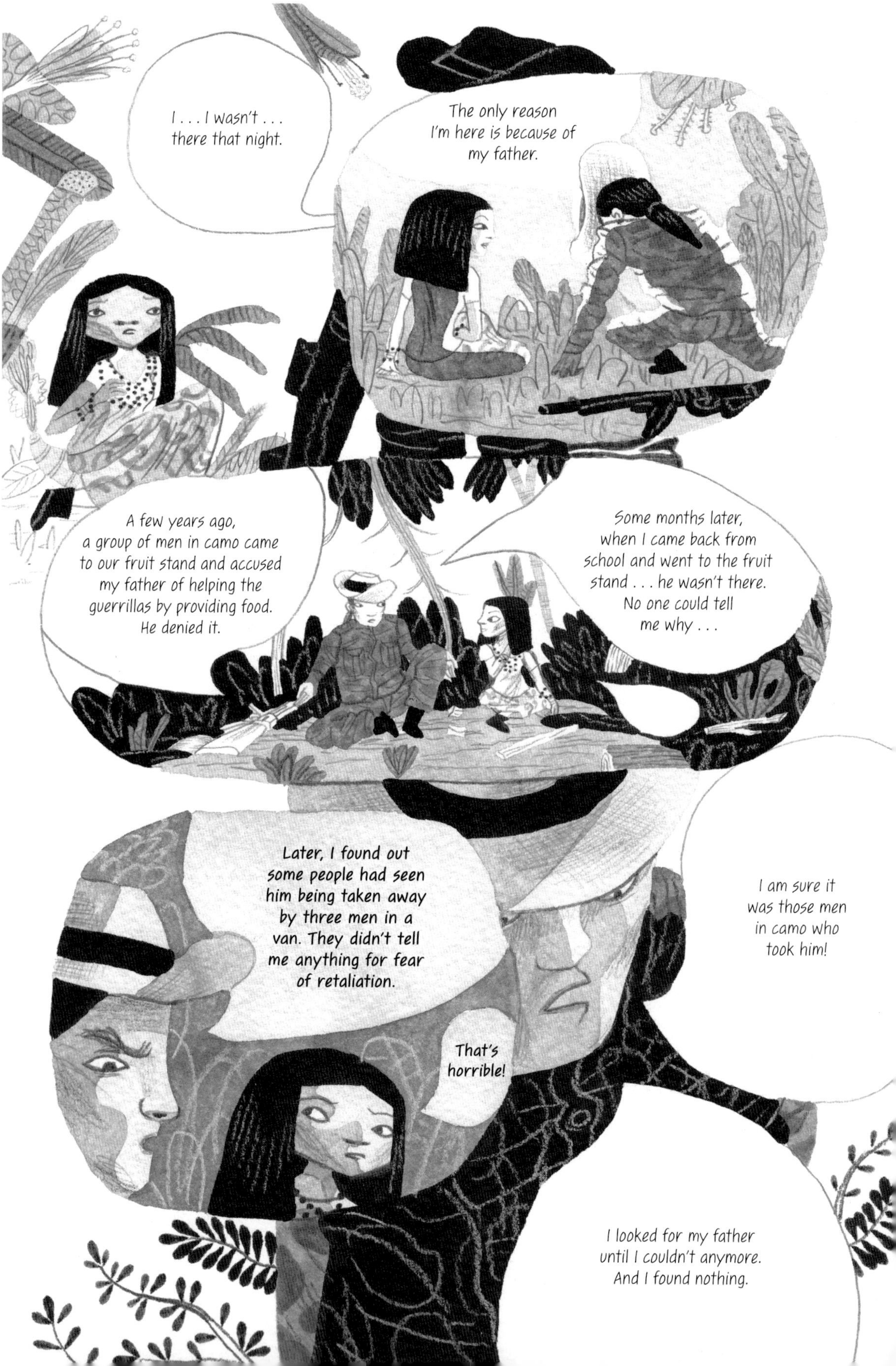

I . . . I wasn't . . . there that night.
The only reason I'm here is because of my father.
A few years ago, a group of men in camo came to our fruit stand and accused my father of helping the guerrillas by providing food. He denied it.
Some months later, when I came back from school and went to the fruit stand . . . he wasn't there. No one could tell me why . . .
Later, I found out some people had seen him being taken away by three men in a van. They didn't tell me anything for fear of retaliation.
I am sure it was those men in camo who took him!
That's horrible!
I looked for my father until I couldn't anymore. And I found nothing.

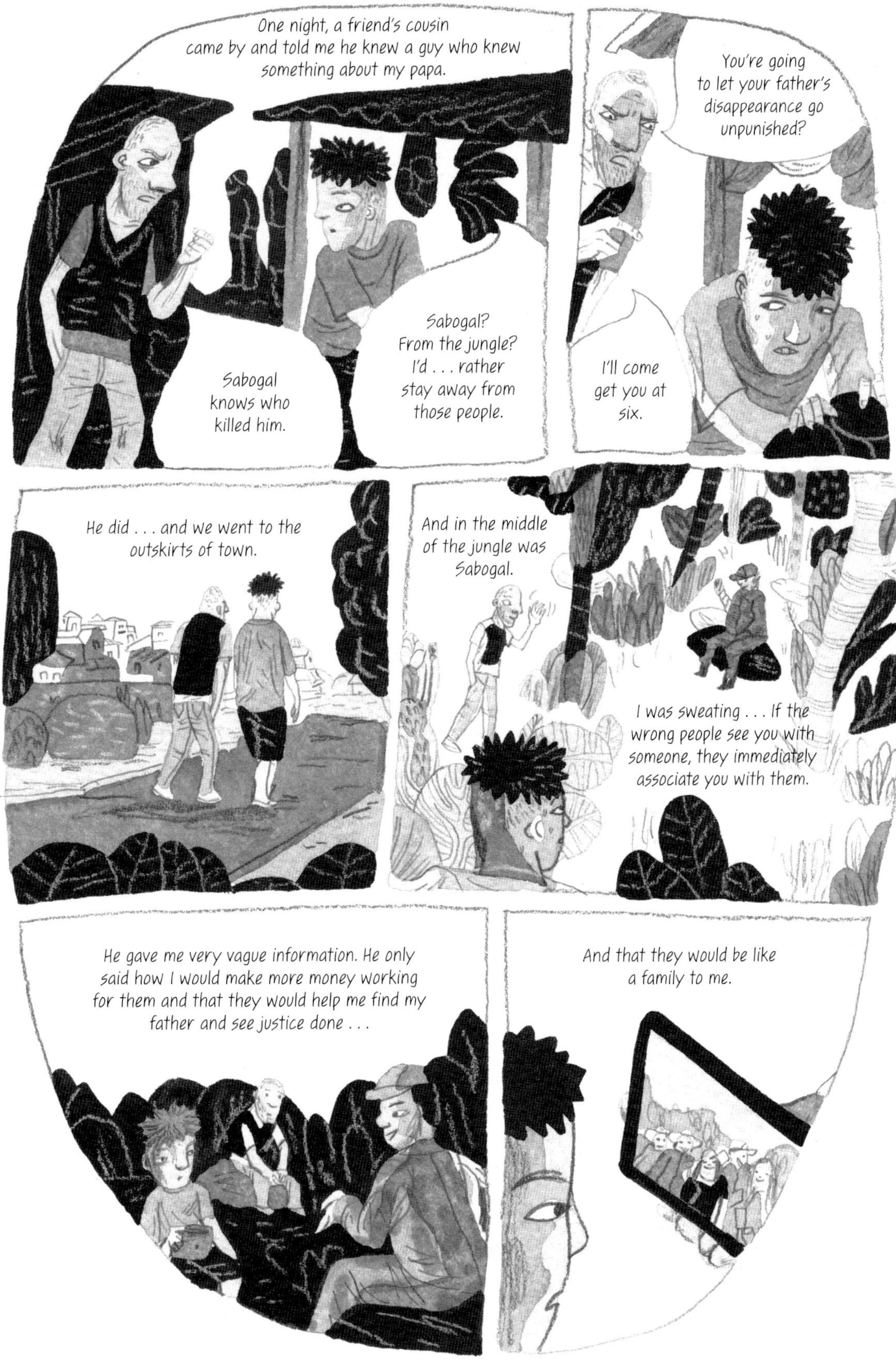
One night, a friend's cousin came by and told me he knew a guy who knew something about my papa.
Sabogal knows who killed him.
Sabogal? From the jungle? I'd . . . rather stay away from those people.
You're going to let your father's disappearance go unpunished?
I'll come get you at six.
He did . . . and we went to the outskirts of town.
And in the middle of the jungle was Sabogal.
I was sweating . . . If the wrong people see you with someone, they immediately associate you with them.
He gave me very vague information. He only said how I would make more money working for them and that they would help me find my father and see justice done . . .
And that they would be like a family to me.

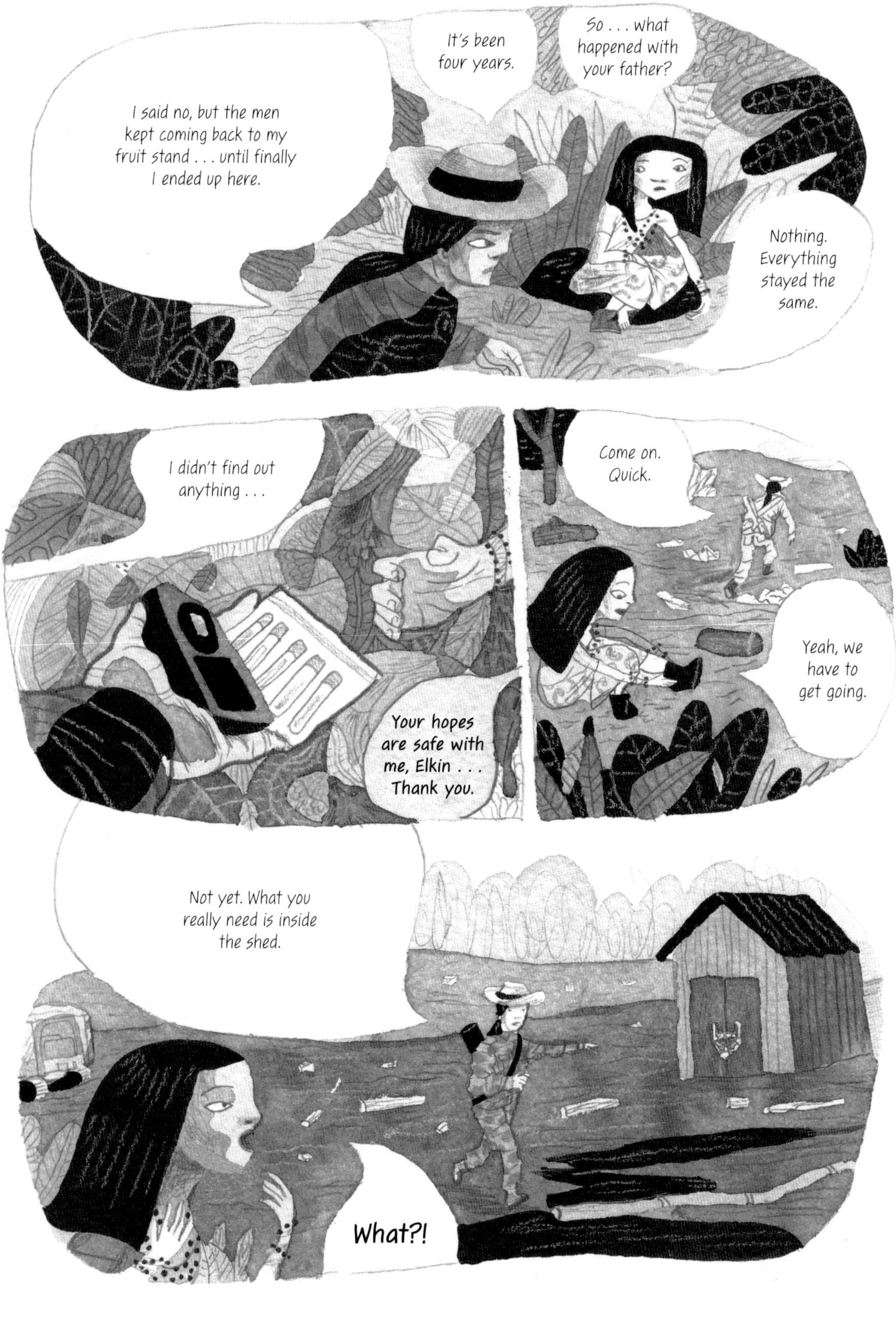
I said no, but the men kept coming back to my fruit stand . . . until finally I ended up here.
It's been four years.
So . . . what happened with your father?
Nothing. Everything stayed the same.
I didn't find out anything . . .
Your hopes are safe with me, Elkin . . . Thank you.
Come on. Quick.
Yeah, we have to get going.
Not yet. What you really need is inside the shed.
What?!

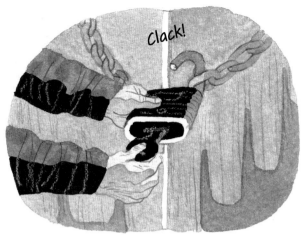

Clack!

What is all this?!

Hurry up, Andrea! We've only got a couple of minutes!

Incredible!

Contracts and invoices . . .

This is worth more than the gold they're after!

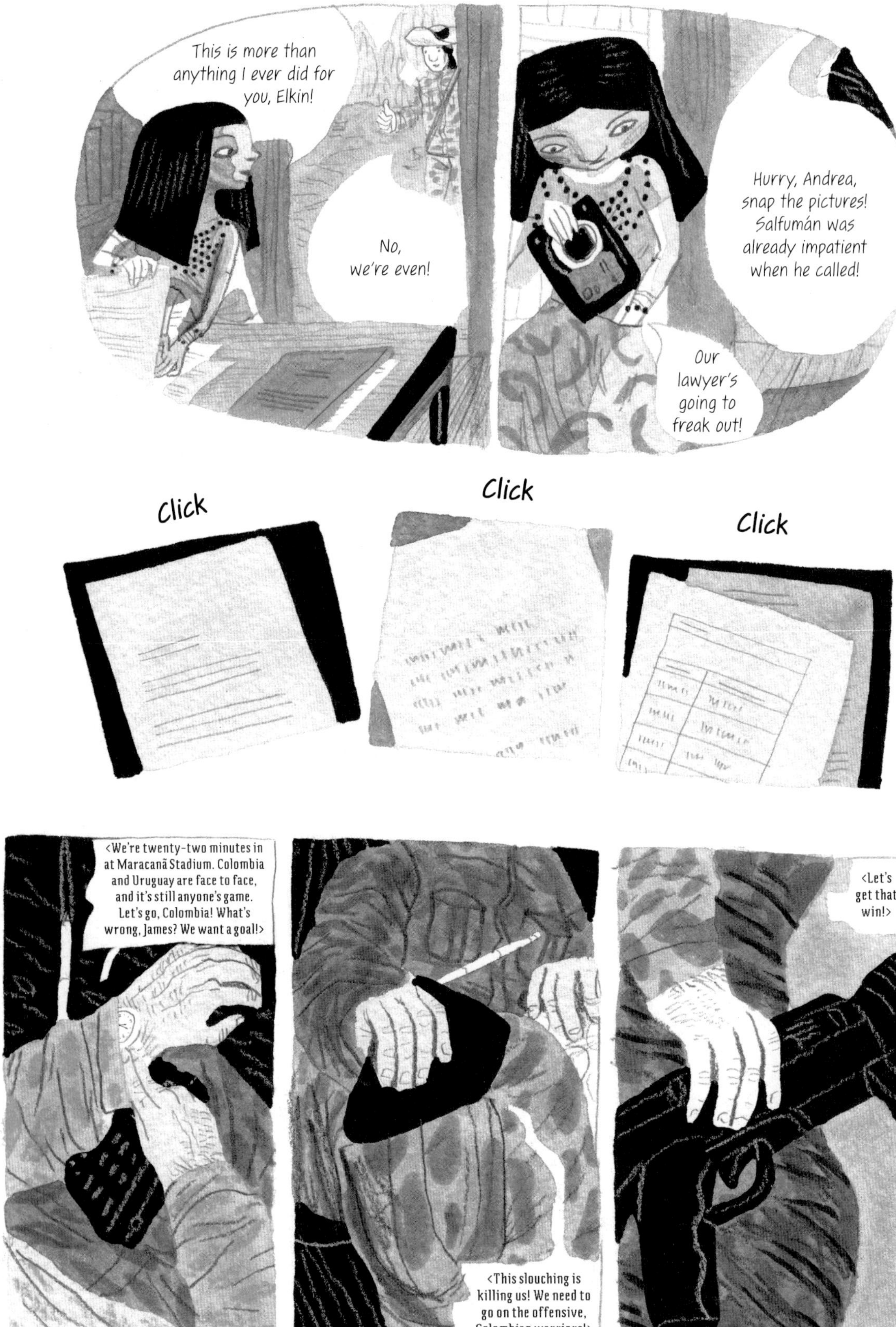

This is more than anything I ever did for you, Elkin!
No, we're even!
Hurry, Andrea, snap the pictures! Salfumán was already impatient when he called!
Our lawyer's going to freak out!
Click
Click
Click
<We're twenty-two minutes in at Maracanã Stadium. Colombia and Uruguay are face to face, and it's still anyone's game. Let's go, Colombia! What's wrong, James? We want a goal!>
<This slouching is killing us! We need to go on the offensive, Colombian warriors!>
<Let's get that win!>

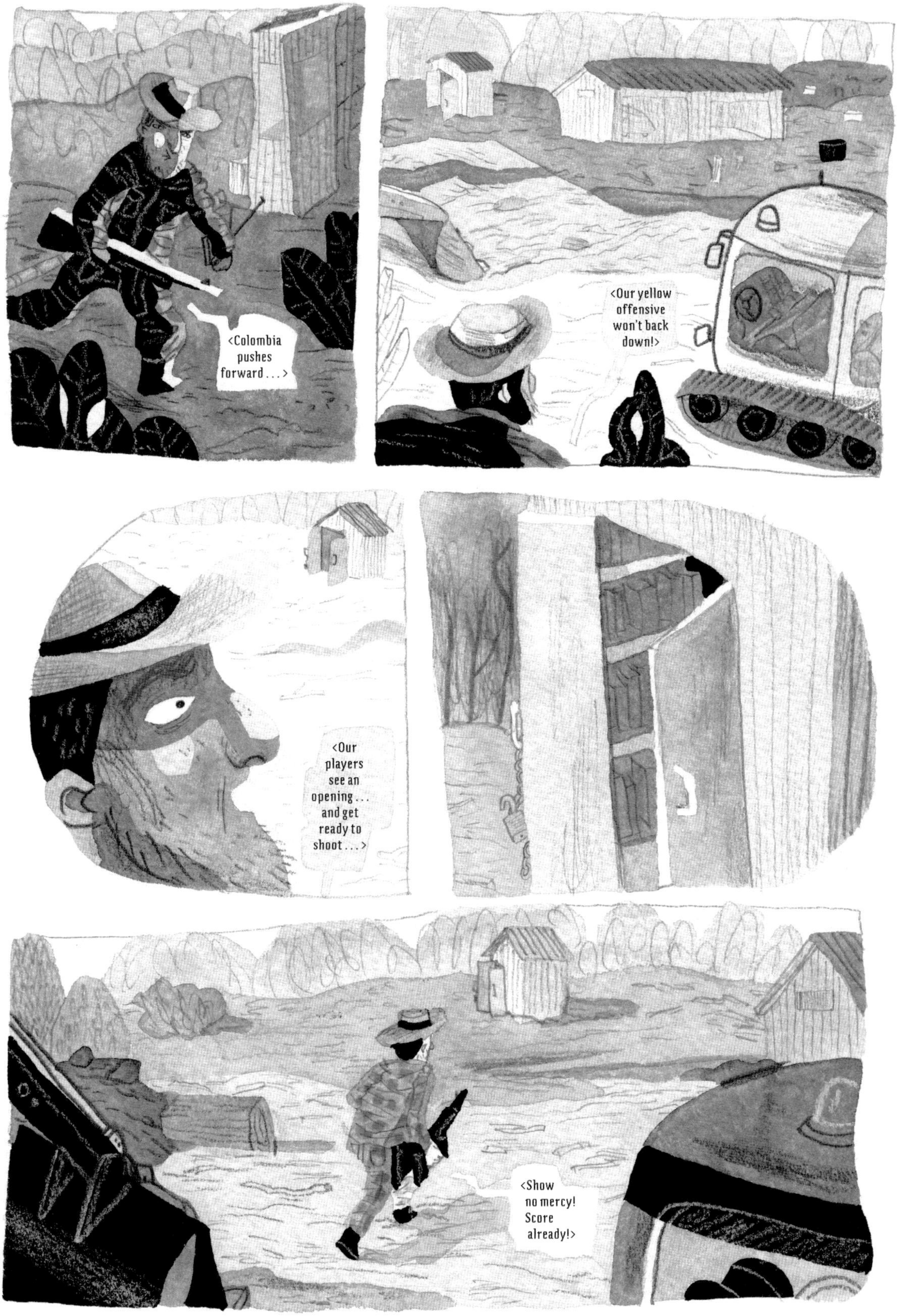
<Colombia pushes forward . . .>
<Our yellow offensive won't back down!>
<Our players see an opening . . . and get ready to shoot . . .>
<Show no mercy! Score already!>

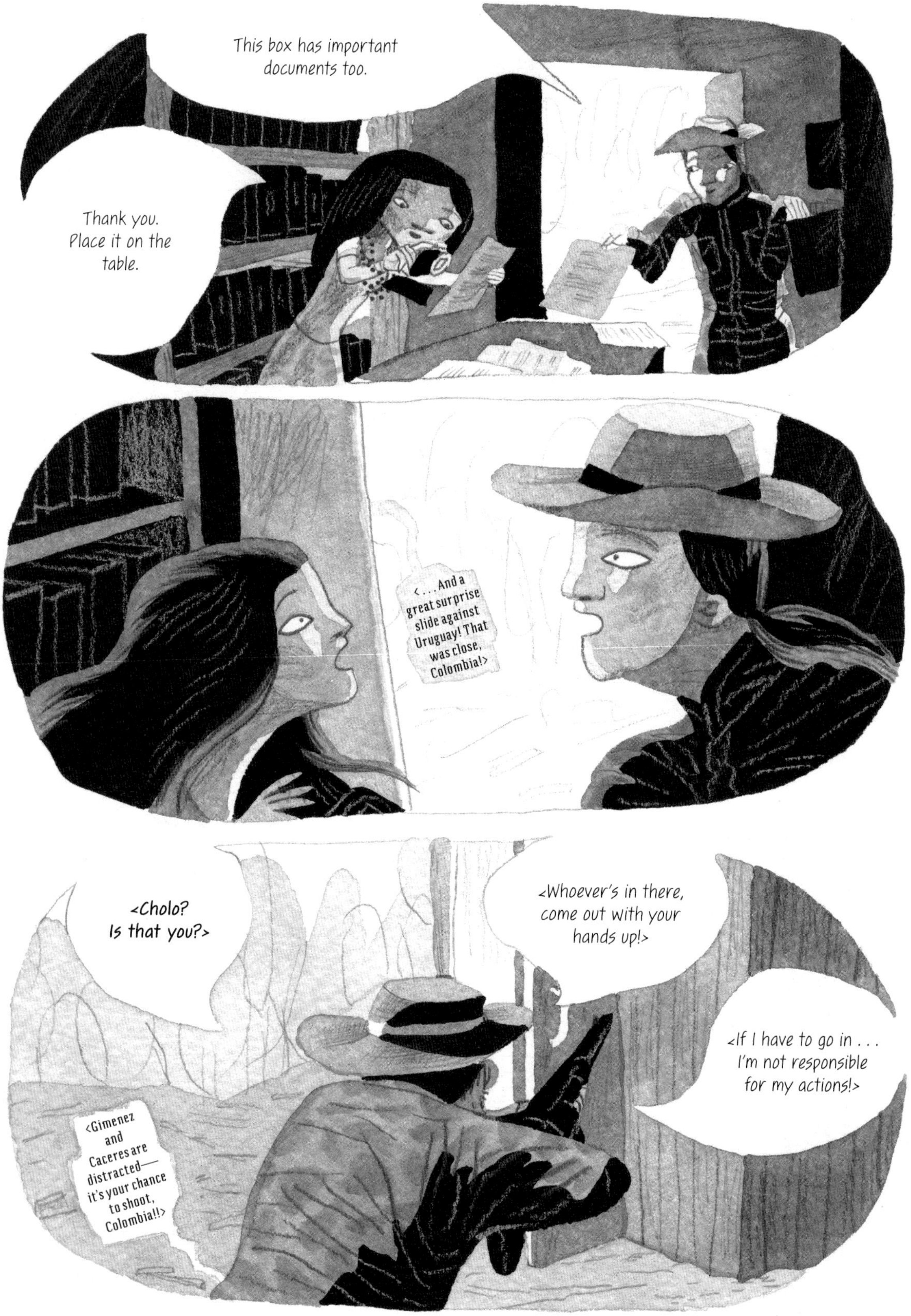
This box has important documents too.
Thank you. Place it on the table.
<... And a great surprise slide against Uruguay! That was close, Colombia!>
<Cholo? Is that you?>
<Whoever's in there, come out with your hands up!>
<If I have to go in . . . I'm not responsible for my actions!>
<Gimenez and Caceres are distracted— it's your chance to shoot, Colombia!!>

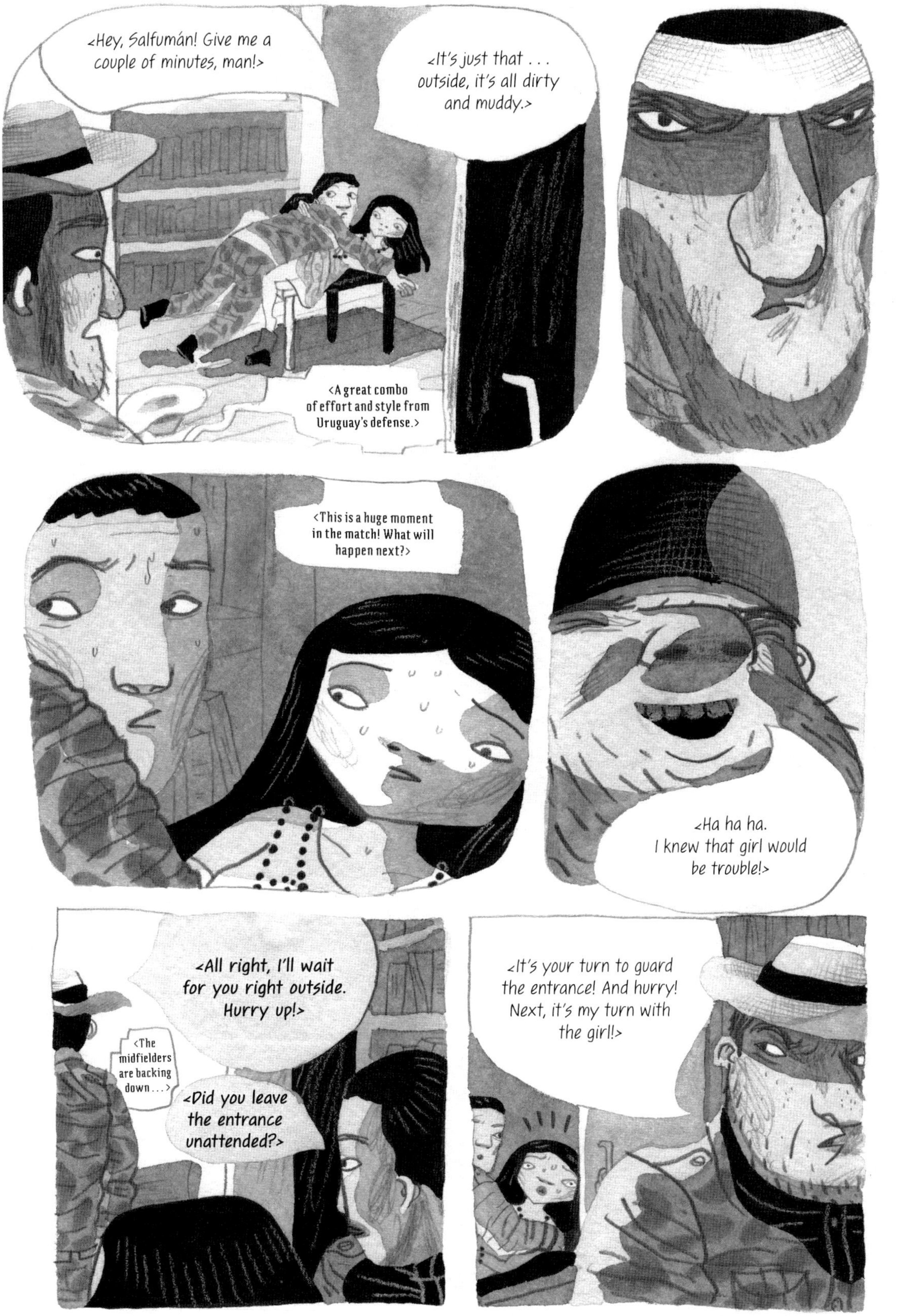

<Hey, Salfumán! Give me a couple of minutes, man!>
<It's just that . . . outside, it's all dirty and muddy.>
<A great combo of effort and style from Uruguay's defense.>
<This is a huge moment in the match! What will happen next?>
<Ha ha ha. I knew that girl would be trouble!>
<All right, I'll wait for you right outside. Hurry up!>
<The midfielders are backing down . . .>
<Did you leave the entrance unattended?>
<It's your turn to guard the entrance! And hurry! Next, it's my turn with the girl!>

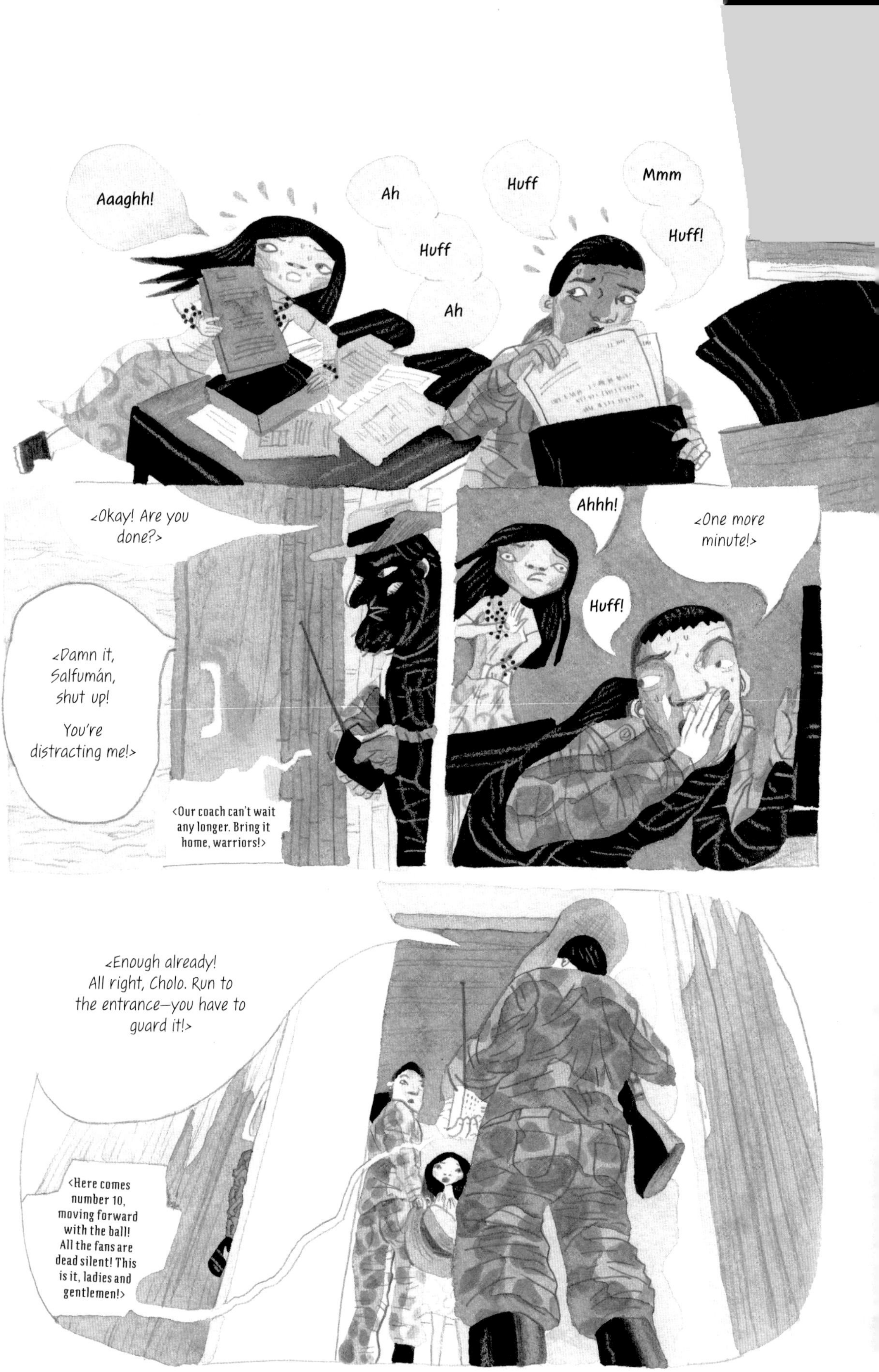
Aaaghh!
Ah
Huff
Ah
Huff
Mmm
Huff!
<Okay! Are you done?>
<Damn it, Salfumán, shut up! You're distracting me!>
<Our coach can't wait any longer. Bring it home, warriors!>
Ahhh!
<One more minute!>
Huff!
<Enough already! All right, Cholo. Run to the entrance—you have to guard it!>
<Here comes number 10, moving forward with the ball! All the fans are dead silent! This is it, ladies and gentlemen!>

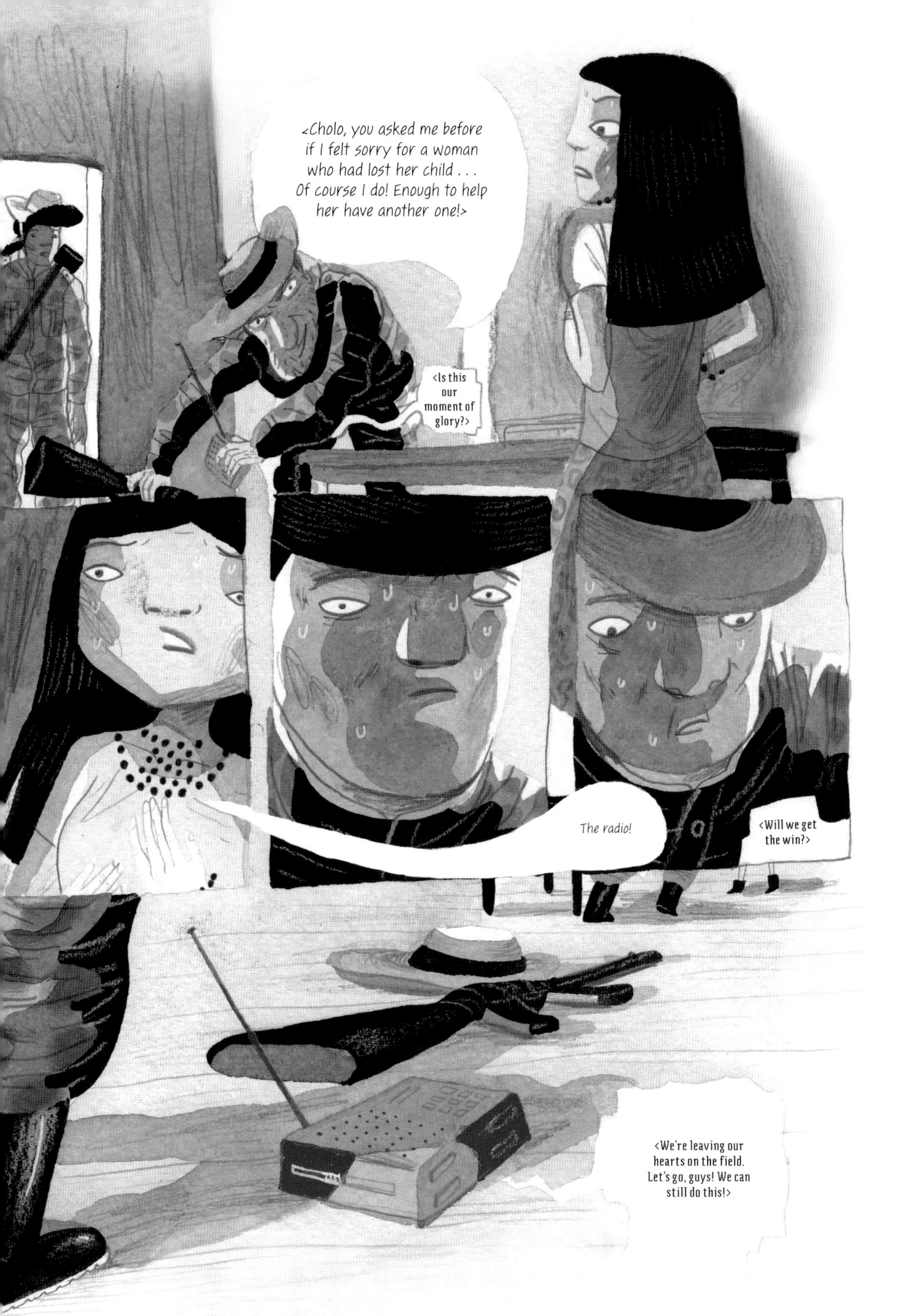
<Cholo, you asked me before if I felt sorry for a woman who had lost her child . . . Of course I do! Enough to help her have another one!>
<Is this our moment of glory?>
The radio!
<Will we get the win?>
<We're leaving our hearts on the field. Let's go, guys! We can still do this!>

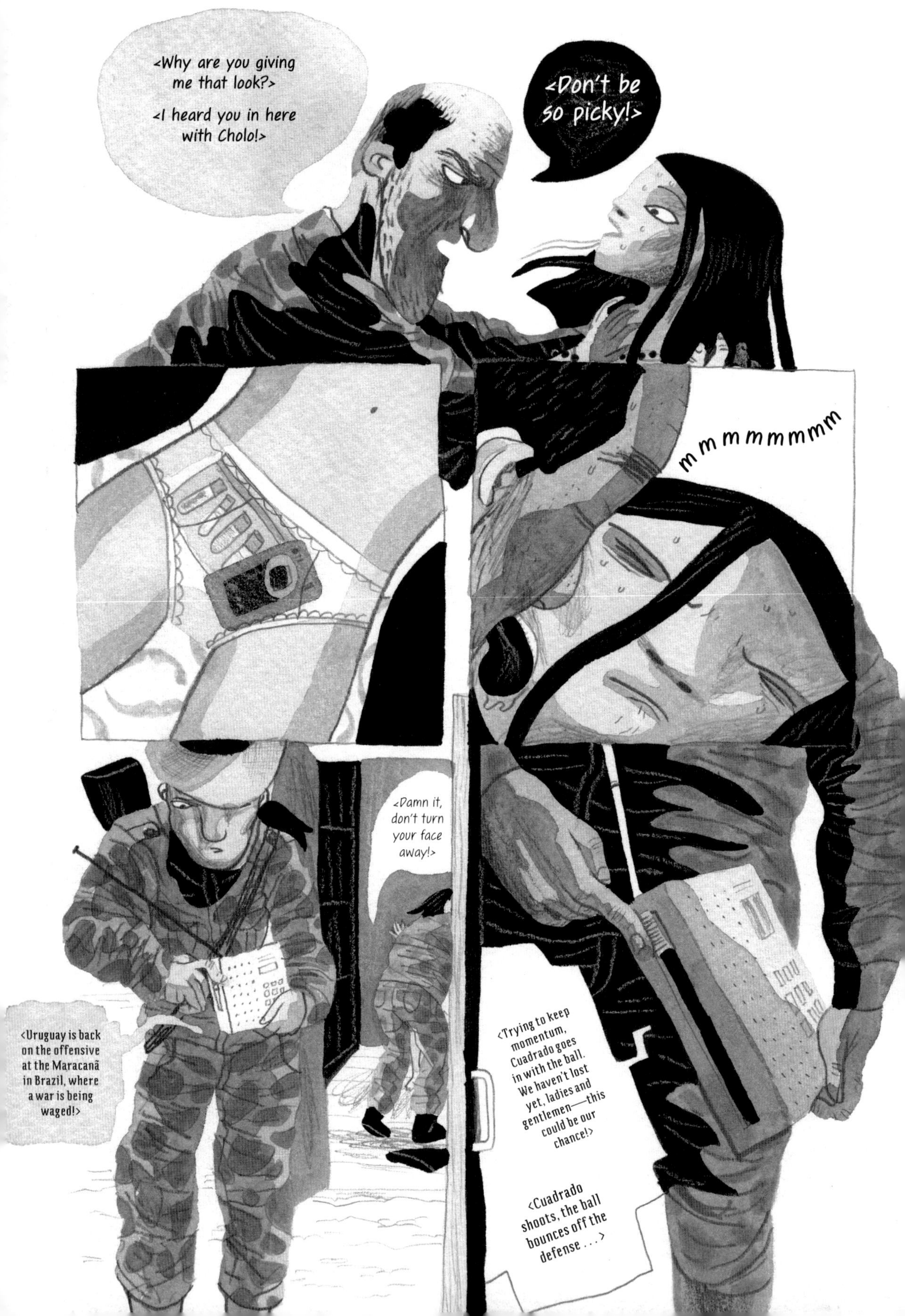

<Why are you giving me that look?>
<I heard you in here with Cholo!>
<Don't be so picky!>
mmmmmmmm
<Damn it, don't turn your face away!>
<Uruguay is back on the offensive at the Maracanã in Brazil, where a war is being waged!>
<Trying to keep momentum, Cuadrado goes in with the ball. We haven't lost yet, ladies and gentlemen—this could be our chance!>
<Cuadrado shoots, the ball bounces off the defense . . .>

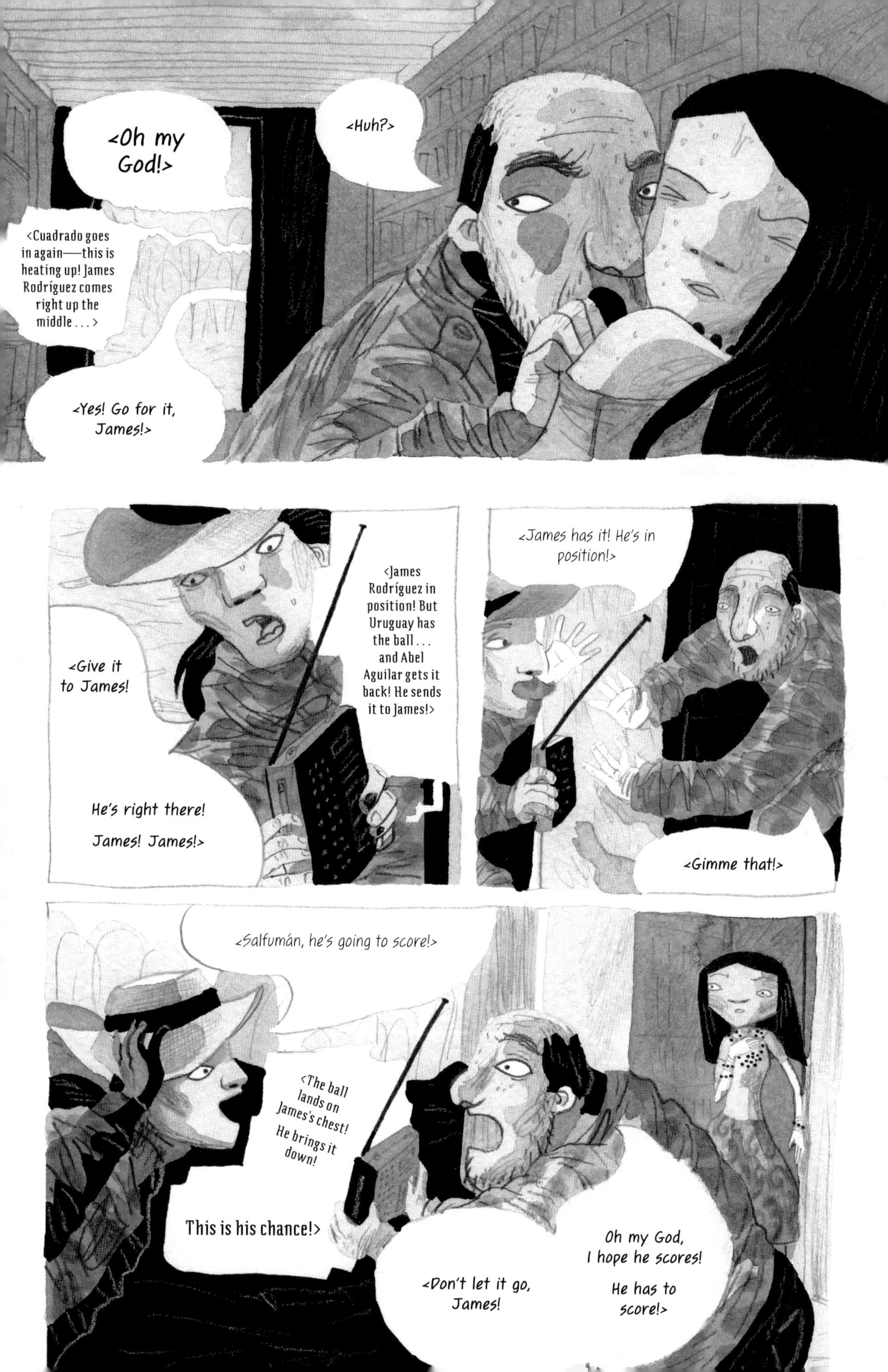
<Oh my God!>
<Huh?>
<Cuadrado goes in again—this is heating up! James Rodríguez comes right up the middle . . .>
<Yes! Go for it, James!>
<James Rodríguez in position! But Uruguay has the ball . . . and Abel Aguilar gets it back! He sends it to James!>
<Give it to James! He's right there! James! James!>
<James has it! He's in position!>
<Gimme that!>
<Salfumán, he's going to score!>
<The ball lands on James's chest! He brings it down! This is his chance!>
<Don't let it go, James!
Oh my God, I hope he scores! He has to score!>

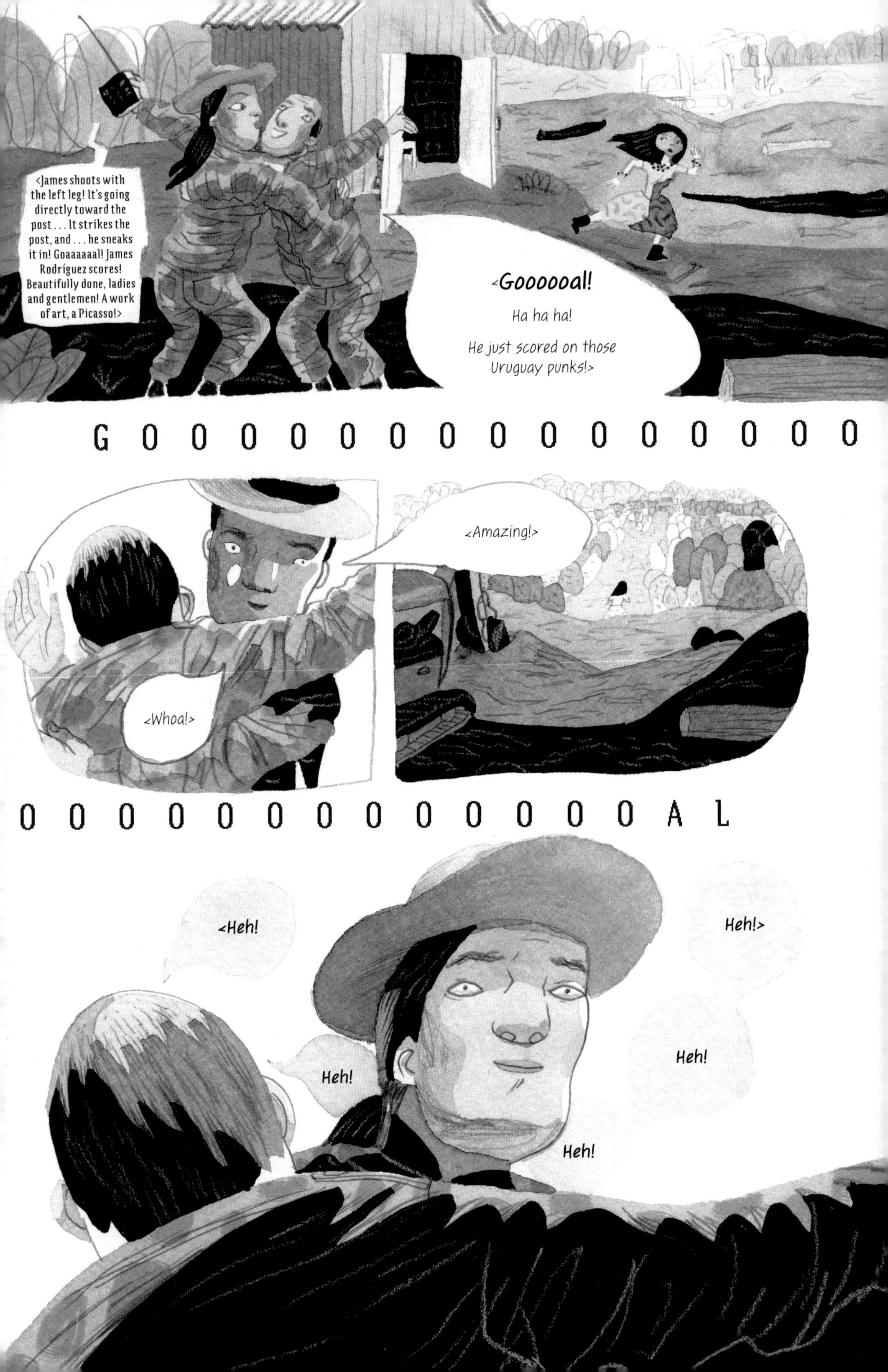

<James shoots with the left leg! It's going directly toward the post . . . It strikes the post, and . . . he sneaks it in! Goaaaaaal! James Rodríguez scores! Beautifully done, ladies and gentlemen! A work of art, a Picasso!>
<Goooooal!
Ha ha ha!
He just scored on those Uruguay punks!>
G O O O O O O O O O O O O O O O
<Amazing!>
<Whoa!>
O O O O O O O O O O O O O A L
<Heh!
Heh!>
Heh!
Heh!
Heh!

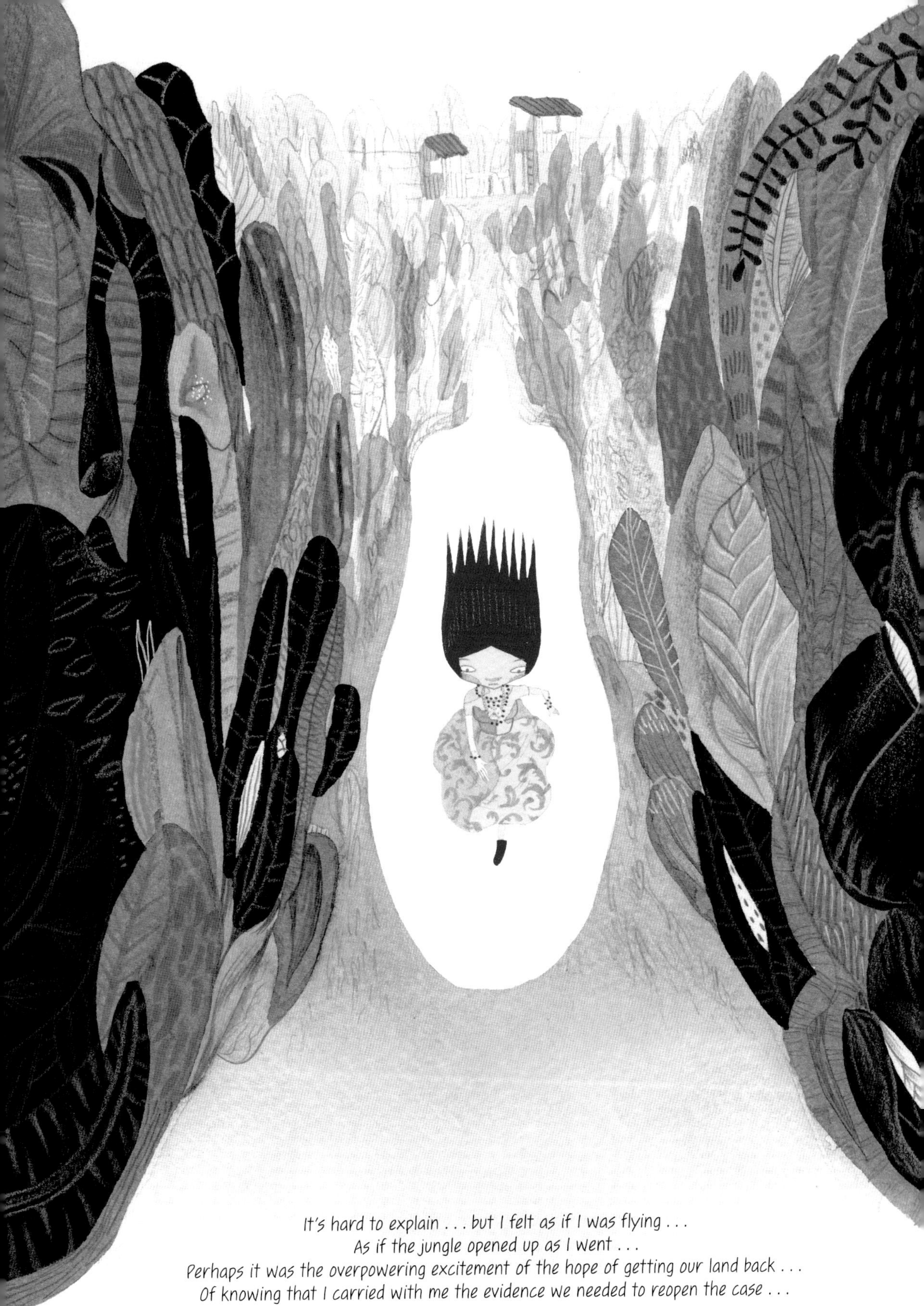

It's hard to explain . . . but I felt as if I was flying . . .
As if the jungle opened up as I went . . .
Perhaps it was the overpowering excitement of the hope of getting our land back . . .
Of knowing that I carried with me the evidence we needed to reopen the case . . .

I love it, Papa!
It's so, so beautiful!

I knew you'd like it.

Here, I'll help you put
it on, sweetie.

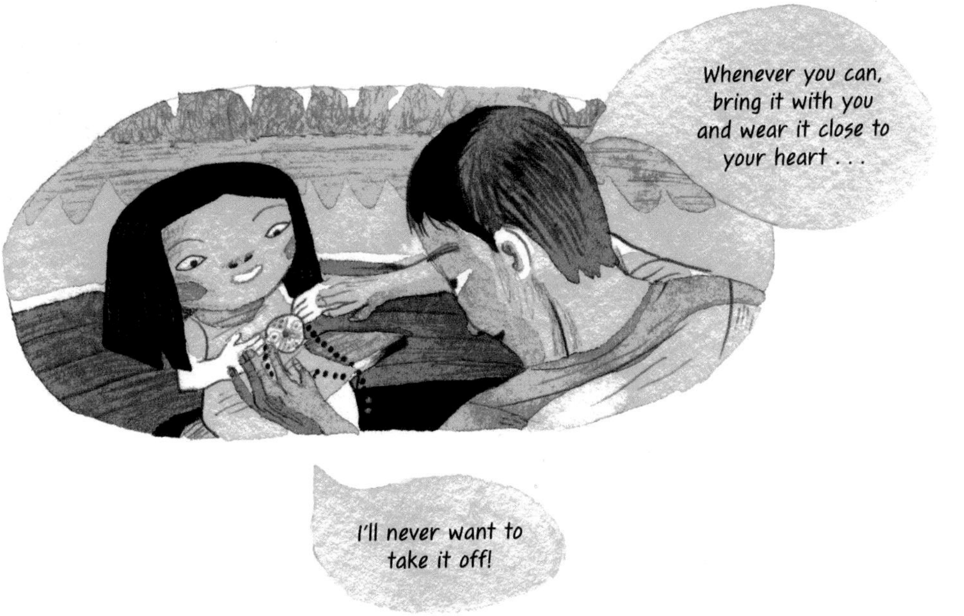
Whenever you can, bring it with you and wear it close to your heart . . .
I'll never want to take it off!

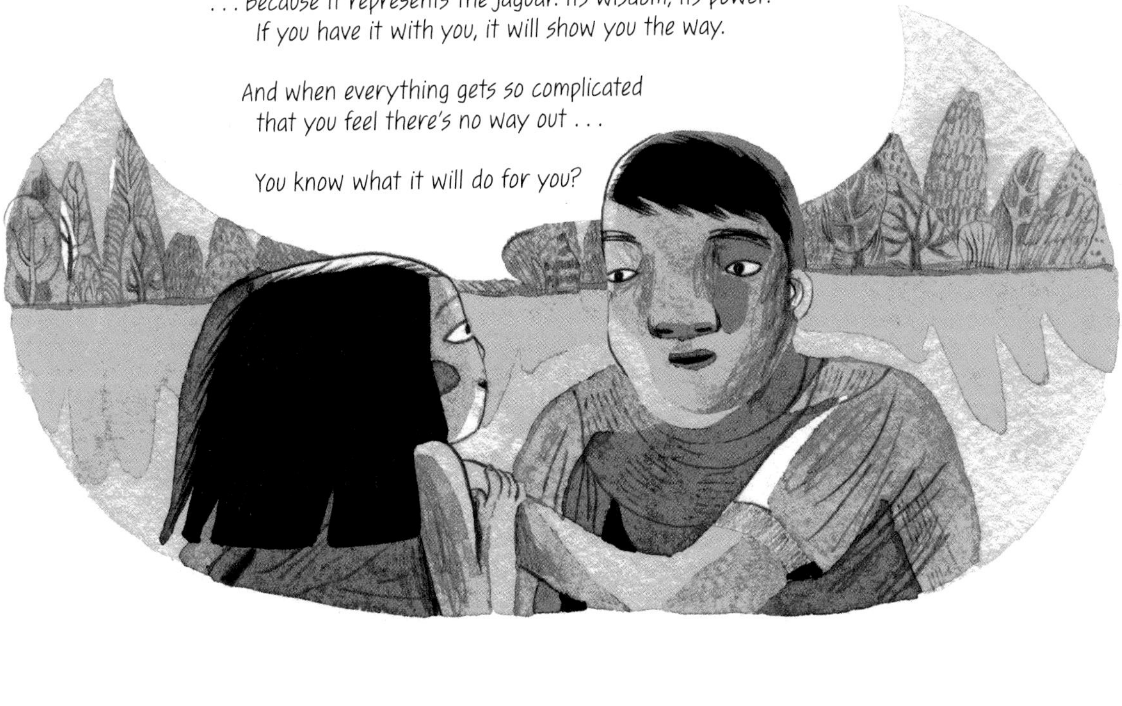
. . . Because it represents the jaguar. Its wisdom, its power. If you have it with you, it will show you the way.
And when everything gets so complicated that you feel there's no way out . . .
You know what it will do for you?

What?

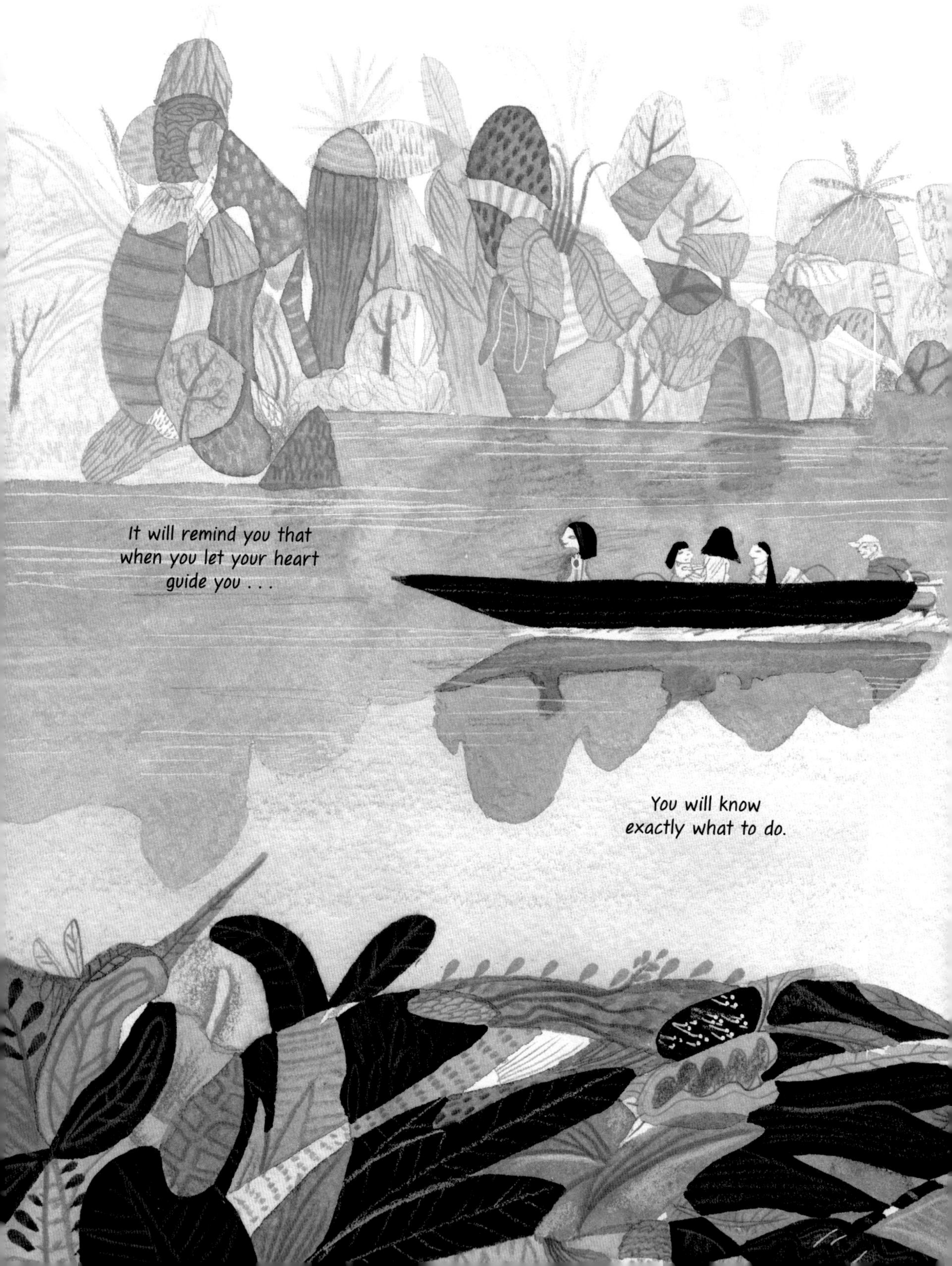

It will remind you that when you let your heart guide you . . .

You will know exactly what to do.

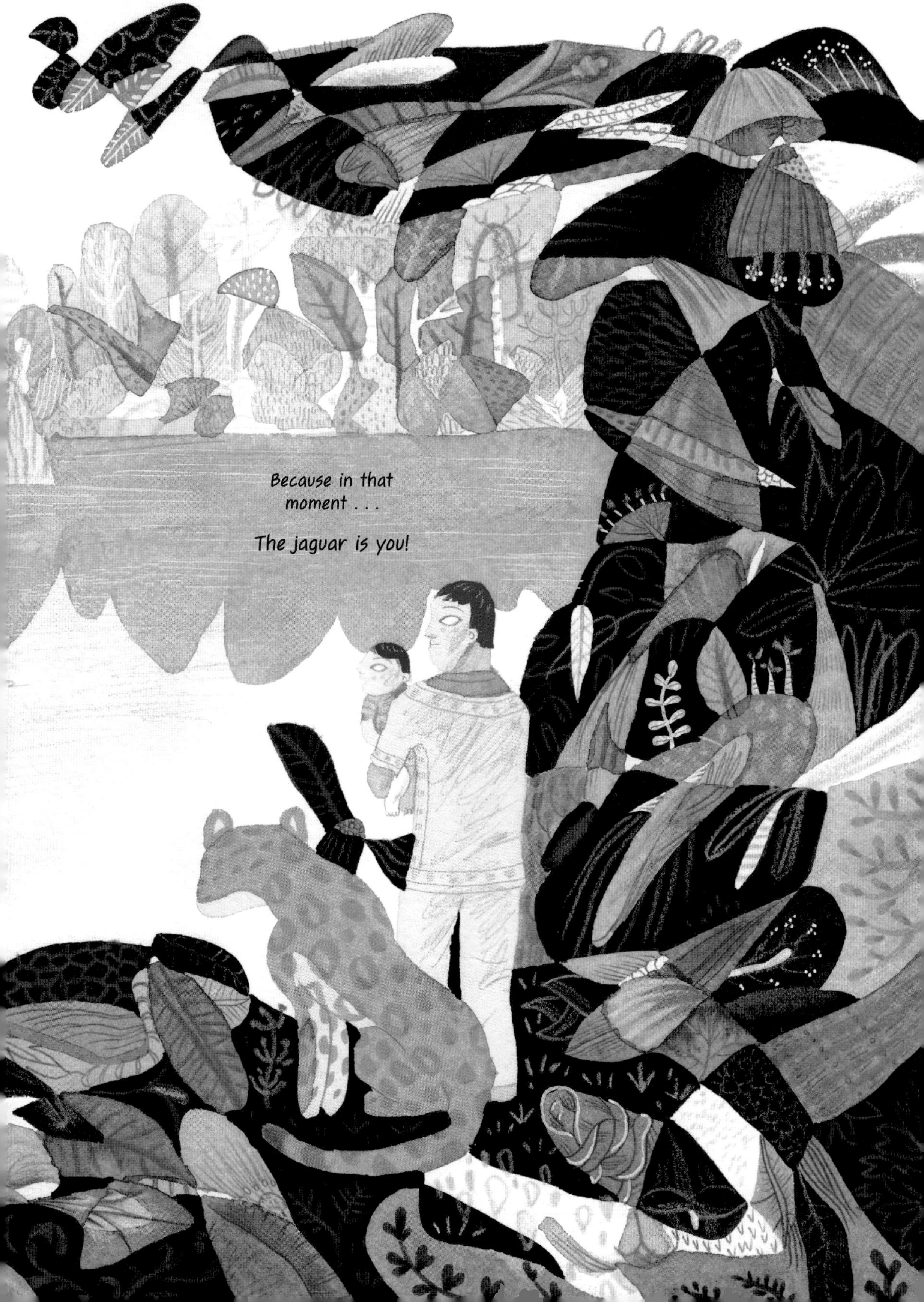
Because in that moment . . .
The jaguar is you!

AFTER *AMAZONA*

Although Andrea is a fictional creation, the story of *Amazona* has been inspired by real conditions affecting the many Indigenous peoples of Colombia. In the years since 2014, when the story takes place, and since 2018 to 2019, when Canizales created this graphic novel, a combination of forces has continued to threaten, displace, and disappear people from Indigenous groups across the country. According to the International Work Group for Indigenous Affairs, the Indigenous population of Colombia includes approximately 1,500,000 individuals; the country's 2018 census places that number at more than 1,900,000 individuals from 115 different native peoples. In a country of more than 50 million people, they are disproportionately harmed by acts of violence and corruption.

Alongside the country's Afro-Colombian peoples, Indigenous Colombians face forced displacement, and efforts to resist are fraught. A variety of organizations consider Colombia the most dangerous nation in the world for human-rights defenders. As of 2019, Colombia's human-rights ombudsman estimated that close to 500 Colombian activists have been murdered since the beginning of 2016, a majority of them Indigenous human-rights defenders. In 2020, hostile actors killed more than 110 Indigenous activists, environmentalists, and journalists across the country.

Colombia is abundant with biodiversity, and forests cover nearly half of its land. This includes approximately 14,000,000 square miles of the Amazon rain forest. Much of this biodiverse area belongs to resource-rich Indigenous reserves. For many Indigenous groups, the concept of home extends beyond their immediate dwellings and to the plants and forests of these territories (or departments). These natural surroundings provide living spaces, sacred spaces, and spaces of healings. Rain forests benefit people outside these territories and cultures as well, producing the oxygen people breathe planet-wide. However, as a result of the areas' resources, both these habitats and their inhabitants are at risk.

In departments such as Cauca, Nariño, Chocó, and others, mining operations—legal and illegal— have encroached on the natural habitat. Indigenous groups in these areas include the Nasa, in Cauca; the Pastos, in Nariño; and the Emberá, in Chocó. Chocó has a substantial Afro-Colombian population as well. Throughout such departments, local peoples who oppose these land-grabbing and extraction efforts often meet with death threats or violence from the armed employees of mining and energy companies. Similar violence has resulted from the seizing of forest land for cattle rearing and from disputes over land on which people grow coca plants. The threat of armed groups is ongoing; according to the Environmental Justice Foundation, 2019 and 2020 were some of the deadliest recorded years for the defenders of these territories. Colombian human-rights activists allege that government authorities have failed to protect these territories and their peoples or to provide humanitarian aid. When mining or similar operations displace Indigenous peoples, safer conditions elsewhere may not be available. More than 40 percent of Colombia's total population lives in poverty, and the overcrowded urban housing depicted in *Amazona* is a reality for some of the displaced. But a return may not always be possible, as these operations can destroy the contested environments.

Indigenous peoples have experienced armed violence not just recently but throughout Colombia's history. For decades, the Colombian military and rebel group the Revolutionary Armed Forces of Colombia (FARC) were engaged in a civil war, putting people who belonged to neither party in the crossfire. This civil war ended in 2016, upon the signing of peace accords between the government and FARC. But new patterns of violence erupted following the peace accords. Other armed groups moved to control the territories formerly occupied by FARC rebels, such as the coca-growing regions of the west and southwest. As a result, peoples of rural communities, especially activists and Indigenous leaders, remain at risk. Deforestation has also accelerated. In the years directly following the 2016 agreement, close to 1.2 million acres of the Colombian Amazon were destroyed.

In spite of these hardships, the Indigenous peoples of Colombia continue to show leadership and resilience. In October 2020, Indigenous leaders launched a gathering known as a minga in response to paramilitary killings in Indigenous communities, government neglect, and the abuses of government-aligned businesses. Derived from the Quechua term *minka*, a minga involves the widespread mobilization of peoples for the purpose of working toward the common good. In this case, it involved thousands of peoples from different Indigenous and Afro-Colombian groups, many of them from the southwestern part of the country.

Participants in the minga gathered first in the city of Cali and requested a dialogue with Colombian president Iván Duque. When Duque did not honor this request, the minga began a move to Colombia's capital city, Bogotá, traveling in a caravan miles long. The minga reached Bogotá on October 19, and on October 21, minga leaders declared their intent to stay in the capital, where they would take part in nationwide strikes against poverty and inequality. These strikes, promoted by a coalition of activists, students, teachers, doctors, and other Colombians, have advanced a protest against government policies—in particular, a change to taxation during the COVID-19 pandemic. Strikers and the Indigenous Minga have encountered violence both from government security forces and from armed civilians acting on police encouragement. Human-rights organizations have reported unwarranted detentions, sexual assaults, and disappearances. However, even under these threats, the national strikes and the Indigenous Minga continued into 2021, voicing demands for equality and a more just future.

SELECTED BIBLIOGRAPHY

Allen, Nicolas. "Colombians Don't Just Want a New Government—They Want an End to Neoliberalism: An Interview with Forrest Hylton." *Jacobin*, May 16, 2021. https://jacobinmag.com/2021/05/colombia -protests-strike-2021-duque-uribismo-neoliberalism-police.

Cultural Survival. "Cultural Survival Condemns the Massacre of Indigenous Leaders in Colombia. " November 1, 2019. https://www.culturalsurvival.org/news/cultural-survival-condemns-massacre-indigenous-leaders-colombia.

Feng, Deon. "Risking Death to Defend Life in Colombia." Globe Post, December 4, 2020. https://theglobepost.com /2020/12/04/colombia-human-rights-defenders.

International Work Group for Indigenous Affairs. "Indigenous Peoples in Colombia." IWGIA. Accessed July 8, 2021. https://www.iwgia.org/en/colombia.html.

Mendoza, Diana. "The Indigenous World 2021: Colombia." IWGIA, March 18, 2021. https://www.iwgia.org/en /colombia/4212-iw-2021-colombia.html.

ProPacífico. "Pacific Region." Accessed July 8, 2021. https://propacifico.org/en/about-us/region-pacifico.

Trent, Steve. "As Indigenous Peoples Protest in Colombia, We Must Rally with Them." Environmental Justice Foundation, November 12, 2020. https://ejfoundation.org/news-media/as-indigenous-people-protest-in -colombia-we-must-rally-with-them.

ABOUT THE AUTHOR

Canizales is a Colombia-born author-illustrator living in Majorca, Spain. His books have been published in Spanish, English, Basque, Chinese, French, Greek, Italian, Korean, Macedonian, Polish, Portuguese, and Ukrainian. Spanish honors for his art include the 2019 Cuatrogatos prize (shortlisted), the 2018 Cuatrogatos prize, the 2018 Ciudad de Palma Comic Awards (honorary mention), and the 2017 Divina Pastora social graphic novel award. He also works as a professor of drawing at Universitat Oberta de Catalunya.

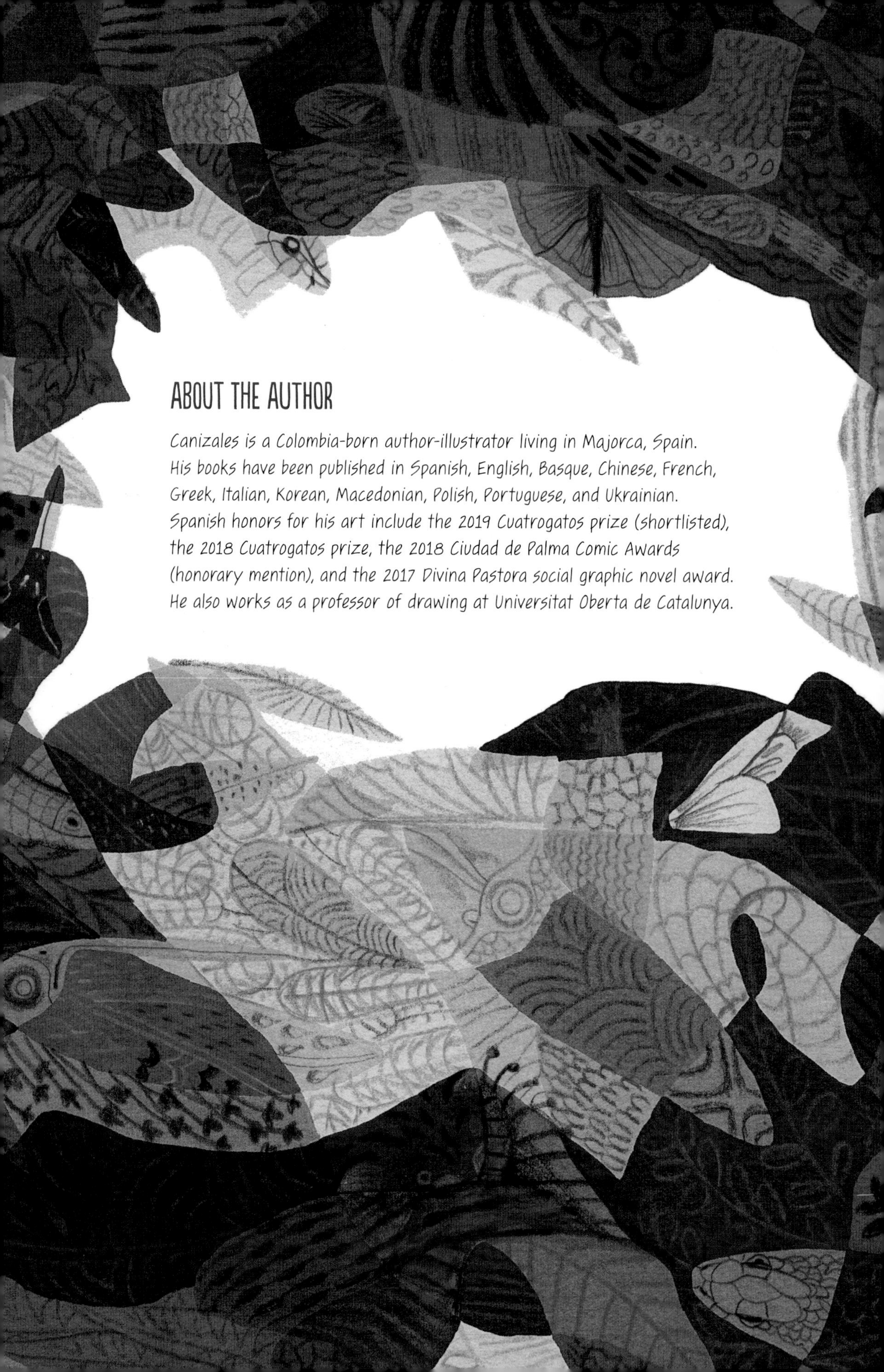

santa clara
county
library district

Renewals: (800) 471-0991

www.sccld.org

ANDREA, a young Indigenous Colombian woman, has returned to the part of the Amazonia region she calls home. Only nineteen years old, she comes to mourn her lost child, carrying a box in her arms. And she comes with another mission. Andrea has hidden a camera upon herself. If she can capture evidence of the illegal mining that displaced her family, it will mark the first step toward reclaiming their land.

With *Amazona*, Canizales presents a suspenseful, socially conscious graphic novel in a stark, singular visual style.

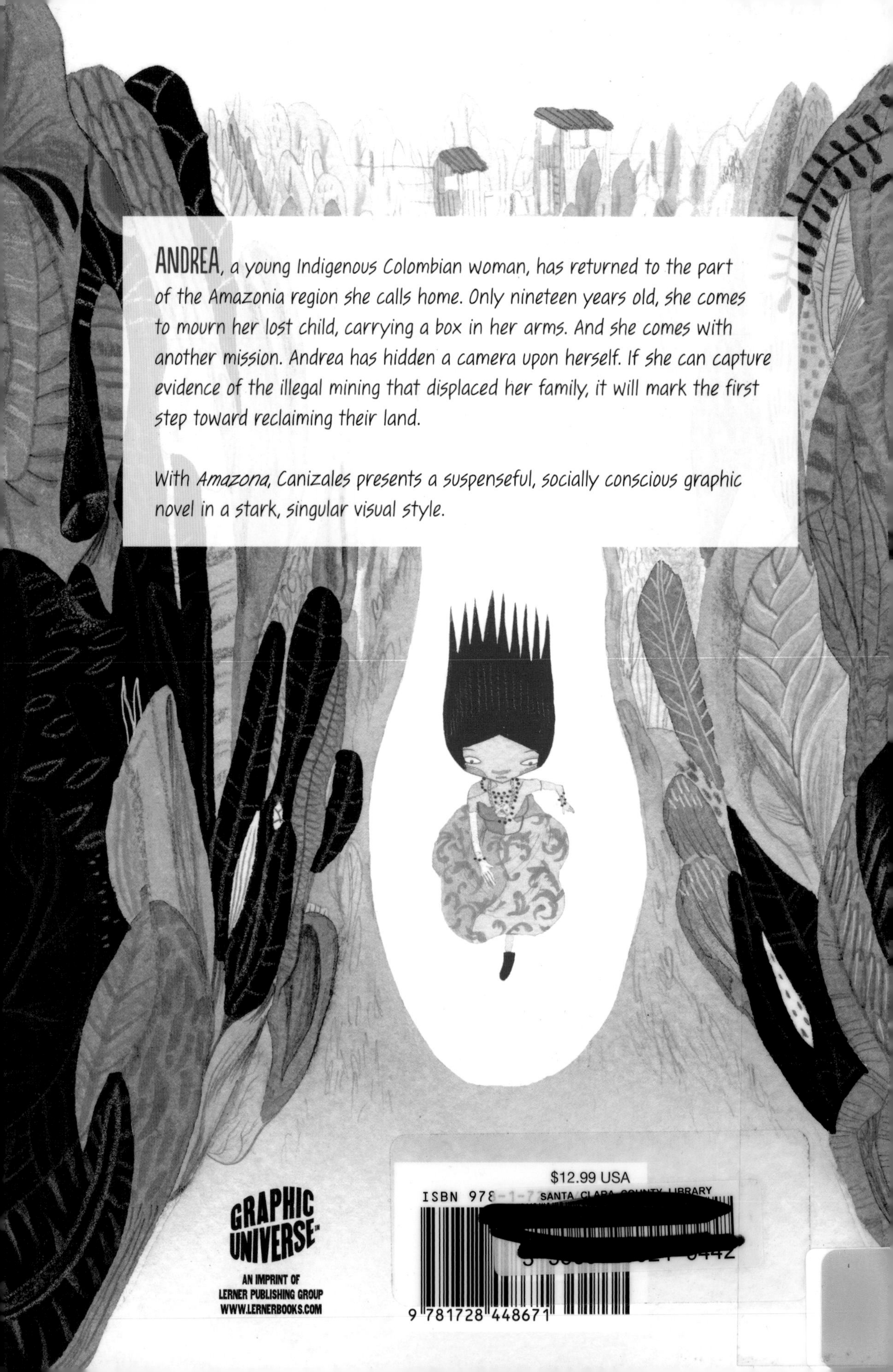

GRAPHIC UNIVERSE™
AN IMPRINT OF
LERNER PUBLISHING GROUP
WWW.LERNERBOOKS.COM

$12.99 USA
ISBN 978[redacted]
9 781728 448671

MAKING POLICY, MAKING LAW

AN INTERBRANCH PERSPECTIVE

MARK C. MILLER AND JEB BARNES

EDITORS